GUARDED LOVE

"Darius—" she began, only to have him take full advantage of the moment to kiss her. His tongue thrust deeply and repeatedly, stroking every inch of her mouth. The act was lusty, wet, and hot as pent-up emotions were released in a savage onslaught. Darius simply held on to her arms as he bruised her soft mouth beneath the passionate possession of his own.

He began to tease her lips with soft wet pecks that made her whimper in anticipation of more. "I want you to stop shutting me out," he groaned in a ragged whisper, before his tongue delved deeply, briefly.

Selena knew what he meant. "It's easier this way," she whispered, when he broke the kiss again. Tears began to pressure her eyes.

"Easier? Why?"

Because I'm in love with you, she silently admitted.

BOOK YOUR PLACE ON OUR WEBSITE AND MAKE THE ARABESQUE ROMANCE CONNECTION!

We've created a customized website just for our very special Arabesque readers, where you can get the inside scoop on everything that's going on with Arabesque romance novels.

When you come online, you'll have the exciting opportunity to:

- View covers of upcoming books

- Learn about our future publishing schedule (listed by publication month and author)

- Find out when your favorite authors will be visiting a city near you

- Search for and order backlist books

- Check out author bios and background information

- Send e-mail to your favorite authors

- Join us in weekly chats with authors, readers and other guests

- Get writing guidelines

- AND MUCH MORE!

Visit our website at
http://www.arabesquebooks.com

GUARDED LOVE

AlTonya Washington

BET Publications, LLC
http://www.bet.com
http://www.arabesquebooks.com

ARABESQUE BOOKS are published by

BET Publications, LLC
c/o BET BOOKS
One BET Plaza
1900 W Place NE
Washington, DC 20018-1211

All Kensington Titles, Imprints, and Distributed Lines are available at special quantity discounts for bulk purchases for sales promotions, premiums, fund-raising, and educational or institutional use. Special book excerpts or customized printings can also be created to fit specific needs. For details, write or phone the office of the Kensington special sales manager: Kensington Publishing Corp., 850 Third Avenue, New York, NY 10022, attn: Special Sales Department, Phone: 1-800-221-2647.

First Printing: December 2003
10 9 8 7 6 5 4 3 2 1

Printed in the United States of America

To Todd,
Thank you for your unending support and love.
You always made me believe this day would come.
I love you so very much.

ACKNOWLEDGMENTS

Alphonso and Carolyn Washington—My great parents. My greatest promotors. Thank you for ALL you do to make my life the joy that it is.

LaWanda Washington—My sister, best girlfriend and best assistant. Thank you for taking the time to attend all my author events. I love you.

To my family at *The Winston Salem Journal* in North Carolina—I love you guys a lot. Thanks for supporting me.

To my REAL friends—you know who you are. Thanks for never doubting me or telling me to put my writing on the back burner.

Sha-Shana Crichton, Tonya Howard, Chandra Taylor—you ladies are truly the best!

To the book clubs and readers who have welcomed my work into your meetings and homes. I can't thank you enough!

ACKNOWLEDGMENTS

One

"All right, Harry, enough with the secrecy, you have to tell me where you found these guys."

Harold Morris smiled and cast a humorous glance toward the petite, voluptuous beauty next to him. "Don't ask stupid questions. You know I've got connections," he bragged.

Selena Witherspoon reclined in her high-backed cushioned chair and sighed. "Are you tellin' me they're all gay?"

Harry rolled his eyes toward the ceiling. "Did I say that?"

Selena's provocative hazel gaze settled on Harry. She looked for some form of aggravation in his deep, black stare but there was none. She smiled, thankful she hadn't excited his quick temper. "I only asked that because I've seen some of your, uh . . . friends and I must say they're pretty . . ."

"Tasty?" Harry finished, shooting her a wicked glare. When Selena burst into laughter, he couldn't help joining in.

The two old friends had been chatting for the last hour and a half. They were seated in the impressive ballroom of the posh Miami Paradise Halls Hotel. Harold, one of the newest clothing designers in the industry, had garnered much praise after the release of his first collection. In the past three years, Harry M, as his label was called, had emerged as a well-respected and popular artist. Now, his second batch of work was generating an equal buzz and had prompted a sneak preview of his fall line. Final rehearsals were in progress for the fashion show to be held at his cousin's hotel. Media hounds all clamored for an advanced peek of the event. Early articles already promised that the show would be quite a feast for the eyes. The grand ballroom stage and accompanying runway that had been installed were packed with gorgeous, sexy men.

Selena was in awe of the fact that she was viewing all the excitement firsthand. She was as impressed as she was happy for her friend. They sat watching the rehearsals and Selena was still struck by all the undeniably attractive males in the room. Selena was the owner and publisher of *Reigning Queens*. The magazine targeted African American women and was famous for its racy and highly opinionated articles. The pieces covered every topic from politics, parenting and travel to beauty, relaxation and men. She was always on the hunt for handsome faces and toned bodies to feature on the magazine's pages for her annual Heavenly Bodies issue. It was safe to say that Selena was having an extraordinary time, her lovely eyes feasted on the smorgasborg of gorgeous physiques as the models strutted around the room.

"Goodness," she breathed, "I have got to get in touch with some of these guys," her voice low and determined.

Harry shrugged. "Hell, if it means the chance to get in that magazine of yours, I know they'll talk to ya."

A small frown marred Selena's smooth caramel complexion. "You really think some of these guys would accept an offer to pose for *Reigning Queens?*" she asked, referring to her magazine.

Harry shrugged. "Why wouldn't they?" he challenged, his onyx gaze still focused on the stage.

Selena toyed with one of her thick dark brown curls and debated. "Well." She sighed. "Ever since I started the magazine, I've noticed how difficult it is for some black men to actually believe they're wanted for spreads."

Harry shook his head. "Now *that's* something I can't believe. Especially when we're sooo delicious."

Selena couldn't help laughing at her friend's sincere statement. "I fully agree!" she managed to respond through her laughter.

"Mmm-mmm . . . no . . . no, sweetie!" Harry called out to

one of the models on stage. "'Scuse me a minute, Selena," he said, before leaving to step toward the runway, where he offered one of the handsome young men there a few suggestions on how to present his attire.

Selena scooted down in her seat and leaned back in the comfortable chair. Seated there, with her shapely legs crossed and her hands dangling over the arms of the chair, she pondered her latest endeavor.

One look at the gorgeous men of Miami had been incentive enough to assure her. The decision to open a branch magazine in the upbeat, sensual town probably wasn't so foolish after all. The branch would be second to the main office in New York. *Reigning Queens* magazine had already earned Selena acclaim and recognition many times over.

A rueful smile tugged at her full lips as she repeated the word in her head. *Acclaim.* That same acclaim, though wonderful and heady, had also served to highlight a reputation she wanted to downplay. She grimaced, recalling the sexual innuendo and rumor that often surrounded her. True, much of the attention was a result of the magazine she published. There were, however, certain past events she wished she could erase from her heart and mind.

"But that's exactly what they are. *Past* events," Selena tried to convince herself.

Of course, Selena would never deny her love for men. Especially black men. Why should she? She was, after all, a black woman who felt that her male counterparts had been given a rough time of it for far too long. While that may have been a strong viewpoint, Selena would point out the obvious. There was an unmistakable absense, or shortage, of black men as objects of love, romance, and desire. Whether on television, in movies, or magazines, the black men were scarce. Selena simply wanted to show them in all their glory.

"Ms. Witherspoon? Excuse me, Ms. Witherspoon?"

Selena pulled her thoughts back into the present and focused her attention on the waiter who smiled down at her.

"You all right over here?" he asked.

Selena returned the young man's smile. "Yeah. Yes, I'm fine. Thank you," she assured him.

"Well, let me know if I can do anything for you," he offered.

Selena, forever on the job, took that as her cue. "Actually, I may be able to do something for you," she said, enjoying the expectant look coming to the waiter's handsome face. "Have you ever heard of *Reigning Queens* magazine?" she continued.

The man graced Selena with a dazzling smile. "Yeah, I heard of your magazine, Ms. Witherspoon. My mother tries to keep it on the 'DL' that she subscribes, but I know better."

Selena set her mouth into one of her sultry pouts and shook her head. "Well then, I guess since your mother subscribes, you wouldn't be interested in posing for us?"

He flushed a bit beneath his light complexion. His bright smile grew more luminous. "Are you kiddin' me?" he asked.

Selena toyed with the thin gold chain around her neck and shook her head again. "I never 'kid,' " she informed him.

He ran one hand across the back of his neck. "Damn, Ms. Witherspoon, that sounds unbelievable, but I don't know when I'll be able to take a trip to New York. Isn't that where the magazine is published?"

"It is, but you won't need to go to New York."

"Oh? Are you guys gonna be doing something down here?" he asked, a frown beginning to appear.

Selena reached into the black portfolio leaning against the leg of her chair. "Actually, I'm in Miami to open a branch office to the one in New York. We're in the final stages, but it'll probably be another six to eight weeks before we're fully operational," she explained, jotting a hotel number on the back of a card before passing it to him. "Call this number and make an appointment with my assistant . . . That is, if you're interested," she added.

"Ms. Witherspoon, I'm way past interested," he promised her.

She waved her hand. "Listen, why don't you call me Selena?" she insisted, pleased by his eagerness.

He took her by the hand. "Thanks, Selena. Uh, my name's

Barry Garner," he stammered, his excitement threatening to boil over. In the next second, he'd leaned over and pressed a kiss to her cheek. Instantly, he regretted the action. "I'm sorry, I, um, I don't know why I did that."

Selena responded with a slight shake of her head. "That's okay," she drawled, her long lashes fluttering. "I assure you that I'm used to it."

Barry's dark gaze grew intense as he watched her. "I can easily believe that," he told her, before taking the card and leaving her with a lingering stare.

A slow, knowing smile warmed Selena's lovely features as she leaned back in her seat. She removed a speck of lint from the black cotton T-shirt she sported and nodded several times in acknowledgment of the male glances she received.

In her business, Selena forbade herself to become infatuated by all the attention directed her way. The strict rule came by way of necessity. She had been burned several times in her past and had finally learned her lesson because of those times. The experiences made her much wiser, fortunately. Selena was beautiful and she knew it. Of course, her looks brought many men to her door. Thankfully, she finally realized how dangerous it was to accept every opportunity with open arms.

Selena was a caramel-complexioned beauty with wide, stunning hazel eyes. Those who didn't know her from childhood always assumed that her mane of thick curly dark brown hair was processed. Everything about Selena Witherspoon, however, was natural and open. Besides her having self-confidence and an awareness of her own sensuality, her greatest key to success was her comfort with the opposite sex. She never allowed herself to lose control. The last thing she wanted was to become too involved and have her heart broken when a man betrayed her or realized that he couldn't handle certain aspects of her life.

"Selena! Selenaaa! I'm goin' to check on some things backstage, and then we'll go see my cousin!"

Selena smiled and waved to Harry, who'd called to her from

the rear of the stage. Just then, she spotted another interesting prospect across the room. "Take your time!" she told her friend.

Velma Morris closed her eyes and relished the strong embrace that enveloped her. Reluctantly, she pulled away and gazed up at the tall, strikingly handsome man who held her. "Thank you again for coming all the way down here from Brooklyn," she whispered.

Darius McClellan smiled down at his old friend, his warm cocoa gaze narrowing. "Did you really think I wouldn't come?" he asked, his soothing deep voice as warm as the stare he sent her way.

Velma nodded slowly, wanting to swoon over the way his entrancing eyes slanted at the corners. "I just know how busy you must be," she finally told him.

Darius's broad shoulders rose in a slow shrug toward the comment. "Hell, by now my business almost runs itself and you're crazy if you think I'd turn down a free trip to Miami," he teased, flashing her his double-dimpled smile.

Velma laughed and took his hand. "Y'all follow me," she called, leading Darius and his two associates to a cozy corner table in the elegant restaurant of her hotel.

As Darius settled his lean, athletic frame into his seat, he studied Velma closely. His hypnotic chocolate stare traveled across her pretty face and he could tell there was a lot on her mind.

"Why don't you tell us what's going on down here?" he urged, leaning back in his chair. The mellow baritone of his voice never failed to coax a response.

Velma cleared her throat. "A while back, I started getting these calls—uh, *unfriendly calls,*" she clarified, with a nervous laugh.

Darius's thick brows drew closer. "Do you know who it was?" he asked.

"My ex-husband," she quickly admitted with a nod.

"What's the problem?" Darius continued, trailing one finger along his temple.

"Charles Herbert's been brooding ever since we divorced over a year ago," Velma shared, her lips tightening into a thinner line.

"Damn, haven't I heard that name once or twice since I've gotten to Miami?" Darius whispered, frowning as he concentrated.

Velma shrugged. "I'm sure you have. Charles is responsible in some way for almost half the shopping centers in this part of the city."

"Well, why would a man so well known resort to some petty crap like this?" he asked.

"Charles always was a jealous son of a bitch. He's got three times as much as me, but he doesn't want me to have *anything* of my own."

Jerry Kent, one of Darius's associates, leaned forward. "Couldn't you get any local help, Ms. Morris?"

Velma grimaced and shook her head. "No one around here would dare side with me over Charles. Even if my hotel is one of the hottest spots in town."

"Has he made any serious threats, Velm?" Darius asked, watching her nod in response.

"I really can't afford *any* negative publicity. Especially in the next two weeks."

"Why not the next two weeks?" Max Richardson inquired.

Velma nodded toward Darius's other associate, before reaching into the gray leather book she'd brought to the restaurant. After handing each of them an agenda, she leaned back in her seat. "In less than two weeks, my cousin Harry Morris is having the fashion show for his new line here at the hotel."

Jerry's head snapped up. "Hey, Harry M's your cousin?" he asked, watching Velma nod. "He's got some tight gear out there. I even got a few pieces in my closet."

"I'll make sure I tell him," she promised, giving Jerry a weak smile.

Darius was silent as his intense brown gaze scanned the agenda. A soft smirk tugged at the curve of his mouth when he reached the end of the page. "Velm, is this last event what I think it is?" he asked.

Velma smiled, without looking at the sheet, and clasped her hands. "Mmm-hmm. Miami Bass is still huge, especially down here. The record company is having; some kind of bash and the hotel's already booked solid for it. As you can see, I really can't afford any shake-ups."

Darius reached over and smothered Velma's smaller hand beneath his. "Listen to me, everything's gonna be just fine," he promised her, before looking at Max and Jerry. "Get a team on the next flight down here," he firmly instructed, nodding as the two men left the table.

Velma turned grateful eyes on him. "Darius, thank you. I—"

"Could you please cool it with the 'thank yous'? My security firm is one of the best, if not *the* best. The least I can do is help out a friend . . . hell, an old flame."

Velma shook her head and smiled at his concern. "Why did we ever break up?" she asked him, watching Darius shrug one shoulder.

"We were way too young to know what the hell we were doin'. At least we're still friends."

The look on Velma's dark, pretty face said she wanted to add something more to their current topic, but she didn't have the chance. At that moment, one of the waitresses tapped her shoulder and told her she was needed in the kitchen.

Nodding at the young woman, Velma turned her gaze back to Darius. "I guess I'll just have to meet you back in my office. Do you remember where it is?"

Darius sent her a wicked grin and nodded. "Yes, I do. I'll probably get something to drink out of here before I go."

Velma sighed and stood from the table. "Well, take your time. I could be a while."

Darius sat alone for only a moment. Soon, the waitress who'd approached Velma earlier had returned to the table.

"Mr. McClellan, could I get you anything?" she lightly offered, her eyes lingering on his dark, devastating features.

Darius favored her with one of his sexy, dimpled smiles. "If you'd bring me a glass of grapefruit juice I could take with me, I'd appreciate it."

The woman hung on to every word Darius uttered. Her eyes lingered on his gorgeous mouth as she stood rooted to her spot. After a second or two, Darius grew concerned.

"Are you all right?" he whispered, touching her hand as he smiled.

She blinked. "I'm sorry," she gushed, shaking her head as she backed away from the table. "I'll be right back with your drink."

Left alone again, Darius took the time to enjoy the plush beauty of the hotel. Paradise Halls had a cool, airy elegance that was unquestionably relaxing. Darius recalled Velma telling him that Charles had bought her the hotel during their marriage. He'd hoped it would give her something to do while he was occupied with business. No one was more surprised than Charles when Velma made such a success of the dilapidated establishment.

Darius ran one hand across the soft wavy hair, which he wore in a close cut. Four women were passing his table just then. They each cast repeated glances toward him. Darius nodded, making eye contact with each of them. He pressed his lips together and looked away to keep himself from chuckling when they bumped into one another while their eyes remained focused on him.

Always the first to admit his mild arrogance, Darius was well aware of his looks and the affect they had on the opposite sex. Women were at times so impressed by his physical appearance, they tolerated the subtle cockiness he sometimes displayed.

Fortunately, that cockiness didn't override his naturally soothing demeanor. Darius McClellan always knew just the right thing to say and the way to say it. He communicated just as effectively with his baritone voice as he did with his gorgeous brown eyes. Those features, combined with the sexy dimpled smile, neat trimmed mustache, and the well-built muscular body, always worked in his favor.

"Here's your drink, Mr. McClellan," The waitress said as she set the juice to the table.

Darius stood and reached into one of the front pockets on his sagging jeans. "Thanks, but call me Darius." He pressed a crisp ten-dollar bill into her hand.

Harry knocked lightly on the heavy oak door leading to his cousin's office. "Velma? Velma, you in here girl?" he called, before stepping into the room. He checked the luxurious washroom at the rear of the office. "Damn, I guess I'll have to go hunt her down," he told Selena, while slapping his hands to his sides in frustration.

"Don't worry about it," Selena said, taking in her impressive surroundings as she walked farther into the room. "You think Velma will mind if I use her phone?"

"Hell no. Go 'head," Harry urged, waving his hand. In the next second, he had disappeared out the door.

Selena crossed the thick white carpet covering the spacious office. She perched on the edge of the desk, unconscious of how high her flaring white skirt rode over her thighs. She dialed the digits and, after a few rings, a rushed voice answered the call.

"Reigning Queens magazine. Selena Witherspoon's office."

"Hey, Anna, it's me," Selena identified herself to her executive assistant, Anna Edwards.

"Hey! How's it goin'?!" Anna cried, eager to hear about her boss's trip.

That was all the encouragement Selena needed. "Girl, I truly believe this is one of the best ideas I've ever had."

Anna giggled. "Well, I'll take that to mean that everything's going great."

"Anna, this Miami office is gonna be so incredible. I can't wait to get it off the ground."

"Well, the rest of the staff will be down in a day or two to help set things in motion."

"Is Carla coming down with them too?" Selena asked, referring to her managing editor, Carla George.

"Yeah, she'll be with them," Anna assured Selena. "I take it you've found some good prospects for those layouts we're so famous for?"

Selena couldn't prevent the tiny scream of excitement that slipped past her lips. "Anna, girl! I wish you could be down here with us. The men . . . Honey, the gorgeous creatures I've seen since I've been down here. And that's just *inside* the hotel."

"Stop it!"

Selena laughed. "I swear to you I am not lying!"

"Nooo, Selena, stop before I jump through this phone to see for myself!" Anna warned, knowing what an eye Selena had for gorgeous men.

Selena was most certainly enjoying her conversation. She hadn't even noticed the office door opening.

Darius's slanting gaze narrowed a bit more when it landed upon the luscious sight atop Velma Morris's desk. He finished his drink and took in every inch of the voluptuous beauty on the phone. His intimate appraisal began at the tips of her strappy black heels, moving over the lush, sensual length of her legs and thighs, the curve of her derriere, the tiny waist, and an outstanding pair of breasts. His wickedly seductive smile remained fixed as he took in her very lovely face and hair. The sexy smirk he wore threatened to become a full-blown grin, once he caught on to her conversation.

"I tell ya, Anna, if you weren't pregnant, not to mention a happily married woman, you could come down here and have yourself a ball," Selena taunted, tossing back her head as she laughed uncontrollably.

Darius chose that moment to make his presense known. He stepped farther into the room and set his beaded glass on an end table. The clatter caught Selena's attention and she whipped her head in the direction of the sound.

Seeing the tall, dark giant across the room rendered her

speechless. Her lips parted in surprise and mild embarrassment as the phone almost slipped from her weakened grip.

"Selena?" Anna called. "Selena? Somethin' wrong?"

Selena could only stare at the magnificent dark male not ten
feet away. Her lovely eyes traced every inch of his devastating
frame and she almost gasped at the stab of arousal she felt
simply by looking at him.

Meanwhile, Darius allowed himself to take an even closer
look at the caramel-complexioned beauty. When the devilish
smirk reappeared on his gorgeous face and his softly suggestive stare connected with hers, Selena felt her lashes flutter.
She willed herself to heighten her self-restraint.

Remembering Anna on the other end of the line, she
pressed the phone to her ear. "Sweetie, let me call you back,"
she whispered, impressed by how calm she sounded.

Darius trailed one finger across his mustache and nodded
toward the phone. "I didn't mean to interrupt your call."

Slowly, Selena pulled her hazel gaze away from his mouth
and looked into his deep brown eyes. "Don't worry about it,"
she said, punctuating the statement with a lazy shrug.

Darius leaned against the cream-colored wall, hiding his
hands inside his pockets. "It sounded like a very good conversation."

"It was only business," she explained, the deep sound rumbling from his throat producing chills along her spine.

"I wish my business was so much fun," he complained.

Selena allowed the soft inviting smile to tug at her mouth. Before she could say anything more, Harry returned with Velma.

"Selena!" she cried, rushing toward the stunning younger
woman.

Selena held her arms open wide. "Lookin' good, girl!" she
said, just as excited.

Velma shook her head, her long ponytail swinging merrily.
"I can't believe you came all the way down here just for
Harry's show."

"Hey!" a wounded Harry called from across the room.

Selena laughed. "Well, I'm also down here to start a new magazine."

"*Another* one?" Velma asked, completely surprised and impressed.

"Well, a branch to the one in Manhattan," Selena clarified, watching the woman nod.

Meanwhile, Harry had caught sight of the tall, intense-looking man leaning near the wall. Of course, his interest was piqued. "Velma? Who's your friend?" he inquired with deliberate slowness.

Velma smiled, hurrying over to Darius and bringing him to the center of the room. "Darius McClellan, this is my cousin Harold Morris I mentioned earlier. And I'm sure you've already been introduced to Selena," she surmised.

Selena felt her heart drop right to her stomach when the man cast his penetrating cocoa gaze in her direction.

"Mmm-mmm," he corrected Velma, slowly shaking his head.

Velma didn't seem to notice the electricity crackling between Selena and Darius as she continued the introductions.

Darius had taken Selena's hand in a light, friendly hold. Still, she could feel the power surging in the simple touch.

"Darius owns a huge security firm in Brooklyn," Velma explained. "I've been having a few concerns here at the hotel and asked if he'd come down and give me a hand," she told Harry, before refocusing her attention on Selena. "Are you finding everything okay with the hotel, girl?"

Selena ordered herself to stop drooling over Darius and fixed Velma with a refreshing smile. "Everything's just fine, but . . . what I wanna know is, have you started subscribing to my magazine yet?" she teased.

The blood rushed to Velma's cheeks at the mention of the sexy magazine. "I, uh, still pick it up from the newsstand every month," she admitted.

Selena tossed a silky brown lock of hair across her shoulder. "Well." She sighed. "I tell ya, girl, I could probably get layouts for the next six months from this hotel alone."

"You've seen *that* many prospects?" Velma asked, her eyes wide.

Once again, Selena's seductive gaze came to rest on Darius. "Oh yes," she cooly assured the woman. "But anyway, duty calls," she announced, ordering herself not to lose herself in Darius's eyes again. "I only wanted to stop by and say hello."

"Anytime," Velma said as she fell in step next to Selena. "Don't be a stranger while you're here," she playfully ordered when they approached the door.

"Oh, don't even worry about that," Selena countered, before turning to Darius. "It was nice meeting you." She spoke in a soft voice, placing her hand in his.

"I assure you the feeling is mutual," Darius told her, smiling as he watched her eyes trace his mouth.

With effort, Selena pulled her gaze away. "Harry, we'll, uh, get together later," she promised her friend. All the while Darius still held her hand, his strong fingers caressing her palm so lightly the touch could have been imagined.

"I'll give you a call," Harry was saying.

Selena found it difficult to focus on the words, though. Turning back to Darius, she reluctantly extracted her hand from his and left him with a lingering stare before she walked away.

Darius's mouth curved into a deeper smile, his coffee gaze appraising Selena's derriere pressing against the airy fabric of her skirt. He sighed, finding himself regretting the fact that she was leaving, and went to take a seat on one of the suede office sofas.

Harry had stepped over to the bar and was preparing a stiff drink. No one noticed the change in Velma's demeanor as her eyes shifted from Darius to the door Selena had just exited through.

Two

Max Richardson downed a bit of the gin and cranberry juice he'd ordered, then smiled as though he was quite pleased with himself. "It was so smart of me to come on down a few days ahead of the team," he said.

Darius chuckled. "You sound happy about it, dog. *Too* happy. I was under the impression you wanted to get a head start on all the work we got ahead of us," he told his right-hand man.

Max snapped his fingers. "That too," he replied with a grimace.

"Hmph."

"Man, what is it with you? I know even a workaholic like you can't turn a blind eye to all the dimes runnin' around this hotel."

"No, I can't. Never said I wasn't gonna look. No harm in lookin'," he said in a resolved tone.

"D man, I know you ain't gonna deny yourself a *little* flirtation while you're down here?"

Darius swirled the Courvoisier in the glass he held. "I got every intention of denying myself," he grumbled.

Max's wide grin brought to life the dimples in his cheeks. "You know you ain't down here to find Mrs. D. McClellan?"

"You're right, I'm down here to work."

"And have a good time," Max interjected. "Man, enjoy yourself. If anybody deserves to, it's you."

Darius raised his glass in the gesture of a mock toast. "'Preciate it, man."

"Hell," Max continued, "hard-nosed New Yorkers like us rarely get time to enjoy such lushness and I'm definitely gonna take advantage."

Darius's rich, honest laughter turned more than a few heads. "Man, I never knew you were such a playa."

"That's 'cause I'm always workin', brotha," Max countered with another raise of his stout glass. He took a sip, eyeing Darius closely. "Seriously, though, this decision to ward off women got anything to do with Tenike Harris?"

Darius tensed visibly at the unwelcomed memories the name evoked. "I'm not warding off women," he argued.

"But it does have something to do with her?"

"It's a dead issue," Darius snapped, tapping his fingers on the glass table. "A *long*-dead issue."

"That still affects your personal life."

"Max—"

"And the cynical way you look at every woman you've met since that whole drama."

"These are the times I wish I didn't know you so long."

"Hmph." Max smirked. "But you do, and I know what all that crap put you through. I don't want to see you let it bring you down . . . and I know it has been."

"Oh?" Darius prompted, with a raised eyebrow. "You know this, huh?" he probed, signaling the waiter for another drink.

Max wasn't a bit put off by his friend's less than warm attitude. "D, it's no secret you're known to be the 'hit it and quit it' type. For lack of better phrasing, of course."

"So are you. So are most of the brothas we know."

Max chuckled, looking around for the waiter. "Well, at least we do *promise* to call the next day."

Darius's lips twitched under his mustache in a gesture of distaste. "It's all in your approach," he explained. "I believe in being direct. They know what it's all about for me, so there're no misunderstandings."

"And you don't get tired of that, man?" Max asked, shaking his head in disbelief when Darius shrugged. "After all this time," he continued, "you got all this success and no one to enjoy it with."

Darius laughed at what he saw to be a tired perception. "I enjoy my success *more* because I don't have to worry about pleasing a woman who can't appreciate what I went through to get it."

Max could tell how deeply Darius was affected, in spite of his lighthearted expression. "Sorry, man."

"Forget it. I didn't mean to get so emotional there. It's just that I like my life despite what everybody else thinks. There's no drama and best of all, no nasty secrets to come bite me when I least expect it."

Selena gave herself the once-over through the mirrored panels of the elevator. A satisfied smile crossed her lips as she approved her choice of attire for the evening. The black jump-suit hugged her curves in the most adoring manner. A mass of straps crisscrossed over the back of the outfit, offering tantalizing glimpses of her flawless light caramel skin.

The doors swished open and Selena hurried out. Moving too quickly, she slammed right into the stone wall that was Darius McClellan's chest. Before she could steady herself, his large hands rose to cup her hips.

"I'm sorry," she whispered, her small hands resting against the lapels of his wine-colored jacket.

"No problem," Darius assured her, a dimple appearing near the corner of his mouth when he smiled.

Selena could barely think, as she stood there staring up into his incredibly gorgeous face. All she could really focus on were his fingers teasing her skin beneath the straps of her suit.

"So where are you off to?" he inquired, as though there were nothing out of the ordinary about him holding her so possessively.

Selena marveled at how wonderful his voice felt as it rumbled through his chest to vibrate against hers. "I'm meeting Harry for drinks," she explained.

Darius stood there with his strong fingers laced behind her back. For a moment or two, he stood gnawing the inside of his jaw. When his head dipped a bit closer to hers, Selena was certain he was about to kiss her.

"Listen—"

"Darius! Darius!" Velma called from somewhere down the hall, interrupting Darius before he could complete his sentence.

His long lashes shielded his eyes briefly, and then he was looking down the hall. "Yeah, Velma?" he called.

Velma noticed Darius and Selena in the snug embrace, but pretended not to. She chose to deliver her message from her end of the long, deserted corridor. "Max and Jerry need to see you. They say it's important," she announced, waiting for him to join her.

Selena, who was enjoying the scent of Darius's cologne, finally looked up at him. When she tugged at the knot in his gray tie, she recaptured his attention. Darius reluctantly relinquished his hold on her. His soothing brown gaze remained riveted on her face.

Selena cleared her throat and stepped away from him. She attempted to still her hands from shaking by smoothing them across her hips. She turned to leave, waving to Velma before heading on down the corridor.

Darius muttered a hushed curse as he watched her leave.

"No, thanks, but maybe later," Selena said, smiling sympathetically at the fifth man who had asked her to dance.

Just then, Harry was returning to their table with the drinks. He frowned, placing a Long Island iced tea before Selena. "Since when do you turn down offers to dance?" he inquired.

Selena toyed with the gold chain around her neck. "Just not in the mood, I guess." She sighed.

"Hmph," Harry said, taking a sip of his champagne cocktail. "I'll bet you're in the mood for all those free drinks you get after dancing with these muthas," he guessed, rousing Selena's laughter. A knowing look crept across his handsome face then as he studied her more closely. "So . . . what do you think about Darius McClellan?"

Selena's eyes narrowed in suspicion and surprise. Immediately, she was on the defensive. "Why are you asking me about him?" she snapped.

Harry's mouth fell open at the blunt reply. His dark gaze was knowing as he watched her.

"I'm sorry, I'm sorry," Selena said, realizing how edgy she was.

The knowing look on Harry's face intensified as he leaned across the small round glass table they shared. "I only wanted to know what you thought of him."

"I think the same thing that *you,* and every other *woman* who ever met him, thinks," she retorted, toying with a lock of her hair.

Harry's gaze turned expectant when she said nothing further. Once it was obvious Selena had no intentions of elaborating, he slammed his palm to the table. "And that is?" he insisted.

"Look, Harry," Selena drawled, "I think Darius is fine, sexy, and all . . . but that's all. I'm not looking to get involved right now."

"Who said anything about getting involved?" Harry asked, appearing completely honest.

"I know what you're getting at."

"Girl, what in the world is wrong with that?"

Selena waved her hands in the air. "I just don't need the aggravation right now."

"Selena, how long are you gonna fool yourself into believing the single life is for you?"

"Why the hell are you even asking me that question, Harry, when you already know why?"

"Selena—"

"Harry, how long have you known me? You know how every last one of my relationships has turned out. They've all failed and now . . . I'm just sick of trying."

Harry's brows rose a notch as he leaned forward in his high stool. "So you *are* thinkin' about Darius McClellan on another level besides the most basic?"

This time, it was Selena's turn to sit with her mouth hanging open. Harry's statement had rendered her momentarily speechless. "I can't believe this, I just met the man and already you're trying to marry me off to him."

Harry propped his chin against his palm and regarded his friend with probing eyes. "I didn't say a thing about marriage, but there is an obvious chemistry between y'all and I just figured . . ."

"What?" Selena spat, her lovely face marred with a fierce glare. "What did you figure, Harry? That I'd just sleep with him? Thanks."

Immediately, Harry reached across the table and took Selena by the hands before she could pull them beneath the table. "Love, I'm sorry and . . . I didn't mean to imply that. I know you hate it when people think that way about you."

Selena shook her head. "Harry, I'm no saint. There are things I'll always regret. . . . Just forget it," she decided, unable to look her friend in the face.

Harry wouldn't let it go. "You've just been hurt so much and I hate to see you let it—"

"Now hold on, Harry," she ordered and tugged her hands free of his. "I'm not carrying around any old baggage here. I'm just not in the market for any *new* baggage."

"But there was a spark between you and the brotha."

Selena rolled her eyes before fixing Harry with an exasperated look. "I'll admit it, all right? There was a definite attraction toward your cousin's gorgeous security specialist," she confided, her expression turning serious. "It was so strong it almost scared me, but I think it had more to do with the fact that work has been my man for the last two years. It's been a while since I met anyone who . . ."

"Curled your toes by doing little more than looking your way?"

Selena couldn't help laughing at the summation. "Still, Harry . . ."

"Yes?" he drawled, sipping on his drink.

Selena gave a quick shrug. "That quick meeting was enough to tell me that Darius McClellan is not a man who would or could tolerate a relationship with a woman with a busy life like mine."

"Love, is there anyone out there who could *totally* tolerate it?" Harry asked, his tone as sarcastic as his expression.

"I doubt it," she confirmed. "There're very few people in this world who can truly accept a person as he is."

"All right, guys, let's get this thing started," Darius announced, standing before the table of men. He'd called the breakfast meeting to order. The team from his office in Brooklyn had arrived in Miami the night before.

"Now our client is Velma Morris. She's the owner of this hotel. She's afraid that her ex-husband is trying to sabotage the place."

"Has he threatened her?" Kevin Amons, a captain for McClellan Securities asked.

Darius nodded. "She says he has, but hasn't put anything into action yet. He's a powerful guy down here, responsible for a lot of the shopping centers in this area of the city. We're expecting a lot of traffic down here in the next couple of weeks, so we really gotta be on top of things."

"You got that right, D," Hamilton Adams, another captain, commented, taking a look around the impressive restaurant. "This is a big son of a bitch," he noted.

A round of laughter rose from the table over Ham's statement. The table full of well-dressed, handsome black men drew several stares from everyone who entered the dining room.

Chief Captain Maurice Starks leaned back in his seat and enjoyed the view. "Can y'all imagine all the honeys that must be up in this piece?" he asked.

"Just remember what you're here for," Darius advised. He tried to sound firm, but was unable to stop a smile from tugging at his gorgeous mouth.

"Oh, I know what I'm here for," Maurice assured his boss. "But you can't help being flattered by all the stares we're getting. Look at this, man."

"Hell, dog, that's just because we're dressed up," McClellan Securities Vice President, Max Richardson commented with a lazy chuckle.

"D, are we gonna have to keep up this three-piece-suit routine for the entire trip?" Stiney Carlyle, assistant to the chief captain, asked.

Darius sighed and smoothed his fingers across his mustache. "I think it's important during most of the events, but on your own time and in meetings like this, it won't be necessary."

"Good Lord," Max breathed.

Darius looked over at his friend; then, following the line of his gaze, he saw what had captured his colleague's interest. Watching Selena Witherspoon as she entered the restaurant, he almost uttered the same phrase.

Selena stepped into the elegant dining room looking breezy and lovely in a figure-flattering peach empire-waisted dress with a flaring hemline and capped sleeves. The frock emphasized her full bottom, tiny waist, and very full breasts. She'd captured the attention of every man who worked for McClellan Securities, including the boss himself.

Selena smoothed her hands across the dress as she rushed over to the maitre d'. "Milt? Please tell me you have a table for me and Joni?" she begged.

Milton Lyles smiled at the unease on her face and nodded. "Look around at this place," he urged, gesturing toward the barely filled dining room. "Where's the other half of the team?"

Selena waved her hand across her shoulder. "Oh, she'll be down in a second," she explained, referring to her assistant Joni Sams.

Milton nodded and reached for a couple of menus. "Well, I not only have a table for you, but I'd be pleased to show you there," he said, motioning for Selena to take his arm.

She laughed at his galantry, the slight gesture causing the curls to dangle from her high ponytail and bob uncontrollably. Placing her hand in the crook of Milton's arm, she allowed him to lead the way. The day was just beginning and the restaurant had not reached a fraction of its capacity. The lack of bodies made it easier for Selena to spot the table of onlookers following her every move.

Lowering her lashes demurely, she tilted her head toward her escort. "Milt, I see someone I'd like to speak with. Could we stop by that big round table over there?"

Milt responded with a knowing grin. "Why am I not surprised that it's filled with men?"

"I don't know . . ." she drawled, flattering Milton with a lingering look.

"Oh, please, everybody sit down," Selena was urging the group who stood as she and Milton approached the table. "Good morning," she whispered to Darius as her gaze moved over his devastating length.

"Morning," Darius greeted, his own provocative stare taking a leisurely appraisal of her curves.

"Aren't you gonna introduce us, boss?" Cameron Davenport, assistant V.P., asked, his eyes twinkling with mischief.

Darius, who had remained standing, waved his hand toward his team. He introduced Selena to the seven men and fought to smother his grimace over their eagerness to shake hands with her.

"Nice to meet you all," she was saying, smiling when they enthusiastically returned the sentiment. Her hazel gaze settled upon Darius once more. She left him with a cool smile before turning to Milton and allowing him to escort her from the table.

The team watched her walk across the dining room. There wasn't one who hadn't been captivated by her refreshing confidence and the undeniable sensuality that seemed to float around her.

"Damn," Team Captain Jesse Phelps muttered as he watched Selena easing into the chair Milton held for her.

"She is fine as hell," Co-Captain Owen Nellus chimed in, while shaking his head in disbelief. His colleagues fully agreed.

"D, if there's nothin' else we need to discuss right now, I need to go take a cold shower," Curtis Gordon, apprentice to the team captains, announced, pulling the tie free of his collar.

"I second that," someone called.

Darius laughed. "That's all for now. Later we'll meet to discuss strategies and take a tour of the hotel."

The group quickly filtered out of the restaurant, no one wanting their workaholic boss to remember something else they needed to cover. Darius stood there gathering his papers, then turned his head and watched Selena getting settled at her table. He finished collecting his things, then headed in her direction. The confident smirk tugging at his mouth added something more alluring to his already devastating features.

As he approached, Darius couldn't help admiring her appearance. To say she was beautiful again would simply be stating the obvious. Her petite lovliness reminded him of a child's doll. He wondered if her curls were as soft as they appeared. She had a natural look that was instantly provocative. Still, her appeal went deeper than that. Much deeper. There was something true about her—something open—he couldn't quite grasp what held his interest so intently. Although he'd taken a vow to distance himself from any potentially serious involvements, he felt no hesitation in wanting to get to know her better.

Selena had just taken a small sip of her apple juice when she noticed Darius walking up to her table. In an unconscious gesture, she smoothed her hands across her legs in an effort to still their nervous movements.

Once Darius stopped before her, Selena felt her eyes lowering to once again appraise his form. She studied the long length of his legs beneath the crisp, perfectly tailored legs of his trousers, the strong arms that had held her so gently the night before, his lean waist, and the broad, unyielding chest. The mocha-colored, three-piece suit only enhanced the definition of his chiseled form. Clearing her throat, Selena finally let her hazel stare meet his chocolate one.

Darius tapped his black portfolio to the table and lowered his gaze. "I want you to know that you just ended a very productive meeting," he shared, his voice deep and relaxing.

Selena's eyes widened. "How?"

"My team took one look at you and had to head for the showers. Literally," he explained, his incredible eyes focusing on the pout of her lips.

The statement caused Selena to laugh unexpectedly. She stopped abruptly, however, when she noticed the intensity of Darius's stare.

"Are you eating alone?" he asked, even as he pulled a chair away and took a seat.

Selena, focusing on the ease with which he angled his tall frame into the chair, took a moment to answer. "No . . . no, I'm waiting for my assistant."

"Mmm . . ." He gestured, nodding as his long lashes closed over his bedroom eyes. "I bet I can guess how this 'assistant' looks."

Selena folded her hands in front of her and fixed him with an expectant look.

"He moonlights as a dancer for Chippendales?" Darius

teased, his gorgeous smile reappearing when her laughter touched his ears.

The intensity of his stare, however, belied the smile and Selena apologized for laughing.

Darius simply shook his head. "No problem. I like the sound," he assured her.

Selena wiped a tear from the corner of her eye. "For your information, my assistant is a young woman, twenty-two years old and about to graduate from college."

Darius snapped his fingers and winced playfully. "Damn, and I thought I had you pegged as a woman who surrounded herself with nothing but men."

Selena quickly masked her unease at his observation with a naughty look. She closed her eyes as though she were conjuring up an idea. When she opened them and focused a dreamy gaze toward the ceiling, Darius clenched his fist in order to resist touching her.

"That sounds very nice," she finally admitted, enjoying the potency of his charm. "So . . . why would you think that about me?" she heard herself asking.

Darius tugged on the gray silk tie, leaving it to hang loosely around his neck. "Velma told me you run your own magazine?"

"That's right," Selena chimed in a proud manner.

"Well, I'm sure you don't use cover-to-cover talkin' about fashion or hair?"

"Your ears aren't deceiving you," she confirmed, the natural arch of her brows rising a notch. "Did you pick that up from what Velma told you?" she teased.

"I picked that up from the conversation I overheard yesterday," he confided, tapping a finger against his mustache.

Selena pressed her lips together as she recalled the conversation. "Well, as I said, your ears didn't deceive you," she replied, almost bursting into laughter again.

"My magazine is geared toward black women but it's filled with handsome men."

Darius tapped his strong fingers along the white tablecloth. "I take it you weren't satisfied with what the other magazines had to offer?"

Selena threw her hands in the air. "Well, I'll give props to those publications, but even *they* fall short when it comes to black men."

"And by that you mean?" Darius asked, his lips twitching slightly in acknowledgment of her unconsciously suggestive comment.

Selena recognized the pun and smiled in spite of herself. "There never are enough black men featured in them," she clarified.

A wolfish grin spread across Darius's handsome face. "So you're here to flush 'em out?"

"I am," Selena declared without hesitation. "'Cause they're out there. Take your associates, for instance."

Darius frowned. "What about them?"

"All wonderful prospects for possible spreads," she said with a nonchalant shrug.

Darius massaged the bridge of his nose. "I tell ya, those heads don't need to get any bigger than they already are. So I won't be passing your views on to them," he decided, joining in when Selena laughed. "Is that why you do it?" he asked.

A tiny sigh passed her lips as her hazel gaze flitted around the restaurant. "Well . . . yeah. That and the fact that black women need to see what's out there," she said, enjoying the look of surprise that appeared on his gorgeous face. "We hear all the time that all our good men are married, gay, or in prison, so my magazine features handsome, intelligent black men for them to look at and dream about."

"Are you speaking for yourself?" he queried, his seductive brown eyes resting momentarily upon the cleft between her full breasts.

Selena noticed the direction of his gaze and smiled. "I never have trouble putting faces to my fantasies," she assured him, while silently ordering herself to curtail her honesty.

"You fantasize a lot?" he asked in a soft, coaxing manner.

"Only when I'm trying to figure out how to get something I want badly," she answered just as softly.

The look in her eyes left no doubt in Darius's mind as to what she was talking about. Just then, something caught her eye across the dining room and she waved.

Darius followed the gesture and noticed a petite young woman heading toward them. "This is your assistant," he guessed, glancing at Selena.

"It is," she confirmed, watching as he stood and tapped the portfolio on the table.

"I'll leave you to your business then."

Selena pretended to pout. "Shoot, and I didn't even get the chance to ask you any questions."

Darius's gaze narrowed and he shrugged while pushing one hand into his pocket. "If you let me take you to dinner tonight, you can ask me whatever you like."

Selena nodded, pretending to ponder his proposal. "That sounds like a nice idea," she said after commanding herself not to scream the word *yes*.

Darius nodded and smiled as though he knew she would accept his offer. "I'll call you later," he promised, reaching out to squeeze her shoulder when he passed her chair.

Joni's eyes widened at the sight of the tall, chocolate-dipped male leaving her boss's table.

"You all right, Selena?" she tentatively inquired.

Selena could only shake her head in response.

"Will you just get the hell off my phone and stop callin' me!" Velma cried into the receiver, running a shaking hand through her hair as she paced her office.

"What the hell are *you* so upset about when it's my name you're crushin'?" Charles Herbert's mellow voice rose over the line.

Velma sucked her teeth. "I don't know where you got that

idea. I don't even want to hear your name, much less waste my time tryin' to trash it!" she retorted.

"Cut the crap, V!" Charles demanded, threatening to break his phone receiver in half. "Why'd you bring Darius McClellan down here from New York? As if I didn't know already!" he added.

Velma frowned. "What's that supposed to mean?"

"I haven't forgotten how caught up you still are about your ex," Charles drawled.

"That was a long time ago and Darius is only here on business."

"What business?"

Velma offered no reply.

"Mmm-hmm," Charles said. "Well, I'll take that to mean two things, V. One, you're tryin' to pin something on me, and two, you're probably tryin' to hop back in the sack with McClellan."

"You dirty son of a bitch!" Velma spat, almost too angry to express the words. "We're just friends," she added, forcing herself to sound calm.

Charles muttered a curse. "I guess I don't need to remind you that your feelings for Darius McClellan were one of the things wrong with our marriage."

Velma's laughter was harsh. "Hell, Charles, there were many things wrong with our marriage. It's just too damn bad I don't have time to run over the entire list with you!"

"I'm not sure what you're up to yet," he said, deciding not to press the issue further. "But don't think this helpless-victim act is gonna fool Darius or anyone else for long. I know what you're really like."

Velma slammed the phone down and leaned against her desk. Her eyes were wide with fear . . . and worry.

Three

"Now the rooms on this floor are mostly occupied by the executives and associates of some of the larger corporations."

Darius and his team followed Velma from the elevator and onto the tenth floor. She had chosen to conduct the hotel tour herself, and was leading the group along the wide glassed-in corridor.

"There are suites toward the opposite end, but the conference rooms are down here," she explained.

Max Richardson jotted something into the black notebook he carried, then glanced toward Velma. "Ms. Morris, you said these rooms are mostly occupied by the executives and their associates, but can anyone else use them?"

Velma sighed, smoothing her hands across the coral silk blouse she wore. "Well, we don't discriminate. However, the offices have to be reserved so we know who's using them at all times. We like to make sure we can accommodate everyone, so there are a couple of general meeting rooms that many organizations can use at the same time. Those don't have to be reserved."

"Could we see them?" Owen Nellus asked, and Velma was happy to lead the way.

"Joni, where did you find this one?" Selena asked, marveling over a photo she selected from the stack in the middle of the table.

Joni favored her boss with a smug smile. "He's a construction worker out of Maryland. His name and address are on the back. I've got the phone number in my private book."

Selena cast a knowing look in the younger woman's direction. "I bet you do," she whispered.

The two women had decided to conduct part two of their morning meeting in one of the general meeting rooms Velma had been discussing. It was afternoon and Selena and Joni had been studying photos for the past forty-five minutes.

Velma had just arrived with Darius and his team. The large meeting area was already filled to capacity, so the security experts parted ways to get a better look at the room. When McClellan Securities Captains Kevin Amos and Stiney Carlyle spotted Selena, they walked over.

Selena noticed Darius's associates approaching her table and her smile brightened.

"Hey, Selena."

"What's up, you guys?" she greeted. "Is it time for another meeting?"

Kevin waved his hand. "Nah, Velma's giving us a tour of the hotel."

Selena nodded slowly, then turned to Joni. "Guys, I'd like for you to meet my assistant Joni Sams. Joni, this is Stiney Carlyle and Kevin Amos."

"How'd you do that?" Kevin asked, appearing completely surprised as he glanced at Stiney.

Selena didn't pretend to misunderstand. "I never forget names . . . or faces," she assured them.

Kevin and Stiney were obviously impressed and admitted how flattered they were. Stiney noticed Selena several times as she glanced around the room. A knowing look spread across his handsome face.

"Darius is around here somewhere," he told Selena, smiling at the embarrassment coming to her lovely face.

"Really?" Selena managed, after clearing her throat.

Joni propped her chin in her palm and observed Selena.

"Was that the man at your table this morning?" she asked, watching her nod.

Kevin rubbed his hands together. "Well, we'll let you ladies get back to your meeting. We just wanted to stop by and speak," he said, nodding once again before he and Stiney walked away.

"Lord, Selena, they're all so gorgeous," Joni commented once the men had moved on.

"Mmm . . . tell me about it," Selena heartily agreed.

Kevin cast a quick glance back toward Selena's table and shook his head. "Man, I can't believe they live right in New York and I've never run into 'em."

Stiney chuckled at his colleague's naivete. "Man, don't you know how big New York is? Hell, you don't even run in circles with women who look like that."

"Forget you, man," Kevin muttered. "Say, did you see how D was starin' at Selena this morning?"

Stiney rolled his dark eyes toward the ceiling. "Man, can you blame him?"

"Not a bit. I only mentioned it because he was so quiet at breakfast after she walked in, and you know how rare that is."

Stiney shrugged. "Well, if D's been struck by lightning or some crap like that, it's about time. The man spends too much time workin' as it is."

"True, but you know the brotha's still a playa," Kevin pointed out, watching Stiney nod in agreement. "You know, I wonder if even a diehard ladies' man like D could handle that?" he asked, referring to Selena.

Stiney laughed. "That would be somethin' to see. I know you noticed the way she was checkin' him out."

"Yeah, I noticed. I was hoping she'd turn that look on me!"

The twosome walked on, unaware that their conversation was being overheard. Velma, who had been walking along behind Kevin and Stiney, heard their interesting words. Her dark gaze was pensive as it followed them to the other side of the conference room. She spotted Selena's table then and headed over to speak.

Joni and Selena were busy scheduling an informal itinerary for the remainder of the trip.

"Hi, Selena, Joni," Velma greeted, returning the smile the two women turned on her. The look in her eyes, though, belied the insincerity of the gesture.

"Hey, girl, how's it goin'?" Selena asked, pushing papers aside and urging Velma to take a seat.

"I should be asking you that," Velma countered, accepting the seat Selena had cleared. "Looks like you're buried in work."

"Ha! This is nothin'," Selena assured her, slapping at a curl that had fallen loose to dangle outside her ponytail. "Wait till tomorrow."

A slight frown wrinkled Velma's brow. "What's tomorrow?" she asked, shifting her gaze from Selena to Joni.

"The rest of our team is coming in from New York," Joni explained, as she pushed the rest of the photos into her briefcase.

"And you'd best believe I'll be swamped," Selena added. "Once the bulk of our work is out of the way, I'm gonna relax as much as possible while everything's still smooth."

"Well, are you free for dinner?" Velma asked, her smile still in place.

Selena looked apologetic. "Ah, Velma, I already made plans for this evening."

"Oh," she whispered with a brief nod. "With Harry?" she coolly inquired, attempting to downplay her intense interest.

"No . . . my plans aren't with Harry."

Velma watched Selena for a moment longer, then decided to cease her questioning. "Well, have a good time," she urged, her lips tightening as she spoke.

"Ms. Witherspoon?"

Selena looked up at the conference room attendant who'd approached the table.

"A note for you, ma'am," the young woman said as she extended a small white envelope.

Velma and Joni embarked upon another conversation while Selena tore into the message. Inside, she found a simple, white card. *A Picture is Worth a Thousand Words*. . . .

The note brought a smile to Selena's face. She flipped the card over before peeking inside the envelope, where she hoped to find the aforementioned picture.

"Everything okay, Selena?" Joni asked.

"Yeah." She sighed, replacing the card into the envelope. "One of our prosects believes a marketing gimmick will better his chances," she said, passing the envelope to Joni.

"Sounds like you ladies have your work cut out for you," Velma noted, before she sauntered off.

Melissa Foreman wiped a tear from her eye as she struggled to control her laughter over one of her boss's silly comments.

"You sure you're all right on that end?" Darius asked, teasing his executive assistant. "Maybe I should arrange for a temp to look out for you."

"Please," Melissa said, waving one hand above her head. "You know you're happy to have someone laugh at your tired jokes."

"I don't ever have problems in that area," Daris reminded her, knowing he didn't need to.

"Anyway." She sighed. "How long do you think you're gonna be in Miami?"

Darius reclined on one of the huge suede chairs in the conference room. "I know it'll be until after this party for the record company."

"Damn, you are so lucky to be goin' to that thing," Melissa said for the fifth time.

Darius only groaned.

"So, what's it like down there?" Melissa asked, full of curiosity about Miami.

"Well, the weather's nice," Darius said, his lips twitching a bit as he deliberately misunderstood the context of his assistant's question.

Melissa sucked her teeth. "Stop. You know what I mean."

"The women are unbelievable," he finally confirmed.

"Mmm, I'll take it that goes for the men as well?"

"No comment."

"So you say the women are unbelievable, eh? Should I suspect you're referring to one woman in particular?"

Darius sighed and shook his head. Melissa's instincts were always keen where his love life was concerned. Though she was years younger than her moody boss, Melissa Foreman had a sixth sense when something intense was going on in that area of his life.

"Sorry to disappoint you, Mel."

"Oh, please, when you left here, I told you you'd meet somebody special."

"Melissa—"

"Darius, all I wanna know is if you're willing to give it a shot."

"Good-*bye,* Melissa," Darius said, before he set the receiver in its cradle. He'd done a fine job of not answering her questions, though he could admit to himself that she'd been right. He had met someone. Whether or not he would give it a shot was something he didn't know.

Rising from the chair, Darius pressed one finger against his mustache and leaned against a long mahogany table. Starting another intimate relationship was a thought he hadn't seriously considered in a number of years. Though he may have been interested in the possiblity, he really didn't think he could stomach it. His previous relationship had affected several abilities necessary in order to have a successful relationship—one of those abilities being trust.

Since Tenike Harris, for Darius women had become a source of companionship and pleasure, not love or trust. Five years ago, he was struggling to get his small security firm off the ground. He had a girlfriend and Tenike didn't like being second best to anything, especially her boyfriend's business.

Darius had been so excited by his new venture, seeing Tenike was something he never had time for. It was quite obvious that he would eventually make something of the endeavor, so Tenike decided to hold on to her inevitable cash cow and assured him all was well.

Unfortunately, Tenike had found other ways and other men to occupy her time. Still, Darius, who had been trusting to a fault, tried not to believe what he suspected. Once it finally slapped him in the face, he knew he couldn't ignore it. The relationship came to a devastating end that had soured his outlook toward any future involvements.

His thoughts turned to Selena Witherspoon then and he sighed. She was so beautiful . . . not to mention full of life and sexier than anyone he had ever met. She'd captured his interest immediately and a part of his mind could imagine being in a relationship with her.

"Uh-uh! No way in hell," he voiced, trying wholeheartedly to convince himself. He was determined not to let this . . . infatuation go any further than a simple aquaintance. His lips curved into a doubtful smile as the decision racked his brain.

Moments later, he was shaking his head as if to clear it. He could hear Velma calling out to him from the doorway of the conference room. Slowly, he turned to face her.

"You all right?" she asked as she stepped farther into the room.

"I am, but are you?" he challenged, frowning at her expression. It was clear to him that she'd been worrying over some new situation.

Velma bowed her head and ambled over to lean against the opposite end of the table. Darius frowned more deeply and took her by the hand.

"What's wrong?" he asked, his warm brown eyes filling with concern.

"I got another call from Charles," she finally shared.

"When?"

"Earlier this morning."

"Why'd you wait so long to tell me?" he scolded, the concern in his eyes turning to aggravation.

Velma began to wring her hands as she stepped away from the table. "I'm sorry, but all we did was argue like we always do. It seemed harmless enough."

Darius ran one hand across the back of his head. "So why are you tellin' me now?" he asked with a low sigh.

Velma's expression relayed pure fear. "He called back just before lunch and he didn't seem so harmless then."

"Exactly what did he say?" Darius asked, pulling his tie loose.

"He wasn't specific," she quickly replied, staring out of the huge windows that skirted the far wall of the room. "Charles is too smart to put all his cards on the table right off the bat."

Darius closed his eyes for a second or two, then stood. "It'll be all right, Velma. The guy's probably just blowin' smoke." He hoped to reassure her.

Velma reached for his hand as he stepped past. She stared up at him for a full thirty seconds before speaking. "Would you have dinner with me tonight?" she blurted. "I'm such a wreck, but I know I have to keep myself together for my guests. It would really help if I had someone to lean on tonight."

Darius expelled a soft sigh, but he nodded anyway. He couldn't turn Velma down when she was going through something so unnerving. Unfortunately, making a date with her meant he couldn't keep his plans with Selena.

Harry hummed along with the beat of the slow groove vibrating through the speakers and tossed back the rest of his drink. "I tell ya, Selena, if there's one thing I've done since I been here, it's get my drink on."

Selena laughed and took another sip of her peach daiquiri.

She and Harry had decided to meet in her room for drinks that evening. "I know that's right," she agreed. "And it's even better when they deliver 'em right to your door."

"Hell yeah," Harry drawled. "I could do this all night."

"Me too," Selena declared, before she leaned forward to set her glass on the coffee table. "But I have a date."

Harry frowned. "What the hell is wrong with you?"

"Huh?"

"Hell, I figured you'd be swinging from the chandeliers over this one," he said.

"Mmm," Selena absently replied.

"Girl, what is your problem?" Harry asked, setting his empty shot glass on the table.

Selena shrugged and ran both hands through her loose curls. "I'm just not sure about this."

"It's dinner, not marriage."

Selena rolled her eyes toward him. "I know that, Harry, but we're gonna be here for quite a while and I already want to sleep with the man," she admitted.

"So?"

"Harry, you know how I get when I get caught up over a man and I know I'll get hurt," she predicted.

Harry massaged his eyes. "Girl, it's time for you to let go of that stuff."

"It's not that easy," she argued in a small voice.

"Damn, Selena, you don't even know where the hell Ramon Harmon is now and you shouldn't even care."

"I don't! But that doesn't mean I can forget what happened between us! We did a lot to hurt each other. I did just as much as he did."

Harry shook his head, his aggravation mounting. "Selena, you shouldn't forget, but you can't let that crap rule your life. Do you wanna live this way forever?"

Her full lips curved downward into a pout. "Nothin' wrong with the way I live."

Harry waved his hand in the air and leaned back in his

chair. "Screw it. I am *not* Montel, and givin' you advice is the last thing I feel like doin' tonight, so make your own decisions," he said, smoothing both hands across his bald head.

The two friends were silent for a while. Then Selena stood and slapped her hands to her sides.

"Okay, I'm gonna cancel the date," she announced.

Harry didn't bother to look at her. "You're a fool," he grumbled.

Selena heard him, but headed over to the phone anyway. It rang just as she reached for the receiver. "Hello?"

"Selena? It's Darius."

Her knees weakened, threatening to give beneath her. She took hold of the edge of the message desk and waited. "Darius," she whispered, glancing back at Harry.

He sighed heavily over the other end of the line. "Listen, Selena, I've got something to . . . handle so I'm going to have to cancel our date. I hate having to do this, but it's business."

Listening to his words rumble through the phone, Selena thought she could detect the slightest harshness beneath the soothing bass of his voice. She could tell that he hated to cancel as much as she hated to hear him do it. At once she regretted her decision to back out of their date.

"I promise to make it up to you," he was saying.

"It's okay, Darius, I understand. Really."

"I'll talk to you tomorrow."

"Good night," she whispered, gently setting the receiver down. Her nails tapped the white handset, and then she turned to Harry and spread her arms wide. "Wanna have dinner?" she asked her old friend.

Gibraldi's was one of Velma's favorite restaurants. The small Italian, family-owned establishment boasted a relaxing, darkly intimate atmosphere. It was as popular for its food as it was for the soothing aura that drew scores of people to its oceanfront location.

Velma had decided to treat Darius to an authentic Italian meal instead of the quick dinner he'd suggested they have in her hotel's restaurant.

"I'm sorry for asking you out on such short notice, Darius," she was apologizing once the waiter had placed their orders on the table.

Darius toyed with one of the forks on the table as he shrugged. "No problem," he replied, trying not to sound short with her. Selena and the date he had to break with her had been on his mind since he telephoned her earlier.

Velma lowered her gaze to her own side of the table. "Did you have to break an engagement?" she asked, certain that he did.

"Velma, I already told you it was no problem."

Finally, Velma rested her elbows on top of the table and leaned forward. "Listen, Darius, I know you're here on business. But I also know that this is Miami. There are a lot of women here and I know they haven't wasted any time making you aware of that."

Darius's sleek, dark brows rose interestedly. "What's that supposed to mean?"

"You know what I mean," Velma said, toying with her thick ponytail. "A handsome man, *sexy,* like you? I know the women have probably been dropping at your feet."

Darius laughed, revealing a perfect set of teeth to complement his double dimples. "You're goin' overboard, Velma."

"I don't think so," she said, glancing at him from beneath her lashes. "I'm surprised you didn't have a date tonight."

"Hmph," he grunted, leaning back in his chair. "Well . . . I did."

Velma snapped her fingers. "I knew it," she said, her expression turning serious. "I'm sorry you had to cancel. I wish I had known."

Darius cleared his throat. "Don't worry about it," he ordered, while shaking his head.

Velma, however, wasn't done with her subtle interrogation.

"So, uh, who was it with? Someone who works at the hotel? I know all the waitresses have been dying to get to know you. A guest, maybe?" she inquired.

Darius didn't appear to be growing suspicious by the barrage of questions. His thoughts were focused on Selena.

"It was with your cousin Harry's friend."

"Who? Selena?"

"Mmm-hmm . . . Selena."

Velma positioned her chin against her palm. "I know you hated to cancel that."

You'll never know how much, Darius confirmed below his breath. "We'll get together some other time," he decided.

"Hmm . . . it seems that every man who meets Selena Witherspoon wants to 'get together' with her," Velma noted, her eyes taking on a dreamy look as she stared off into space, and hoped her comment sounded flattering enough.

Darius smiled in spite of his souring mood. "How long have you known her?" he asked.

A discussion featuring Selena Witherspoon was not her ideal way to spend the evening. Still, Velma was pleased to finally have some time alone with Darius.

"I met Selena, oh, I guess about eight years ago," she recalled. "She and Harry started hangin' together in college. Harry's parents live down here too and sometimes Selena would come with him during their breaks and stuff."

"Is that when you met her?" Darius asked.

"Mmm-hmm. . . . Yeah, I was already married to Charles by then." She sighed.

Darius couldn't help noticing the tired frustration clouding her face. He knew she was thinking of her troubled marriage. "Were y'all ever happy?" he asked.

Velma replied with a slight wave, "For a while . . . I guess. I mean, we *did* get married. Charles was from a family with money and it was easy for him to sweep me off my feet. I think that's what I really fell in love with."

"So? What changed?"

"Charles," Velma answered without hesitation, then frowned. "Well . . . maybe not Charles. I mean, he never stopped buying me things, but maybe, after a while, I just wanted more."

"Such as?"

"His time, or maybe somethin' to do with *my* time."

"That's why he bought you the hotel?" Darius probed.

Velma's nod was slow and deliberate. "Mmm . . . that's when he bought me the hotel," she reminisced. "You know, Darius, Charles and I really had some great times. But, in spite of all that and everything I have, I wish I had never met him. I woulda been better off."

Darius sighed and tugged on his earlobe. "I hear ya."

Velma fixed him with a sheepish grin. "I'm sorry. I didn't mean to bring you down. I know you went through some stuff of your own."

"That, my friend, is an understatement," Darius assured her, the sensual curve of his mouth twisting into a cold smile. "What happened with me and Tenike was low, but I'm glad it happened, you know? It smartened me up."

Velma's smile was bittersweet. "I'm sorry, honey. You may be smarter, but I know it still hurt," she said. "Has there been anyone else since Miss Thang?"

"No, I don't have the nerve," he admitted. "That kind of soured me on relationships."

Velma chose not to comment on his outlook and grew silent. She reclined in her comfortable armchair and regarded him with an intense stare. Darius, meanwhile, allowed his chocolate stare to travel around the dim dining room. Though he hated having to cancel his plans with Selena, the mellow environment of the restaurant was doing wonders for his mood.

Velma sipped a small amount of the spring water. Two hands settled on her shoulders just as she placed her glass on the table.

"Harry! What're you doin' here?" she cried.

Harry's dark gaze settled briefly on Darius and he smiled. "I'm here with Selena," he announced.

"Well, where is she?" Velma asked, not seeing Selena anywhere in the room.

"She went to park the car," Harry said, turning to the waiter who had come to inform him that the table was prepared. "See y'all later," he called.

Just as Harry walked away, Darius spotted Selena entering the dining room with a double escort. He smirked, watching as she laughed and talked with the two waiters who towered over her small, curvaceous frame.

Selena glanced around the room, her hazel gaze searching for Harry. She did a double take when she spotted Velma at a table with Darius. Selena felt her knees weaken a bit as he sat there watching her with his warm, chocolate stare. Reflexively, she squeezed the arm of one of her escorts.

"Ms. Witherspoon, if you'll walk this way."

She managed to tune into the waiter's soft words and responded with a brief nod. Thankfully, Darius and Velma's table was on the other side of the room, so she didn't feel the need to walk over to greet them. It was for the best, she figured, since her heart was racing uncontrollably. She predicted she would only wind up making a fool of herself.

Harry's eyes widened appreciatively as he watched Selena's escorts bring her to the table. "Mmm . . . do you think I could get an escort like that when we leave?" he asked, once the two handsome Italians had walked on.

Selena rolled her eyes toward her friend. "I seriously doubt it."

Harry appeared disappointed, but quickly recovered. "Did you see Darius with Velma?" he asked.

Selena only nodded and pulled a menu before her face.

"And he told you it was business?" he smuggly inquired.

"That's what he said," Selena sang.

"You believe him?"

Selena groaned and slammed the menu to the table. "Why should I care?" she snapped. "After all, he *is* working for her."

Harry's dark eyes narrowed dangerously. "Don't even try it," he warned.

A deep furrow wrinkled Selena's brow. "Don't even try what?" she asked, completely innocent.

"You're steamin' over there."

"I am not."

"Admit it. You can't stand it that he turned you down."

Selena shook her head and concentrated on the raised pattern in the red tablecloth. "He didn't turn me down," she muttered.

Harry propped his cheek on the back of his hand. "So why are you out with me?"

"It was business, Harry!" she said, between clenched teeth.

"Yeah . . ." he drawled, rolling his eyes toward his cousin and Darius laughing at their table. "They look loaded down with work."

"Will you stop it?" she demanded, rapping her knuckles against the table. "What's wrong with you?"

"I'm just tryin' to get you to admit that you like the guy," he said, shrugging his broad shoulders as though the entire situation were of little importance.

"I like him, Harry. Are you satisfied?"

"And you're steamin' 'cause he canceled your date. Even if it was for . . . business?"

"Did it just slip your mind that I was about to call and cancel just as the phone rang?"

"But *you* didn't cancel on him. He canceled on you."

"And?"

Harry's dark brows rose a few notches. "And you're mad as hell. Admit it!"

Selena leaned forward, her light eyes shooting daggers into Harry's face. "Drop it. I don't want to waste my time talkin' about this all night."

Harry spread his hands out before him. "That's all right, you've answered me." He sighed.

Selena rolled her eyes and took a sip of ice water. When she glanced up to find Harry shaking his head and smiling, she felt the strongest urge to dash the remainder of the cold liquid into his lap.

Before she could carry out the plan, the waiter returned.

"I have a note for you, Ms. Witherspoon," he announced.

"I'm this close, Harry," she threatened, while opening the envelope the waiter handed her. *Soon all will be revealed.*

"What?" Harry called, noticing the soft smile curving her mouth.

"One of the guys trying to get into the debut issue," she said, setting aside the envelope. "He's marketing himself like crazy. This is his second note. He hasn't sent a photo, but these little blurbs are supposed to heighten our anticipation."

"You think he'll be worth the hype?"

"Well, if he's not, he's got a job in my promotions department. I think he'll reveal himself soon enough."

"You've got good taste in restaurants, girl." Darius sighed, tossing his napkin to the table.

Velma rubbed her hands together, pleased by the compliment and the fact that they'd had an uninterrupted meal. "Well, we'll have to do it again before you leave," she suggested.

"That sounds good," he agreed, reaching for his wallet. "You ready?"

"Mmm-hmm, but don't do that." She waved her hand toward his wallet. "It's on me."

"Uh-huh."

"Sweetie, you're already chargin' me an arm and a leg to do security here. This dinner isn't gonna make much difference," Velma insisted.

Darius watched her for a moment, his gorgeous brown eyes twinkling mischievously. "All right, I won't beg."

Velma signaled for the waiter and took care of the bill,
while Darius waited, his chocolate stare searched the dining
room for Selena. He found her across the room laughing with
Harry, and his gaze narrowed. He'd wanted to see her that
night. He knew he was breaking one of his solid rules: not to
be taken in simply by a lovely face and even lovelier body, but
he couldn't seem to prevent what was happening.

"Darius? Darius, are you ready?" Velma was asking.

"Hmm?"

"Ready?" she repeated, standing and watching him follow suit. "I guess we should go say good night?" she asked,
nodding in the direction of Harry and Selena's table.

Harry set his fork aside and sighed. "Well, looks like
you're gonna get your wish. Here he comes."

Selena frowned and glanced over her shoulder. She could
feel her heart dashing to her stomach and gave a noticeable
swallow.

"Calm down," Harry cautioned from across the table.

"Shut up," Selena growled, before smiling brightly at the
couple approaching the table. "Hi!" she greeted.

Velma smiled and patted Selena's hand. "Hey, girl, we just
wanted to say good night."

"We were just about to order dessert. Y'all wanna join us?"
Harry invited.

Selena noticed the devilish gleam in her friend's dark eyes.
"They probably have to get goin' Harry," she reminded him
through clenched teeth.

"Oh, we do," Velma said. "I've got so much to do and I
can't keep my top security man out all night."

Selena's cool stare met Darius's penetrating one and she
held her tea glass in a death grip. "Told you, Harry."

"Maybe some other time," Darius suggested, one corner of
his sensual mouth curving upward into a smile. The deep

dimples caught and held the attention of the two women watching him.

Of course, Velma didn't miss the electricity crackling between Darius and Selena. She cleared her throat and curled her hand around one of his solid biceps.

"We'll see you guys back at the hotel," she chimed, before whisking Darius out of the dining room.

"Ten."

Selena pulled her hazel gaze back to Harry and frowned. "'Scuse me?"

"I'll bet you ten dollars he'll be knocking on your door tonight."

Selena gave a nervous chuckle and waved her hand. "You are makin' way too much out of this."

Harry shrugged and returned his concentration to the remaining corner of his lasagne. "If you don't have ten dollars, all you had to do was say so," he murmured.

When Harry left Selena's hotel room after they returned from dinner, it was well past midnight. After such an exhausting day, however, Selena was still energized. She decided to wind down with a long shower, hoping it would relax her and offer an opportunity to think.

As the powerful spray of steamy water coursed over her skin, she allowed her thoughts to turn to Darius McClellan. What was it about him? she asked herself. True, he was tall, dark, gorgeous, and intelligent, but so were many men whom she knew. Yes, he did have charm, class, and money, but so did a lot of men she knew. Of course, she admitted that it was rare for her to meet one with so many attributes rolled into a single, well-built package. Then, there was that underlying tug of sexual attraction. Yes, she'd felt it before, but never had it been . . . so strong. Almost tangible. She could feel it every time he looked at her. The message those warm browns sent was unmistakable.

Shaking her head, Selena decided to put Darius out of her mind. She knew all too well how easy it was to lose sight of reality when a handsome man was involved. For her it had usually meant an open invitation to be hurt. Selena knew she could not allow her body to control her actions in a situation like this. These days, that sort of carelessness could prove fatal. Though she never took chances and always played it safe, she did not trust herself when it came to Darius McClellan.

Shutting off the shower spray, Selena hurried out of the spacious champagned-tiled stall. In the bedroom, she applied lotion before slipping into an empire-waisted, cocoa-colored nightie. The moment her head touched the pillows, she was asleep.

Darius debated whether it was too late to be waking Selena as he stood in the corridor outside her door. He felt he owed her some type of explanation for canceling their date even though he had told her it was business related. He could see the question in her eyes earlier that evening when she had walked into the restaurant and seen him there with Velma.

Leaning against the door, he wondered if he should even be making the effort. After all, he'd told himself time and time again that he was done with relationships. Especially with women like Selena. Exactly what type of woman was she? he asked himself, realizing he didn't even know the answer to that question. He knew what he saw on the outside though, and he liked it very much.

It couldn't hurt to get to know Selena Witherspoon a little better, he decided. They certainly didn't have to be a couple to do that. Smirking, he traced his neat mustache. Natural arrogance told him she wouldn't object. Still, Darius warned himself to keep his cool. As incredible as she was, he could easily envision having her in bed in a matter of days and he refused to allow the promise of that sort of involvement to rule his actions. Clearing his throat, he pulled one hand from the pocket of his trousers and knocked.

The loud rapping on the door, woke Selena easily. She jerked from her slumber, a frown marring her face. She wasn't altogether certain that she'd been hearing knocking at such a late hour, but left the bed anyway. Pressing her hand to the loose ball of riotous curls atop her head, she stumbled toward the living room. When she looked through the peephole and saw Darius McClellan, her hand jerked off the knob as though it burned to touch. Now she was certain she'd been dreaming. She looked through the peephole again. No, he was actually there—this was no dream. She was wide awake and thought she looked a mess!

Selena heard determined rapping again as Darius knocked once more. Since she certainly didn't want him to think she wasn't in, she whipped open the door.

Darius's gorgeous brown eyes widened just slightly as he took in Selena's appearance. Her tousled hair and sexy sleepwear held his attention. His deep-set, slanting gaze narrowed as it traveled over her tiny, voluptuous body and he leaned against the doorjamb for support.

"Good evening," Selena whispered, as she cut her gaze away from his face. She could imagine the sight she must've made and wished she'd remained dressed awhile longer.

Darius tapped one finger to his chin and smiled. "Am I interrupting you and Harry?" he playfully drawled.

Selena pressed her lips together to keep from laughing. "Uh-uh, we finished about two hours ago," she replied, taking part in the teasing.

"I can tell," Darius whispered with a slow nod.

Selena's mouth fell open. "That was cold," she criticized, wagging a finger in his direction.

"Mmmm . . ." Darius gestured, caressing the light shadow forming on his jaw. "Unlike your bed, right?"

This time, Selena didn't bother to stifle her laughter. "Well, you've just answered my first question," she said, the natural arch of her brows rising a notch.

"What's that?" Darius asked, a slight frown coming to his handsome, dark face.

"If you had a sense of humor," Selena stated simply.

Darius couldn't keep his gorgeous smile from shining through. "Only when the joke is at someone else's expense," he smoothly confided.

Silence dominated the conversation after that point. Darius couldn't keep his delicious warm gaze from caressing Selena's chest. Her full breasts heaved slowly against the thin material of her attire, and with effort he managed to keep his stare from lingering.

"How long are you going to keep me in the hall?" he asked, pushing himself away from the doorjamb to tower over her.

Selena, lost in the sound of his voice, took a moment to respond. Finally, she stepped away from the doorway. "Sorry . . . come in," she invited, waving him inside.

The uncertainty Selena felt when she'd seen Darius earlier returned fully. She could feel the nerves churning in her stomach and reminded herself that he was just another man.

"I apologize for canceling out on you tonight," he was saying as she stepped farther into the living room.

"Oh, that's okay," she drawled, tossing her hands into the air.

Darius shook his head, signaling that he wasn't satisfied. "Uh-uh, Velma was in bad shape about everything that's goin' on with the hotel and she needed somebody to lean on. Canceling our date was the last thing I wanted to do, but I wouldn't have felt right leavin' her out there like that."

"Darius, will you stop? I'm fine about it. I don't hold any grudges about you canceling. It's forgotten," she tried to assure him.

A slow grin spread across his face as he took a seat on the arm of one of the wingback chairs. "Well, since you won't let me apologize, will you let me try to take you out again?"

A tiny voice inside Selena's head screamed, *Yes!* Another, louder voice, warned her that a date would only make her more infatuated.

"All right, we can try this again," she heard her own voice saying as she accepted his offer.

Darius nodded, once again taking a leisurely appraisal of her lovely form.

"So, can I get you anything?" Selena offered, hoping to break through the tension filling the room. When Darius raised his eyes to hers, she realized how the question could have been misinterpreted. "Would you like something to drink?" she clarified.

"No, thank you."

Unsure of what to do with herself, Selena smoothed her small hands across her bare thighs while taking a seat on the sofa.

"So, what would you like to do?" Darius asked.

"'Scuse me?" she squeaked.

Darius chuckled and shook his head. "On the date," he explained.

Selena grimaced. "What'd you have in mind?"

"Just dinner," he answered, with a shrug.

"Well, that's fine, just tell me when."

Darius tilted his head to the side and watched her. "You mean, you don't want to know where we're going?"

Again, Selena shook her head. "No, why?"

Darius chuckled. "Just to be sure you don't get all dressed up to go out for a burger or something like that," he teased.

Selena laughed as well. "I trust you."

The sexy, devilish grin that Darius revealed so easily warned her to rethink that statement. "You sure you want to do that?" he asked.

"Why shouldn't I?" she challenged, her low voice a bit shaky.

Darius watched her for a moment, then pushed himself off the edge of the chair. He walked over to where Selena sat perched on the couch and pulled her up. Immediately, she could feel herself melting against his chest. His strong embrace was snug around her waist, as he dipped his head and pressed his mouth against hers. The smooth yet firm texture of his lips was such a sweet surprise that Selena gasped. Accepting the opportunity, Darius slowly thrust his tongue into the darkness of her mouth.

"Darius . . ." she whispered during the kiss.

A deep sound was his only response as his large hands ventured beneath the flaring hemline of the nightie to cup her bottom. As though she were weightless, he pulled her high against his chest and settled her more snuggly against him.

Again, Selena gasped, feeling the rigid evidence of his manhood against her tummy. Breathing was barely an option, due to the tremendous force of the kiss. It was almost as if he were starved for her. Selena wound her arms about his strong neck and eagerly reciprocated the action. She relished the tingle of his mustache against the delicate skin above her lip. In response, she moved her legs and thighs up and down over the smooth material of his trousers.

Sadly, the pleasure was short-lived. Darius was releasing her mouth and pulling back to look at her.

"Does that answer your question?" he whispered, his coffee stare turning darker with arousal.

Selena had no idea what he was asking. She was too caught up in the kiss, still feeling his lips against hers, his tongue stroking the inside of her mouth . . .

"I'll pick you up here tomorrow at six," Darius said as he placed her back on the sofa.

Selena was still speechless as she watched him go. Her light eyes almost fluttered closed as she ordered herself to calm down. Not even one date and she was already completely drawn to him. Groaning, she buried her face in her hands.

Four

"Oooh, I'm so happy to see you guys!" Selena cried as she hugged the members of her executive staff. The group had just arrived in Miami and were obviously quite taken with the impressive city.

"Girrrl, this place is unbelievable!" *Reigning Queen* Senior Editor, Carla George shouted over the sound of the wind whipping around them.

"You mean, *you* haven't ever been down here?" Selena playfully asked, referring to Carla's reputation as a world traveler.

Carla shook her head in regret. "Nah, Miami has somehow escaped my travel plans," she said while hugging Selena.

"Mmm-hmm, I bet that won't happen again."

A skeptical look crept into Carla's green eyes. "I don't know, I'll have to see if you've been exaggerating about all the good-looking men down here."

Selena laughed and pushed a lock of her windblown hair behind her ear. "Hell, just take a look around!" she ordered, leading them all inside.

Carla and the rest of the group took a look at their surroundings. To say that Selena had been exaggerating would have been grossly unfair. The group of lovely young women appeared to be starstruck as they observed the sea of beautiful people filtering in and out of the hotel.

"Well?" Selena asked, propping one hand on her hip.

"Where'd you find this place?" Advertising Director, Monica Dees asked, smiling at a passing bellman.

"A friend of mine owns it."

Carla rolled her eyes toward the high ceiling. "Hmph, figures."

"Don't even try it. I'm only staying here because Harry suggested it."

Again, Carla rolled her eyes. "Hmph, figures," she repeated in an even more playful, sarcastic tone.

Selena laughed and pushed Carla's shoulder. "Stop. It's his cousin's place."

"Well, I know you don't have any complaints," Carla said.

"Are you crazy?" Selena blurted. "But if you guys are uncomfortable staying here—"

"Hush, Selena. Don't even let that come out of your mouth." Vice President Synthia Witherspoon ordered.

Selena giggled and looked over at her cousin Synthia. The two women were spitting images of eachother and always in agreement when it came to the opposite sex.

Again, however, Carla rolled her eyes. "Hmph, figures."

"Do you have jet lag or somethin'?" Selena asked, sending her friend a skeptical look.

"I never felt better. I just wanna know what's on the agenda so we can get to it."

Selena frowned. "Girl, what's the rush?"

"Hell, I wanna get this mess over with so I can get down to the beach. Can you imagine what's down there?"

Everyone laughed and Selena shook her head. "Hmph, figures," she said, repeating Carla's statement.

"Funny," was Carla's unamused response.

Selena rubbed her small hands together. "I made arrangements for us to have a business lunch on one of the patios. I think we can get started on the bulk of the work from there and then the rest of the trip can be focused more on . . . pleasure."

"Amen, the girl's finally thinking," someone commented.

"So, what time you wanna meet for lunch, Sel?" Synthia asked.

Selena glanced at her gold wristwatch. "Around one. We'll

meet at the front desk." She pointed to the huge mahogany desk directly in front of them. "You ladies can get your keys there and lounge a little beforehand," she suggested.

"Sounds good," Carla said with a nod. "All right, I'm out!" she added, following the others to the desk.

"Selena!" Joni called, hurrying over to where her boss stood with Synthia. "This was delivered to the front desk with the rest of the messages," she explained, handing Selena one of the familiar white envelopes.

"Hmm, maybe our mystery writer is finally ready to reveal himself," Selena decided as she tore into the small package. *College is the best time of your life.*

"What is it, girl?" Synthia asked.

"Yeah, Selena, what does it say?" Joni asked, noticing her boss's reaction.

"Strange," Selena admitted, tapping the white card against her palm, before handing it to her cousin.

"What's this about, Sel?" Synthia asked, while Joni peered over at the note. Both women listened as Selena explained.

"So why is this one so strange?" Synthia further inquired.

Selena tucked a few glossy tresses behind her ear. "Well, the first two notes gave me the impression this guy was tryin' to get a spot in the magazine and wanted to get our attention."

"But you're thinking differently now?" Joni guessed.

"Well, this one is just . . ." Selena trailed off, reaching for the note. "It's off the mark, doesn't follow somehow."

"You think it's something to be worried about?" Joni asked.

"Nah," Selena drawled, sliding the note into her leather tote. "Probably just some wild gimmick. After all, we *are* in Miami."

"And that reminds me, I have a meeting with one of our prospects," Joni announced.

Selena eyed the young woman with a look of playful suspicion. "You sound awful excited about this meeting."

"I swear it's business," Joni vowed, though obvious mischief played on her face. "But, you never know, we are in

Miami," she reiterated, laughing wildly with Selena and Synthia before she rushed off.

Selena waved off her assistant, then turned to her cousin, who had lagged behind. "What?" Selena finally asked, not caring for the knowing look on the woman's face.

"So who is he?"

A frown marred Selena's lovely light caramel face. "Who?"

"The man you've captivated down here," Synthia clarified.

"No one, why would you think that?"

Synthia toyed with the thin wavy brown braid that dangled outside her curly ponytail. "Honey, this is me, remember? You've been here over a week and I'll bet you've got your eyes set on somebody."

"Have you been talkin' to Harry?"

Synthia snapped her fingers. "I knew it."

"Listen, I've met a lot of men since I've been down here, but nobody for you to get excited over."

Synthia shook her head in regret. "Girl, how long will you hang on to that excuse?"

Selena shrugged her slender shoulders as though she were confused. "What excuse?"

"That you don't want another relationship? A real one this time."

"Ha! That's no excuse. I don't want another one."

"Selena . . ."

Selena knew exactly what, or who, Synthia was referring to. Still, she refused to let that unpleasantness interfere with business or . . . anything else while she was in Miami.

"You know, you're beginning to sound just like Harry."

Synthia shrugged. "We both know you very well."

"Mmm-hmm," Selena replied, unconvinced. "Then you should *both* know that women like me don't get the opportunity for a husband and family."

"Excuse me? Who made *that* rule?"

"It's just the way things turn out."

"Sel." Synthia sighed, fixing her cousin with a rueful look.

"You know you always cop out because you won't risk putting your feelings out there again."

"Hell, Synth, can you blame me?"

"You're just scared."

"I'm just honest. Synth, look at my track record," Selena pleaded with outstretched hands. "My track record with men *and* women. Have you ever wondered why I have a staff of women on my executive team?" she asked, watching her cousin shrug. "I've never had any close female friends. *You're* my cousin and Nelia, I've known her since nursery school, so she feels like family," she said, citing her best friend, Nelia Cannon. "Having a staff of women has been like having a circle of friends who share a common interest and who, more importantly, *like me.*"

Synthia took her cousin's hands and gave them a tiny shake. "They like you because you're a wonderful person."

Selena's eyes misted with tears as she looked out over the gorgeous view of the Atlantic in the distance. "I know . . . I know what you're sayin', Synth." she replied as though she were trying to convince herself. "But sometimes . . . I can't help thinking about those who may feel differently."

Synthia's brown gaze narrowed. "Sel, does this have anything to do with those notes you've been getting?"

"No." Selena was honest in her reply. "But it has caused me to think about some pretty foul stuff that's happened to me over the years."

"Then stop," Synthia ordered, cupping Selena's face in her palms. "Because the lady I see before me is one I'm proud to call my friend, my cousin, *and* my sister," she whispered in a fierce tone, before pulling Selena into a tight hug.

That afternoon, Selena and her team were seated at a long glass dining table on one of the oceanfront patios. The setting was beautiful. The sky, filled with the fluffiest white clouds, rivaled the ocean for its blue color. For the first five or six minutes of the meeting, the women simply sat there in awe of the magnificent picture before them. Soon, though, they managed to focus their attention on the business at hand.

The idea to have a huge working lunch appeared to be the right decision. The group accomplished a lot. Since the most tedious aspect of the new magazine seemed to be the financial matters, they were discussed first. Luckily, *Reigning Queens* had a top-notch investment and accounting team in New York. It had provided the executive staff with well-planned projections that were most satisfactory.

"These numbers are pretty impressive," *Reigning Queen* Marketing Assistant Samantha Aptman was saying.

"Very," Selena agreed.

"You think we can make a go of it?" Carla asked.

Selena sighed and leaned back in her chair. "Well, we far exceeded last year's projections. I know this is a new pub, but I believe its appeal will be high. I think we can do it."

"To *Reigning Queens*, Miami style!" Carla cheered, raising her champagne-filled glass.

Everyone followed Carla's gesture and clinked their glasses together.

Selena took a healthy sip from her glass and let the bubbles fizz beneath her tongue for a moment. Then she stood and rubbed her hands together. "Now, it's time for the fun stuff," she announced in a mischievous tone. "Joni," she called, nodding toward her assistant.

Joni gave a curt nod and stood as well. Pulling a thick envelope from her briefcase, she spilled dozens of photos in the middle of the table.

"Now, these are just a few of the contacts that we've made since we've been here," Selena informed her crew, watching the six women at the table as they raved over the pictures.

"Don't tell me these guys had photos already?" Synthia asked.

"Uh-uh, the hotel has a photo shop so I arranged for the guys we spoke with to go have a simple picture taken."

"I'll be damned," the magazine's head photographer, Sabrina Little, breathed as she studied the pictures.

Laura Sheets, her assistant, smiled slyly. "Are you impressed by the quality, Bri?"

Sabrina didn't pull her eyes away from the photos in her hands. "Mmm, yeah, the quality's good too," she murmured, smiling when she heard laughter around her.

"And you found all these guys in a week?" Monica Dees asked in disbelief.

Selena gave her advertising director a smug smile. "Mmm-hmm, some of the best Miami has to offer."

Carla sighed. "Mmm, I'll say, and you even got the phone numbers on the back. Good work."

Selena shook her head. "Don't even try it. These are for business, not your pleasure."

The discussion over the pictures continued and was most colorful. The women were so engrossed by the handsome men in the photos that they were oblivious of everything else. Unbeknownst to the table of beauties, Darius McClellan and his crew were gathering on the opposite end of the patio for their own meeting. The group had already caught sight of the women at the long table.

Like the rest of his crew, Darius couldn't keep his own chocolate gaze from snapping to the other side of the patio. He was focused solely on Selena, enjoying the way the wind whipped her thick hair as she rested her head against the back of her chair.

"Damn," Max Richardson whispered. "Remind me to take a trip to *Reigning Queens* magazine when we get back to New York."

A wolfish grin spread across Darius's handsome face as he nodded his approval.

"Man, why don't you get Selena to introduce us?" Chief Captain's Assistant Stiney Carlyle asked.

"Why me?" Darius replied, pretending to be confused.

Team Captain Jesse Phelps rolled his dark eyes toward the sky. "Aw, man, we have seen the way y'all look at each other."

Darius kept his gaze downcast. "You know what they say about wild imaginations," he grumbled.

"Whatever," Jesse retorted.

"Can we get down to business now?" Darius snapped, grimacing when he heard the chuckles around him.

"What's first?" Max finally inquired, when his laughter had subsided.

Darius cleared his throat and stood. "Well, we've got this fashion show in two days."

Co-Captain Owen Nellus frowned at the agenda he held in his hands. "Are you expecting any shake-ups?"

Darius sighed and ran a large hand over the back of his neck. "There shouldn't be, but Velma did say Charles is getting a little bit nastier."

"So, what's the plan?" Apprentice Curtis Gordon asked, watching Darius expectantly.

"Nothin' fancy," Darius decided. "Posts at every entrance and exit should be enough. We'll sweep the place beforehand just to make sure."

The crew spent the next several minutes going over the layout of the ballroom where the show would be held, as well as the surrounding areas. While his men were busy assigning posts, Darius scribbled a few words on an index card and handed it to a passing waiter.

"Okay, we'll meet in the morning in the main conference room to start on the cuts," Selena said.

"Oooh, do we have to?" Joni whined.

Selena nodded, her expression just as regretful. "I'm afraid so, we can't keep everyone, but we *can* put them away for future reference."

"Mmm . . . the *immediate* future."

"Be good, Carla," Selena warned when she heard her

friend's statement. She was about to adjourn the meeting when a waiter approached her. The handsome young man was all smiles as he handed her a folded index card. By the time he'd walked away, he was absolutely beaming from all the brash compliments he'd received.

"I can't take y'all anywhere," Selena muttered in mock aggravation as she watched everyone gathering their things. Settling back in her seat, she opened the small card. *I will see you tonight at six! I promise! D.*

The brief note wasn't very revealing, but it was enough to set Selena's heart racing in anticipation. Her hazel eyes scanned the note several times before a small frown clouded her face. She wondered how he knew she was there and gazed across the patio from behind her sunglasses. She spotted him at a long table similar to her own. From the looks of things it was a business meeting, judging from all the papers crowding the glass-top surface of the table. Darius was massaging his forehead as he gazed fixedly at something in a folder. The set look to his features made him appear even more devastating. Selena couldn't pull her eyes away.

A few of her associates noticed her unwavering stare and focused their attention in the same direction. Of course, the table full of attractive men brought dozens of comments from the group. Soon, the conversation was completely focused in that direction.

"You know any of them?" Carla asked, smiling at the fixed look on Selena's face.

Selena waved her hand and shrugged. "Yeah, but not very well," she said, clearing her throat.

"How?" Carla questioned, a smirk tugging at her full lips.

"What?"

"How?"

"Oh! Velma Morris, the owner of the hotel, that's her security team."

Carla's perfectly arched brows rose impressively. "Well,

well, maybe I *will* make a few more trips down here," she crooned.

"Well, before you make any reservations," Selena continued, raising one hand, "those guys are out of New York. Darius is just doin' a favor for Velma."

"Darius?"

Selena closed her eyes as she realized her mistake. "Synth—"

"So, I guess you know one of them pretty well?"

"We've met in passing," Selena hurriedly explained, hoping that would pacify her cousin. It didn't and soon she was sharing everything. "He asked me out," she blurted.

"I knew it," Synthia whispered, snapping her fingers.

"It's just *one* date, Synth."

"Mmm-hmm . . ."

Selena rolled her eyes and sighed. She'd tried to sound convincing, but obviously Synthia wasn't falling for it. Selena realized she wasn't convinced either.

On the other side of the patio, Darius appeared to be wrapping up his meeting. When they all stood and began gathering their things, Selena's gaze was helplessly drawn to Darius. Her long lashes almost fluttered closed as she recalled their heated encounter the night before. She'd been warning herself to play it cool, but that warning was proving to be very difficult to obey. If Darius hadn't pulled away last night, she was sure they would have made love. No . . . they would've had sex. The only thing that could possibly come from the involvement was sex, Selena told herself.

Darius McClellan reminded her of what could happen when too much was expected. One date, that was it. She refused to let herself be hurt again.

Synthia gave an appreciative whistle and leaned close. "Velma Morris certainly has good taste in security teams. They are gorgeous."

Selena could only nod.

When the security team passed the table, they each made a

point to speak. Of course, Darius walked right over to Selena. Bracing one hand along the arm of her chair, he leaned down.

"Did you get my note?" he asked close to her ear.

"Mmm-hmm," Selena replied, loving the deep bass of his voice filling her ear. "I'll be ready. How should I dress?" she asked, pulling away her sunglasses in order to look directly at him.

The deep dimple in Darius's cheek appeared as his eyes slid away from Selena's face to the scoop-neck peach T-shirt she wore. For a moment, his cocoa gaze was focused on her full breasts pressing against the snug material.

"Don't make me answer that," he whispered, his eyes finally returning to her face.

Selena laughed and shook her head. "Do you know what discretion is?"

"Uh-uh. See ya at six," he promised, leaving her with a sexy wink before he walked away.

Selena bowed her head and gripped her bottom lip between her teeth to stop it from trembling. *Don't get carried away,* she ordered herself.

"Very nice, Sel," Synthia complimented, her eyes following Darius as he left the patio.

"Mmm-hmm . . ." was Selena's only response.

"Look, everything is gonna be cool. We're not anticipating any problems, so relax." A concerned frown clouded Darius's face as he watched Velma pace her office. He was trying to reassure her that his team had everything under control. Unfortunately, it didn't appear to be working.

Velma almost became unglued when she heard the hard knocking on the door. "Come in," she called in a weak voice.

Max Richardson strode into the office. Velma visibly tensed and Max noticed. He too grew concerned by the strained look on her face. "What happened?" he asked, glancing at Darius.

"This woman's a nervous wreck and I'm tryin' to tell her there's no need to be," he replied, pushing himself out of the chair he occupied.

"Here, man," Max said, handing Darius a folder. Rubbing his large hands together, he took a step closer to Velma. "He's right, Ms. Morris. Charles Herbert sounds like a smart man. I really think these threats of his are empty."

"Hmph, well, they're still doin' the trick," Velma argued, wringing her hands.

The doors opened as if on cue and Charles Herbert walked in. He and Velma stared each other down for a full minute before either of them spoke.

They began simultaneously.

"Charles, what—"

"Velma, we—"

Velma took a few steps back, her eyes wide with fear.

"What are you doin' here?" she finally whispered.

"You know what I'm doing here!" Charles roared back, unbuttoning his navy blue designer coat.

"Excuse me?" Darius smoothly cut in.

Velma's gaze snapped from Charles and she raised a hand. "Darius, I'd like you to meet my ex-husband, Charles Herbert."

Darius nodded and Charles returned the gesture.

"It's good to finally meet you," he said, before cutting his dark eyes back to his former wife. "You know, I really wish you'd cease this bull."

"Charles—"

"Why don't you just admit you're lyin'!" he raged.

"Are you forgetting all the conversations we've been havin' over the phone in the last two months? I'm not lying about any of this!"

Charles ran a hand through his wavy dark Afro and shook his head. "You got that many bills to pay, Vel?"

The look in Velma's eyes grew stormy. "You're just jealous."

"Ha! Of what?"

"You never could stand it that I made a go of this place and left you in the dust!"

Charles nodded, massaging his jaw. "Yeah, you made a go of it, but at what price, Vel?"

Velma ran a shaky hand through her hair. "Get out!" she said.

"Happily," Charles sang, turning toward the office door. "But, Vel, stop with the accusations or you'll force me to answer them," he assured her, before looking at Darius. "That's not a threat, Mr. McClellan, it's a fact."

Velma expelled a ragged sigh and held her head in her hands. "Lord, that man . . ." she groaned.

Darius walked over to Max and pulled him to the side. "Look, I don't care how you do it, but set up a system with hotel security to monitor the comings and goings of Herbert."

Max nodded and ran a hand over his bald head. "I'll get right on it," he said, before rushing out.

Darius tapped his fingers on his forehead and turned to Velma. She was braced against her desk, her head back.

"I guess the divorce was messy, huh?" he teased, his smile causing his slanting eyes to crinkle at the corners.

"No. . . ." Velma sighed. "We were so anxious to get rid of each other that it went smooth as silk."

"He's pretty sure you're lyin' on him," Darius said, his brown gaze penetrating.

"Yeah, well, he *did* have an audience," she reminded him. "Just keep him away from me Darius."

"You know I will," he promised.

Five

"Yeah, he walked right in and we can't have that. She's shaky enough as it is."

George Fenton, head of security for Paradise Halls, nodded briskly. "Those people never got along."

Max chuckled as he jotted down information on a pad. "I can believe that. They looked ready to kill each other."

"I know," George assured him, "but I gotta tell ya, this place is huge. How do you suggest we keep up with this guy?"

Max propped his jaw in his hand and thought for a moment. "There are security desks at every entrance, right?"

"Yep."

"Well, my suggestion is to have the guards stay on the lookout for him. We can float some pictures around and have them document every time they see him."

"Good plan," George said, stroking his gray-bearded jaw. "But it's very risky, the guy could easily slip in unnoticed."

Max nodded. "True, but we have to do something. Velma Morris looks like a woman on the edge and ready to jump. We may be going overboard with this entire thing, but we don't want to take any chances."

"So do you want us to call in or something?"

"Mmm, no," Max said, his long dark eyebrows drawn together in a frown. "Excuse me?" he called to the young man behind the front desk. "Have you got a legal pad or somethin' back there, man?"

The gentleman took a moment, then pulled a long yellow pad from a drawer. "Here you go."

Max took the pad and waved it toward George. "This'll do."

George chuckled and shook his head. "No frills, huh?"

"No need. I still don't think anything is gonna come of this."

Max was still talking to George when Synthia Witherspoon stepped up to the front desk. By that time, Max and George's conversation had turned to much lighter topics and Synthia couldn't help smiling when she heard them discussing their predictions for the upcoming basketball season.

"Have you got any messages for the *Reigning Queens* magazine group?" she asked, leaning toward the smiling desk clerk.

The concierge took only a moment before handing her three message slips. Synthia thanked him and turned away from the desk. In doing so, she slammed right into the huge brick wall that was Max Richardson.

"I'm sorry," he whispered, immediately going to his knees to retrieve the messages. "I'm sorry. I should've been watching where I was going."

"That's okay," Synthia slowly replied, struck by the gorgeous giant kneeling before her.

Max was so busy apologizing and being sweet that he didn't really take notice of the lovely young woman smiling down at him. When he finally stood and handed her the messages, his mouth fell open. Synthia's huge brown eyes had him hooked and he was speechless.

"I'm sorry," Max apologized again. His voice was soft and his dark eyes narrowed as he took in Synthia's innocently seductive features.

"No problem," she assured him, waving her hand. "I'm rushing anyway, trying to get to the beach."

Max was still nodding when he snapped his fingers. "You're with the magazine, right?" he asked.

"Mmm-hmm, I'm Synthia Witherspoon," she said, extending her hand.

"Max Richardson," he replied, taking her small hand in his much larger one. "You know, you look just like—"

"Selena Witherspoon? She's my cousin," Synth informed him.

Max was still holding her hand. "Beauty must run in your family."

Synthia smiled, enjoying the shiver his softly spoken comment sent up her spine. "Thank you," she murmured.

"Mmm-hmm . . ." Max replied, still staring.

Synthia cleared her throat. She was slightly unnerved, yet flattered by his gaze. "I, um, I better get going. It was nice meeting you."

Max simply nodded, watching as the tiny lovely lady walked away from him.

As his note that day had specified, Darius was knocking on Selena's hotel room door at 6:00 P.M. that evening. On the other side of that door, Selena was a bundle of nerves. She berated herself for acting like a schoolgirl, when she was a far cry from that.

"Calm down, damn it!" she whispered to herself, smoothing her hands across the short lavender dress she wore. The airy creation reached her thighs and twirled out around her small form. The gold zip front stopped at the cleft of her breasts, drawing attention there, while the long sleeves flared wildly at the wrists. Matching, strappy lavender heels accentuated the casual allure of the outfit. Selena appraised herself quickly in the full-length mirror in the hallway, then opened the door.

"Very nice," Darius complimented when he caught sight of her. His brown eyes roamed the length of her, enjoying the way the dress flared around her thighs.

"Thank you," she breathed, trying to stamp down her excitement over his presence. She'd thought about spending an entire evening alone with him since they met, and it was quite difficult to keep her calm. "Come on in," she said, waving one hand toward the living room.

"So, where are we goin'?" she asked, once Darius was leaning against the back of the sofa.

"It's a surprise," he said, crosing his arms over his chest.

Selena slapped her palm to her forehead. "Don't tell me I got all dressed up just to go out for a burger?" she teased.

Darius looked up at the ceiling as though he were deep in concentration. "Hmm . . . I believe they have burgers there too."

Selena laughed, unable to get over how very sexy he looked in the deep blue denim shirt and khaki Boss slacks that fit him loosely. "You're not gonna tell me, are you?"

"Nope."

"Well, let me go get my wrap and then I'm all yours." She sighed, turning toward her bedroom. Before she got that far, Darius stood and grabbed her upper arm.

His gorgeous, slanting chocolate stare appeared darker as he gazed down at her. "Listen, you should really think about what you say to me, all right?" he warned.

Selena's tempting hazel gaze was wide. "I always think about what I say to you," she whispered, praying he would kiss her. She wasn't disappointed.

A devilish smirk crossed his handsome dark face and Darius lowered his mouth to hers. Selena gasped when she felt his tongue slip past her lips into the waiting cavern of her mouth. The kiss was soothing and caressing, forcing countless moans from her throat as his tongue rubbed roughly all around hers. When he slid his hands beneath the hem of her dress and squeezed her bottom, Selena knew she would have to stop him. After enjoying a few more minutes of the pleasure he was lavishing upon her, she pressed her hands against his unyielding chest and regretfully pushed him away.

"Didn't you make reservations?" she whispered, her chest heaving madly.

Darius smiled at the enticing picture she made and finally nodded. A few minutes later, they were leaving the hotel.

* * *

The club Darius chose for dinner was right on the beach. Though it was filled with people, the place was designed with a series of booths that offered a fantastic view of the sandy strip regardless of where the diners were seated.

Selena couldn't get past how warm and cozy the restaurant was. It was impossible to become bored in such a place. Besides the spectacular view of the beach, there was a soundstage in the middle of the dining room that showcased various forms of entertainment.

"Darius, this place is incredible," she said, once the waiter left with their orders for shrimp jambalaya, hot buttered rolls, and iced tea.

"Thanks. Velma told me about it," he replied, while leaning back in his chair to watch her.

A small frown crossed Selena's face briefly. "That's interesting."

"How?"

Selena shook her head quickly. "Oh, nothing, nothing."

"How?" Darius persisted, still watching her.

"Well, I get the feeling that this is the kind of place she'd want to save for the two of you."

Darius smiled in spite of himself. "We're friends. That's all."

"That's all you've *ever* been?" Selena inquired, propping her hand against her cheek.

Darius chuckled. "We were more in high school."

"Hmph, I figured."

"Why?"

Selena shook her head and raised her naturally arched brows. "I can't imagine her remaining your *friend* all these years."

"Why not?"

"Well . . . I don't think I could."

Darius's gaze narrowed even further. "You always say what's on your mind?"

Selena shrugged, tracing the pattern in the off-white table-cloth. "It's the only way to get what you want."

"I'll remember that."

Selena rolled her eyes over the deeply voiced comment. "Why do I get the feeling my words are gonna come back to haunt me?" She sighed.

After dinner, Darius suggested they take a walk along the beach. Selena had no desire to refuse the offer. The sea air was surprisingly warm, yet the wind whispering over her bare legs still sent shivers down her spine. They'd been strolling for ten minutes when she stopped in her tracks and touched Darius's arm.

"Look," she whispered, pointing toward a thick gray blanket spread out over the sand. In the middle sat an ice-filled bucket and inside there was a bottle of chilling champagne.

Darius pretended to be surprised as well. "I'll be damned," he said, walking closer to the spread. "I wonder who left this here," he said, a wicked smile touching his mouth.

Selena glanced at him and noticed the devilish look in his warm, brown eyes. "You did this?" she asked, though she already knew the answer.

Darius tapped a strong finger to his mustache and studied over the question. "Well, I didn't lay all this out myself, no."

Selena sucked her teeth and pinched his arm. "You know what I mean."

Darius only shrugged and waved his hand toward the blanket. "You wanna sit down?"

Selena didn't think she'd ever forget how thoughtful, sweet, and romantic Darius was being at that very moment. She wouldn't dare tell him that, though.

The rest of the evening was something right out of a dream. The champagne was perfect, the sky was filled with sparkling stars, and the ocean met the beach in waves of crashing white foam. Through it all, Selena and Darius talked about the scenery and the dazzle of the city. The time brought them closer—making them more attracted to each other.

"I don't believe you went to all this trouble," Selena said later, as she leaned back on her elbows and gazed up at the sky.

Darius tilted his glass to his mouth. "It wasn't trouble, but why are you surprised by it?"

Selena looked away from the sky and let her eyes rest on Darius's handsome dark face. "Well . . . most men wouldn't do this unless they, uh . . . *expected* something."

"How do you know I don't?"

"Do you?"

"I'd be a fool if I didn't, but that's not why I brought you out here," he assured her, his deep voice very convincing.

Selena ran her fingers through her silky hair and sighed. "Why'd you bring me out here, then?"

"I made you a promise," he recalled.

"When?"

Darius set his glass inside the ice bucket, then draped his arms across his raised knees. "That first morning at breakfast." He smiled at the confusion still clouding her face. "I told you if you let me take you out, you could ask me whatever you wanted. This seems like the best place to get to know someone. No interruptions."

"You're right about that." Selena sighed, looking around the deserted beach. When she turned her hazel stare to Darius, there was no mistaking the question lurking there.

Darius pulled her close, curling one of his large hands around her upper arm. Selena gasped at the electricity that crackled through her body by the simple touch. Darius didn't move over her. Instead, he pulled her over to straddle him. His hands caressed the lush, silky smooth length of her thighs while he buried his gorgeous face in the crook of her neck.

Selena almost moaned from the intense pleasure of being so close to him. She could feel the rigid power of his maleness thrusting against the finely crafted material of his pants. Her hands caressed the wide, muscular expanse of his back, her long nails grazing the dark denim shirt.

Meanwhile, Darius's strong fingers found the zipper tab resting against the cleft of her breasts. Slowly, he pulled it downward, his fingers pausing to trace the newly exposed, supple skin.

"Darius . . ." Selena moaned, just before she felt his tongue thrusting past her lips. He almost forced her head back from the strength of the kiss, but she didn't mind. She matched him.

Finally, he eased her back on to the blanket, never breaking the kiss. His own deep groans and the expertise of his persuasive hands only heightened Selena's pleasure.

A soft, disappointed moan slipped past Selena's mouth when Darius pulled away. He sought one full breast and cupped it firmly for his mouth.

"Please, Darius . . ." she whispered as he manipulated the hardened nipple with his lips. Her hips moved against him in an unspoken request. Darius continued his sweet torture. Unbeknownst to Selena, he was gaining as much satisfaction by it as she was. He'd wanted to touch her that way since the first day they met. He tugged the nipple between his teeth and farther into his mouth, forcing Selena's moans to grow louder. The feel of his tongue slowly moving back and forth across the firm peak was almost maddening.

"Darius," she whispered again, "Darius, please don't stop."

The soft request slowly forced Darius back to reality. The only thing on his mind had been making love to her. Unfortunately, he knew if he allowed it, he'd be hooked on her. That was the one thing he would not, *could not* let happen. Reluctantly, very reluctantly, he pulled away from Selena and zipped her dress. Her eyes snapped open when she felt him leave her. The look in her lovely, seductive eyes was clearly questioning.

"It's late," he grumbled, standing up. "I better get you back to your room." His clear, deep voice sounded raspy. He offered her his hand and waited.

Unused to being turned down as unused as Darius was to turning down, Selena blinked a few times to make sure she wasn't dreaming. No, the dream was definitely over. Still, she placed her hand in his and let him help her from the tangled blanket.

The walk to the car and the drive to the hotel were silent. Selena wouldn't dare humiliate herself further by asking him inside when he escorted her to her room. Before she could disappear behind the door, Darius cupped her chin and planted a kiss on the corner of her mouth.

"I'll call you," he promised, his gaze narrowed and guarded.

"Mmm-hmm," she replied, without looking up. Clearly, she didn't believe him.

Darius watched her go inside and shut the door. He stood there for a few moments, his head bowed. In his heart, he knew he'd done the right thing in pushing her away. It was for the best, since it was obvious that he could never be "just friends" with Selena Witherspoon.

"Girl, you look like death! What happened?"

Selena leaned her head against the side of the door and sighed. Harry's bellowing was the last thing she needed to hear that morning. "Can you just come back later, please?" she wearily requested.

"No," came the indignant reply, as he hurried past her and into the room. "My show is today or did you forget?"

"Oh, it's not today, is it?" Selena cried, slapping her palm to her forehead.

"It is, but I guess you have more important things on your mind?"

Selena rolled her eyes toward the chandelier overhead. "Confusing things is a better way to put it."

Harry unbuttoned his maroon-colored suit coat and took a seat. "Well, tell me about it and make it fast. I got a lot to do today."

"Thanks for your concern," she drawled. "But there's nothin' to tell."

"Wait a minute, didn't y'all go out last night?"

"Mmm-hmm."

"And?"

"Harry . . ."

"What?" Harry asked, then grew silent as an enlightened expression crossed his attractive honey-toned face. "Am I talkin' too loud? He's in the back sleepin', right?"

"Wrong."

Harry finally lost his patience. "Will you please tell me what the hell is goin' on?" he demanded, slapping his fist to his knee.

"Nothing happened last night. Darius McClellan was the perfect gentleman."

Harry gave a playful cringe. "Ouch. Sometimes that ain't good."

"Hmph, well, he wasn't exactly *perfect,* just damned closed."

"So what happened?" Harry asked, crossing his long legs.

Selena pulled the silk scarf from her head and ran her fingers through her thick mane. "Well, we went to this nice restaurant. Very intimate and cozy. Afterward, we took a walk along the beach."

Harry closed his eyes. "Mmm, Miami's beaches . . . I could tell you some stories, girl."

Selena raised her hand. "Spare me, please," she begged. "Anyway, we were walkin' for a while when I saw this blanket with a bucket of Moet chilling in the middle."

"Damn." Harry sighed, his heavy brows rising. "He did all that and y'all didn't do the do?"

Selena just shook her head. "Uh-uh. We talked and we got very close, but then it was like something snapped and he pulled away right after . . ."

"After . . . what? Selena?"

An uneasy look clouded Selena's lovely face as she averted her gaze. "After I asked him not to stop."

"Oh." Harry's voice fell as he uttered the word. "Mmm," he added.

"What?" Selena demanded, watching him massage his forehead. "You think that's why he pulled away?"

"Nah," Harry said, though his expression said the opposite.

"Yes, you do. It crossed my mind too. He probably thought I was too aggressive and he didn't like it. Darius seems to be a man who likes complete control," she decided, clenching her fists as she turned away. "I can't even believe I said something so stupid."

"Well, what happened after that?"

Selena shrugged and flopped onto the sofa. "He brought me back here. Said he'd call."

"You don't believe him?"

"Ha! Would you? I mean, you've dated enough men to know they don't always mean that."

"The hell you say!" Harry argued, stroking one hand across his smooth jaw. "I always get called the next morning."

The boast almost brought a smile to Selena's face, but she managed to contain it.

"Well, sweetie, I'm sorry you didn't have a good time," Harry said, "but I'm glad it didn't happen. For my sake."

Selena caught his meaning, and this time her laughter couldn't be contained. Soon they were both in high spirits.

Following lunch with Carla and Joni, who were eager to discuss a few more hopefuls for the debut cover, Selena decided to spend some time in the hotel spa. She had to pass the restaurant on the way and caught sight of a curly head of hair similar to her own. Slowing her steps, Selena saw her cousin at a table with a man. A very gorgeous man. With a sneaky smile on her caramel-complexioned face, she headed over to the table.

"Do I know you?" Selena asked, with a confused expression on her face.

Synthia, who was already beaming, appeared more radiant when she saw her cousin. "Sel! I have someone I want you to meet," she said, turning slightly in her seat. "Max Richardson, this is my cousin Selena Witherspoon."

Selena chuckled as she took Max's hand. "Thanks, Synth, but we've met. You work for Darius McClellan, right?"

"That's right," Max confirmed, revealing a gorgeous white smile.

Selena gave Synthia a playful push in the shoulder. "Good goin', cousin, you got the boss's right-hand man," she teased, causing the couple at the table to laugh.

"We just ordered, Sel, do you wanna sit with us?" Synthia asked.

Selena frowned and waved her hand. "No, thanks, I was just passing by on my way to the spa. I want to look halfway decent for Harry's big night, so I better get going. Max, it was good to see you again."

When Selena had rushed off, Max shook his head. "I can't believe how much you two look alike."

"I know, it's scary sometimes," Synthia replied, taking a sip of her daiquiri. "But it can come in handy," she added, with a devious smile playing around her full lips.

Max caught the change in her tone of voice and leaned back in his seat. "How so?" he asked, his dark eyes narrowing intently.

The twosome talked all through lunch. It was difficult getting through the meal, when there was so much to discuss. Conversation flowed easily and neither of them wanted it to end.

"So, what time do we recheck the bathroom?" Co-Captain Owen Nellus was asking as he and Captain Kevin Amos walked into the restaurant with Darius.

"An hour before should be good. Do the best you can, 'cause it's gonna be packed in here," Darius cautioned.

"Well, the audience won't get in there until we've checked the place out," Kevin assured his boss.

Darius shook his head. "I wasn't referring to the audience, I—" He stopped midsentence, his slanting eyes narrowing even further. Across the room, he spotted Max Richardson at a table with a woman. A woman he appeared to be very taken by, judging from the set look on his face. The woman had smooth, caramel skin and a headful of bouncy dark brown hair. She looked just like—*Nah,* Darius said to himself. He couldn't see her face, so he couldn't be certain. Still, he couldn't make himself walk over to find out.

"Darius? Darius?" Kevin was calling, concern etched across his face.

"Mmm? Oh, sorry," Darius whispered, regaining his senses.

"Where'd you go, man?" Owen asked with a chuckle.

Darius shook his head and returned to the subject at hand. "I was saying that the ballroom is gonna be packed with all the people involved with the show."

"Oh yeah, we got that all taken care of," Owen remarked, looking through his portfolio. He and Kevin moved on and Darius followed behind them. He tried to keep his mind on what was being said, but the image of Max laughing and talking with the petite curly-haired mystery woman kept popping into his mind.

Selena's trip to the spa was delayed when she stopped by a dress shop in the hotel and became carried away by all the lovely outfits inside. She did manage to spend an hour in the spa, then decided to relax in a Jacuzzi. She wasn't up to the company of a hoard of people, and it seemed all the tubs were filled with groups of at least six or more. She searched the area relentlessly, until she found a tub occupied by only one person.

Selena didn't know if it was good timing or misfortune that the one person happened to be Darius. Taking a deep breath, she decided not to make too much out of it. His eyes were closed, his head leaned back against the cushioned rest. Selena had to clear her throat several times before he awoke.

When Darius opened his eyes and saw Selena standing before him in a short black towel, he thought he was still asleep. No, he realized, she was actually there, watching him with her hazel eyes.

"I'm sorry, all the other ones were filled. Do you mind if I share this with you?" she asked, pulling her lower lip between her teeth as she watched him frown.

"Don't ask stupid questions," he mumbled, propping his elbow along the back of the tub.

Selena thought his mood was a bit hostile and figured he was upset about the previous evening. She mentally shrugged off the thought, since she wasn't the one who ended things.

Darius, just fresh from a strenuous workout, was far from relaxed. That fact was never more true than when Selena removed her towel to reveal a very flattering blue bikini.

Silence settled over the room, as the two got comfortable in the tub. Selena tried with everything in her to keep her mind off Darius, who was less than three feet away. The last thing she wanted to do was touch him, but that appeared to be a heavy task, since his very long legs were stretched out almost close enough to touch. He seemed to be very content, however, causing her cool temper to rise.

Contentment, though, was just a front. Darius could tell Selena was doing her best to avoid him, and after last night he really couldn't blame her. The way he had left, with no real explanation, after the scene on the beach. He'd felt like a heel for doing it, but to him, preventing—or avoiding—any serious involvements seemed to be tops on his list.

The phone sitting on a cushioned rest near the tub began to ring and they both made a move for it. Water sloshed everywhere as Selena made a play for the receiver. She succeeded only in slamming against Darius's sleek chest. Since the phone was closer to him, all he had to do was reach behind him to grab it.

"Expecting a call?" he asked, smiling down at her.

"Sorry," she whispered, clearing her throat as she pushed herself away.

Darius's slanting coffee stare narrowed a little more as he pressed the receiver to his ear. "Yeah? . . . Mmm-hmm . . . Yeah, hold on. . . . It *is* for you," he said.

Selena kept her gaze downcast as she took the phone. "Yes?"

"What the hell are you doing in there with Darius Mc-Clellan?" Harry's voice rose through the line.

"Nothing," she calmly replied.

"Mmm-hmm. Whatever," Harry said, not at all convinced.

Selena sighed. "What's up?"

"Hmph. I just wanted to remind you that I'm havin' a cocktail party before and after the show. I know how much you're enjoying yourself there, but I expect you to be at *both* parties," Harry ordered.

"I will," Selena promised.

"So what are you doin' in there with him?"

"Good-*bye*, Harry." Selena clicked off the cordless and held the receiver toward Darius. He took it, his eyes never leaving her face. Selena could have kicked herself for allowing him to make her more nervous. "That was Harry," she told him, unnecessarily, since he'd answered the phone. "He just called to see what I was doing," she continued. "I mean, he just called to invite me to his cocktail party. For his, uh, fashion show," she rambled.

Darius didn't bother to respond and simply stared at her with his intense, mellow gaze.

Selena closed her eyes and inhaled deeply, before clearing her throat. "Darius, um . . . about last night . . . my mouth sometimes works ahead of my brain. I guess I said more than I should have."

Darius felt his lips curving upward into a smile, but hid it before she noticed. "You didn't say anything wrong."

"I think I did."

"Because I left so quickly?"

Selena only raised her brows in response. "It's just that it's been a while since I . . . I just don't want you to get the wrong idea about me. People have a knack of doing that where I'm concerned . . ." She let the explanation trail away, unable to ignore the intensity of his gaze. Deciding it was time to leave, she made a move to the other side of the tub.

Darius took her by the arm, urging her closer. Selena felt helpless to stop him, realizing she didn't want to. Darius pulled her atop him, keeping his hands around her arms as he held her fast.

"Kiss me," he commanded.

Selena responded by favoring him with a slow deep kiss. Darius unhooked the fastening of the bikini top and pulled it away. He cupped her full breasts and squeezed the globes mercilessly. Tearing his mouth away from hers, he lavished soft kisses across the caramel-toned mounds. Selena threw her head back and enjoyed the caress. Unconsciously, she pushed herself closer, eager to feel him take the tip into his mouth. Her nails, which had been grazing the chiseled muscles of his back, trailed the taut cords of his torso and disappeared beneath the bubbling water.

Darius's lips finally closed over the hardened peak of her breast and when he felt Selena's fingers teasing him through his shorts, he moaned.

His mouth opened and closed over her breasts, wanting to take as much as he could. Needing to feel her against him, he cupped her bottom and pulled her even closer. Selena cried out softly when she felt the steel length of him against the center of her body.

The moment proved to be just as intense and erotic as before. Still, as the lengthy foreplay grew more pleasurable, Selena knew she should call a halt to the enjoyment. She found that she couldn't. All the reasons why they shouldn't be doing what they were doing seemed irrelevant.

"Selena?" Darius called, his voice sounding muffled with his face buried against her chest.

"Yes?" she whispered.

"I hate to tell you this."

"What?" she said, pulling away as she sought to catch her breath.

Darius appeared entranced by the rapid rise and fall of her voluptuous breasts, before shaking off the effect. "Damn, I hate to tell you this." He sighed.

"Will you please say it? You're scaring me."

Darius tightened his hold on her hips and easily lifted her away from him. "We can't do this."

Selena was shocked by his words, even though the same thoughts had been running through her mind. "Why?" she asked.

Suddenly, he chuckled. "No . . . um . . . no protection," he quietly informed her.

Selena laughed as well, then gave a sigh of relief and tapped her finger against his nose. "Good answer."

"I'm sorry."

"It's just not the right time, I guess," she decided, hoping to keep the moment light.

Darius found her hand beneath the water and squeezed it. "There will be," he assured her. "I promise you that."

Six

Selena arrived promptly for Harry's pre-fashion-show cocktail party. If possible, she looked more radiant than usual. The long black evening gown she wore was a perfect fit. The beautiful material formed to her petite, voluptuous body like a second skin. The halter bodice had an oval-shaped opening that offered a provocative glimpse of cleavage. Her back was left bare while the deep back split in the skirt offered teasing peeks of her shapely legs.

"Now, I know you can't be here all by yourself?"

Selena whirled around and smiled at Cliff Harrison, a mutual friend of hers and Harry's. "What are you doing here?" she asked, clearly surprised to see the man outside of New York.

Cliff shrugged. "Harry sent me an invitation and told me to come on down."

"And so you just dropped everything?" Selena asked, not believing that for a moment.

"Well, he told me how, uh . . . nice the women were down here."

"*Harry* told you that!" Selena shrieked.

Cliff laughed, his gleaming smile a perfect contrast against his very dark complexion. "I know and I said to myself, 'If Harry's givin' the women compliments, then I gotta see for myself.'"

Selena nodded. "I gotcha."

"But if they look half as good as you do," Cliff remarked,

twirling her around, "I made the right choice to come on down." He planted a kiss on her cheek.

The two friends talked for a while, before Selena moved on to mingle more. As usual, she charmed every man she spoke with, but Selena had her sights set on another. Her hazel eyes frequently scanned the private lounge where the party was being held. Darius had yet to make an appearance and she knew he had been invited. Besides, he was security and had access to all parts of the hotel.

Selena almost choked on her rum and cranberry juice when she heard Harry's voice behind her. "What'd you say?" she cried.

"You slept with him, didn't you?" he repeated, a knowing smile on his handsome face.

"Will you hush!" Selena ordered, glancing around to see if anyone had overheard.

Harry was obviously enjoying her discomfort. "You did, didn't you!" he whispered.

"No, I didn't," she smuggly informed him.

"Well? What happened in that Jacuzzi?"

"None of your business!"

"What?"

Selena blinked a few times. "Harry, listen, I love you, but sometimes . . ."

Harry, who knew almost everything there was to know about Selena, wasn't about to be cut out of the loop now. "He turned you down again, didn't he? There's hope for that man yet."

Selena sucked her teeth. "He didn't turn me down. We *couldn't* do that in the Jacuzzi."

Harry pushed his hands into the deep pockets of his tuxedo trousers and studied his friend for a moment. "Well, what was the problem? He didn't have condoms, or something?"

Selena wanted to stop Harry, but she couldn't. Instead, she burst into laughter. Harry covered his mouth, surprised that his question was right on the mark.

* * *

Selena visited the bar for one last drink before the show. Just as the smiling bartender pushed a glass before her, she felt a finger trailing down her bare spine. She tried to keep her glass steady as she turned to look into Darius's gorgeous brown eyes.

"Hello," she managed, her eyes dropping to his mouth.

"Hello," he replied, his baritone voice sounding hushed and very mellow.

"Harry goes all out for his parties, doesn't he?" Selena lightly noted. She was hoping general conversation would keep her mind off how gorgeous he was in the fitted charcoal crew-neck shirt and matching jacket and trousers.

Darius let his coffee gaze roam the room briefly before he looked back at her. "Yeah, it's nice."

Selena pressed her lips together and nodded. She wanted to kick herself for allowing him to make her so jittery. Instead, she tossed her hair and waited.

Obviously, Darius could sense her unease, for a devilish smirk crossed his handsome face. He pulled the glass from her hand and set it back to the bar, then pulled her close.

"I want you so much," he whispered, while bowing his head.

The moment his mouth touched hers, Selena's lips immediately parted. Darius pulled one of his hands from her waist and cupped her chin. The smooth strokes of his tongue deepened, and Selena moaned in response. The delicious friction of his mustache sent shivers up her back and she never wanted the kiss to end. Neither of them cared about the lounge being filled with people or about the tons of stares they received. Insecurities about becoming intimately involved weren't important either.

Velma had been enjoying the party, obviously excited about her cousin's highly anticipated fashion show. When she caught sight of Darius and Selena at the bar, she became absolutely livid. If she had a bit more force in her hand she would surely have crushed the glass she held. Knowing that she couldn't afford to lose her cool that night, or any night, she managed to keep her feelings hidden.

Reluctantly, Selena ended the kiss, not wanting to cause more of a scene than they already had. Pulling away as much as Darius's arms would allow, she looked way up into his eyes. "I guess you're one of those men who doesn't mind showing affection in public?"

Darius chuckled, revealing a set of deep dimples. "I was taught that actions speak louder than words," he informed her, his gaze never wavering.

"And that action was saying?"

"That I want to see you after this party is over."

Selena's fingers curled around the lapels of his jacket and she sighed. "Harry wants me to come to the after party."

"Skip it."

Selena couldn't believe how close she was to agreeing, when she stopped herself. She knew she could beg off on the party, but realized she'd make a big mistake by letting Darius have his way. She remembered all too well how things turned out when a woman made things too easy for a man.

"He really wants me to be there," she finally explained, hoping Darius wouldn't push to change her mind.

He shrugged. "All right. So, where are you sitting?" he asked, pulling his arm from around her waist.

"Harry's got me sitting along the runway. I hope I look okay." She sighed.

Darius chuckled and shook his head. "Unbelievable."

A frown tugged at her silky brows. "What?"

"A woman as beautiful as you has to fish for compliments."

Selena's mouth formed a perfect O and she slapped the side of Darius's arm. "I don't!" she denied.

Darius pretended to be wounded by the slap. "That's okay. If I were as fine as you, I'd fish for compliments too."

"Anyway," Selena drawled, pretending to be unconvinced, but pleased by his comment.

"Will you at least let me walk you to your seat?" he offered, extending his arm.

Before either of them could make a move toward the door, Velma was calling Darius. From the sound of her voice it seemed urgent.

"I'll see you later," he said, sending her a regretful smile.

Selena nodded, returning the smile. "That's fine. Hey, Velma," she called, before walking away.

Velma waved but didn't reply to Selena's cheerful greeting. Instead, her eyes were fixed on Darius. "Do you think this is smart?" she asked.

Darius's heavy dark brows drew closed. "What?"

"Carrying on with Selena the way you are?"

Darius bowed his head and tapped a finger to his mustache. "Velma—"

"I mean, I just don't think it looks good, that's all," she cut in, picking an invisible speck of lint from her auburn Bill Blass pantsuit. "I'm sure Selena didn't mind, but—"

"Velma?" Darius said, pulling her attention off her clothes. "We haven't been around each other in a long time, so you may have forgotten this," he said, easing one hand into his pockets and leaning close to her. "I'm a man who likes to keep my private life *private*. I take offense when someone doesn't understand that, no matter how good a friend she is."

The hard look in his soulful stare belied the softness of his voice. Velma knew better than to push the issue further.

Harry M's fashion show was a complete success. The press clearly loved what they saw. The same was true for the scores of fashion buyers, models, and designers who were on hand. When it was all over, Selena looked around for Darius, but couldn't find him. Before she could get too far, Harry had her by the hand and they were on their way to the after party.

"I've booked the Hotspot for the party," Harry explained as he rushed around backstage. "We're gonna have drinks in the lounge first, so I can talk with the press."

Selena pulled Harry to a deserted corner and hugged him. "I'm so proud of you, baby! I knew you'd shine just like you always do!"

Harry kissed her. "Thanks, hon."

Selena grabbed Harry's hands and squeezed them. "But, I can't go to the Hotspot with you," she said, referring to the posh nightclub in downtown Miami.

"Why?" Harry whined.

"I just don't feel like clubbin' all night. I'll go to the lounge with you, but then I'm out."

Harry shook his head, his gorgeous dark gaze knowing in its intensity. "You got it bad for him, don't you?"

"This isn't about Darius. I already told him I had other plans and couldn't be with him tonight. I just don't feel like more socializing, that's all."

"Mmm-hmm," Harry replied, obviously unconvinced. "Well, I'm here if you need to talk," he sweetly assured her.

"Thank you." Selena sighed, pulling him close again. "But right now, you need to *talk* to the press."

"Ms. Witherspoon?"

Selena turned when she heard her name and found one of the escorts rushing toward her.

"Message for you, miss. The gentleman said it was important," the young man announced.

"Thanks," Selena absently whispered, opening the small white card. *Tenth Floor. Conference Room A1. NOW!*

Selena's heart jumped to her throat. The card wasn't signed, but it didn't need to be. She knew she was going back on her rule not to make things too easy for Darius, but she had to ease her curiosity. Besides, she'd already turned him down once and he'd asked again. That was good.

For now. Selena went to say her good-byes to Harry, and then she left the party.

Since the tenth floor only housed the conference rooms, it was completely deserted at that late hour. When Selena walked into room A1, as the note had specified, everything was completely darkened. Not wanting to spend any more time than necessary on the deserted floor, she started to leave.

"Don't even think about it."

Selena's hand went weak around the silver door lever when she heard the smooth, deep voice behind her. Turning, she softly cleared her throat. "You wanted to see me?" she asked.

"Yes. I'm glad you accepted this time."

Selena nodded. "Well, I was actually on my way back to my room when I got your message." She explained, her voice sounded hollow in the darkened room.

"We have some unfinished business."

Selena smiled, Darius's deep voice settled like a warm blanket around her body. "Unfinished business?" she parroted, "I have no idea what that might be."

"Mmm-hmm. Take off your dress."

Darius was seated at the head of the long boardroom table. Because it was so dark in the room, Selena couldn't see his face, though she was certain he must have been joking.

"Did you hear me?"

"What? Here?" she asked, hating the squeaky sound of her voice.

"Here," he confirmed.

"Here in this conference room?"

"In this conference room."

The rich, baritone quality of Darius's voice was doing wonders at wearing down her defenses. Selena's Chanel purse had already slipped to the floor and her fingers were actually tingling with anticipation. "You can't even see me in the dark," she said, still grasping at excuses.

A lamp sitting on the table was suddenly flipped on. Darius raised his dark brows expectantly, before he leaned back in his seat and watched her with a narrowed gaze.

"Mmm-hmm," Selena said, having no more excuses to offer.

"Anything else?" he asked, smirking slightly as he tapped his fingers to his neat mustache.

Selena's sparkling hazel eyes narrowed and a sultry smile tugged at her mouth. "And what are you going to do while I'm . . . stripping?"

"You tell me."

Selena accepted the silent challenge. Her hands went to the gold snap at her neck and she undid the halter. Since she hadn't worn a bra, when she pulled the straps away, her breasts were exposed to Darius's warm, coffee stare.

The lamp offered soft golden light that more than flattered Selena's flawless caramel complexion. Darius never blinked as his eyes caressed every inch of bared skin. In response, Selena tossed her head back, loving the way he looked at her.

She eased the clinging material of the gown down over her tiny waist and rounded hips to let the garment pool at her feet. Wearing nothing but a pair of strappy, black heels and a lacy pair of black panties, she walked over to the long table.

Darius had to admit that he was surprised by how aroused he was by the sight of her. He swallowed past the lump in his throat more than once as he watched her walk toward him.

"Selena . . ." he breathed.

She moved before him, leaning against the edge of the table, and braced her hands on either side of her. "Yes?" she whispered.

Darius wasted no more time. Standing before her, he grasped her thighs and pulled them apart. Then, he stepped between them and brought his mouth to hers. Selena returned the kiss wantonly, moaning as she wound her arms around his neck. She unfastened the buttons on his jacket and pushed it off his wide shoulders. Darius tore his mouth from hers and rained kisses over her neck and breasts. He pushed her back on the polished table and circled the tip of her breast with his lips. Soft cries filled the room as she enjoyed the soothing tugging and caressing of his tongue against her nipple.

Selena arched her hips slightly when she felt Darius's fingers tracing the lacy waistband of her panties. They eased down to caress the outline of her womanhood. Darius pulled his mouth from Selena's chest to smother her flat stomach with kisses. She could feel herself becoming wetter with each stroke.

Darius finally discarded Selena's lacy lingerie and pushed her higher upon the table. His sensual mouth sought the center of her and she cried out when she felt him there.

"Shh . . ." Darius soothed, raising his head to give her a teasing stare. His gorgeous brown eyes were further narrowed, making him appear even more devastating.

Selena pressed her lips together and tried to stifle her cries when his head lowered again and lavished soft kisses to the mound of silky, curly hair.

"Brown is your natural color, I see," he noted.

Selena could only smile, her thoughts completely focused on the pleasure she was experiencing.

Darius's persuasive lips tugged at the soft petals of her femininity. When his tongue delved deeply inside, Selena arched right off the table. He cupped her hips and held her firmly in place. His tongue continued to stroke her intimately, ignoring her soft cries. A while later, Darius pulled away and Selena moaned her disappointment.

"Please don't say we have to stop," she pouted.

A deep sound rose from Darius's chest as he chuckled. He didn't reply, but lifted her into his arms and carried her to the sofa in the far corner of the conference room.

"Hmm . . . another blanket," Selena noticed, from her cozy position in his embrace. The sofa had been draped with a lovely burgundy quilt.

Again, there was no response from Darius. He simply

placed her on the sofa and stood. Selena's beautiful hazel stare narrowed as she watched him remove the rest of his clothes. Her eyes followed every movement, enjoying the ripple and flex of the cords in his arms and chest. His abdomen was taut with muscles and looked like the perfect six-pack. He stepped out of his shoes, before letting the boxers and trousers fall away. His impressive, hard length and strong well-toned thighs made her want to swoon.

Soft words and moans filled the air once they were both unclothed, really feeling each other for the first time. Darius's huge hands encircled Selena's neck and his thumbs pushed her chin up to meet his kiss. She, in response, raked her long nails across his back and entwined her silky, smooth legs with his heavy, hair-roughened ones.

Once protection was in place, Darius thrust into her exceedingly moist center. Selena's gasp threatened to cut off her air supply as he continued to stroke. The deep, powerful lunges brought her to countless orgasms. Just when she thought it was over, Darius was back for more. He draped one of her shapely legs across his shoulder and trapped the other with his own heavy limb. The position forced him even deeper inside her and Selena surprised herself by becoming more aroused than she'd been before.

Afterward, they snuggled into a warm embrace and fell asleep. Some time later, Darius decided it was time for them to leave. On the way back to her room, Selena asked if he would stay the night. Of course, he didn't refuse.

"Ms. Morris, you have a call. There's a phone at the bar."

Velma nodded at the waiter and headed in the direction of the bar. The gathering was winding down and people were filtering out to the Hotspot for the all-night after party.

"Velma Morris."

"How much longer, Ms. Morris?"

Velma's heart jumped to her throat when she answered the

phone and heard the dreaded yet familiar voice through the line. "How did you know where to find me?"

There was laughter on the other end. "Where else would you be on the night of your cousin's fashion show?"

"What do you want?"

"Ha! Ms. Morris. We want our money."

"I told you, you'd get it," she snapped, her voice rising.

"When?"

"It's going to take a while, but it shouldn't be much longer," Velma replied, struggling to maintain her composure.

"I hope not," the solemn voice breathed through the line. "Don't screw us, Ms. Morris. You won't like the consequences."

Velma slammed the phone down before it had the chance to slip from her hand. Running her fingers through her hair, she looked around the room to see if anyone had been watching her.

Following the night of Harry's very successful fashion show, days seemed to fly. Selena was very involved in preparations for her magazine. Free moments were practically nonexistent, but she made time for Darius. He was becoming increasingly important to her. More than she was willing to admit. Still, she loved being with him and decided to enjoy the moment and see where things would lead.

Darius was feeling much the same way. He hadn't realized how much being with Selena would affect him. He managed to maintain control and not allow past fears to scare her away. It was difficult, considering how comfortable Selena was with the opposite sex and how comfortable they were with her. He knew she often worked with male clients, but that didn't make him feel much better about it. Although Darius was confident, frighteningly so at times, he couldn't stop the twinges of anger and mistrust that sometimes nagged at him.

Such was the case one afternoon when he ended a meeting in the lounge. He recognized Max by his profile. He was at the bar, talking to a small woman. Again, Darius couldn't see her face from the distance, but she looked so much like Selena it was uncanny. . . . It was obvious that Max and his friend were very close, and jealousy, along with disbelief, tore through Darius.

A satisfied smile brightened Selena's face later that afternoon as she relaxed on her sofa. "Marcus, I think you're going to be very good at this."

Marcus Penny smiled, revealing a dazzling set of even white teeth. "Are you serious or just trying to flatter me?"

Selena pressed her hand flat against her chest and fixed Marcus with a hurt look. "I'd never say it if I didn't believe it," she assured him.

Marcus was a distinct hopeful for *Reigning Queens'* Miami premier Heavenly Bodies issue. He and Selena had just finished discussing the magazine and what would be expected of him should he make it to the glossy pages.

"So, do you think I'll get the job?" he asked, propping his hand along the side of his handsome brown face.

"I definitely think you'll get the job," Selena stated, pushing herself from the sofa. "But, I've got six other women I have to answer to," she informed him.

"Are they tough?"

"Yes, but once they see you, I think they'll agree that you're perfect for our first issue."

Marcus's gray eyes roamed appreciatively over Selena's tiny body encased in a form-fitting beige pantsuit. "You certainly are good for a man's ego."

"That's what they all say," she teased, smiling as he moved to follow her to the door. She was laughing at another comment he'd made, when she pulled the door open and found Darius outside. Her light eyes widened appreciatively as they raked his tall form. "I'll call you, Marcus," she absently remarked, her eyes never straying from Darius.

Darius watched Selena for a long while. He appeared calm enough on the outside, though inside he was seething.

"Come in," Selena invited, stepping aside as she waved her hand.

The moment the door slammed shut, Darius turned toward her. His exquisite, sweet coffee gaze was guarded. "What's goin' on with you and Max?"

Selena blinked a few times, before she frowned. "Me and . . . Max?"

"Mmm-hmm. Max Richardson, my first assistant? I think you know him."

The cool, set look on Darius's face unnerved Selena but she would not allow it to completely unsettle her. "Yeah, I know Max. . . ."

"And?"

"And what?"

"Have you been out with him?"

"No!" Selena cried, shocked by the question.

"Don't lie to me," Darius ordered in a voice that was soothing and mellow. His eyes, however, were hard and guarded.

Selena couldn't believe what she was hearing. "Darius, what has you thinking that I've been out with Max?"

Darius winced slightly and shook his head. "Look, I don't care what you do. I know how you can be a big flirt."

"What the hell—"

"And I don't think I can handle that," he slowly finished, his voice never rising.

Unfortunately, Selena didn't feel quite so at ease. "Who the hell are you to come in here accusing me like this?"

Darius pushed his hand into the deep pocket of his olive-green trousers as he moved closer to tower over her. "I know what I saw."

Selena raised her hand, before running it through her hair. "Listen, I don't know what you *think* you saw, but it wasn't me."

Darius pulled his hand from his pocket, heading to the door. "Just like a man to get possessive after you've had sex with him." Her lips tightened into a thin line and she turned her back on him then. "Get out," she whispered.

A moment later, Selena heard the door slam shut behind Darius and she expelled the breath she'd been holding. She spent the next hour going over what had just happened. It was difficult to think clearly, since she felt as though she'd just come through a hurricane.

The next few days were very tense. Though Paradise Halls was a very large hotel, Selena and Darius saw each other at every turn. Selena hated the way things had turned out, especially when she was falling so deeply for him. Darius, on the other hand, behaved as though nothing had happened. Whenever they were in the same room, he wouldn't look at her. As far as Selena was concerned, he had come to her with the accusation about Max for a reason. He'd gotten what he'd wanted and was looking for a way to make her not want to see him again.

Their respective workloads increased as time passed. Darius was up to his ears in security preparations. The party for the record label would be held in two nights and the hotel was already resembling a madhouse. As a result, Velma had also begun to act more secretive. She ceased mentioning any calls from Charles to Darius and he noticed. Since Charles Herbert hadn't been making the calls in the first place, it wasn't difficult to forget. Besides, Velma had more important things to think about. Time was winding down and she had to make money. A lot of it.

"Well, we can't do any more than what we're doing right now. Just keep your eyes peeled."

Darius looked out over his security team to take on any questions from the group. It was the evening before the big party and they were meeting to discuss last-minute loose ends.

"Why do I feel like I've been on a vacation?" Cameron Davenport asked, thumbing through the pages of his portfolio.

A small smirk tugged at Darius's mouth as he shrugged. "See, it's when you start to relax that things happen," he cautioned.

"No offense, D, but we've been relaxed since we got here," Jesse Phelps pointed out.

Darius raised his dark brows in a questioning manner. "Well, if it's too much for you, feel free to go back to New York. I got plenty of work for you there."

"I suddenly remember some exits that need to be checked," Jesse said, pushing his chair from the long table.

Darius joined everyone in laughter, slamming his own portfolio shut. "All right, guys, that's it. I'll see you tomorrow. Have a good time at the party, but remember why we're here."

As everyone hurriedly cleared out of the conference room, Darius noticed Max lingering behind. "What can I do for you?" he cooly inquired.

Max sighed as he stood from his chair. "What the hell is wrong with you, D?"

"What?"

"You know what. Last few days you been walkin' round here with an attitude so cold I could chip ice off your shoulder."

"I got a lot goin' on."

"That's a crock of crap. You ain't been treatin' everybody else like this."

"Max—"

"Out with it, D. What the hell is it?"

Before Darius could utter another word, a petite caramel-complexioned lady walked up to Max. Darius watched as she slipped her arm around his waist and hugged him. She had bouncing, dark brown curls and looked exactly like Selena Witherspoon. Almost.

Max grinned and held the small woman close. "D, this is Synthia Witherspoon. Synth, this is my boss, Darius McClellan."

Synthia smiled and extended her hand. "Nice to meet you."

Darius took Synthia's small hand in his large one and shook it slowly. "Same here."

Synthia turned back to Max and pointed toward the door. "I'll just wait for you outside, okay?"

Max watched her leave before he turned back to Darius. "So? What's this all about, man?"

Darius shook his head, his eyes closing in regret. "Nothin', man, but I am sorry. I mean that," he said and extended his hand. Max finally nodded and shook hands with his old friend as they shared a hug. When he walked out of the conference room, Darius leaned back against the table and began to stroke his mustache. He remained there for the longest time, trying to think of a way to make things up to Selena.

Seven

The knocker rapped against Selena's room door, just as she was about to step into a pair of white spike-heeled boots. She hurried to the front of the suite in her stockinged feet. She found a bellman waiting outside her door.

"Ms. Witherspoon?"

"Yes," she confirmed, watching the stocky young man with an expectant gaze.

"I have a message for you, ma'am."

Selena frowned, watching the freckle-faced redhead pull the note from the breast pocket of his uniform. "It must be mighty important to be delivered to my door," she noted.

"It was a special request, ma'am," he explained, handing her the pad he carried.

Selena shrugged and signed for the message. "Just a sec," she said, reaching into the back pocket of her white short-suit. "Thanks." She pressed a five-dollar bill into the young man's palm.

He smiled and nodded. "Thank *you,* ma'am."

Leaning against the doorjamb, Selena tore into the white envelope. *Mile-High Club. Ride the train. Backseat of my Jeep.*

"What the hell?" she breathed, shaking her head at the suggestive phrases. She had to admit to herself that the cryptic messages were beginning to rattle her nerves. She pushed the door shut and leaned back against it, shrieking when the knocker sounded a minute later. Ordering herself to calm down, she turned to greet her guest.

"Damn, you ain't dressed yet?" Harry criticized, when the door opened.

Selena only smiled and shook her head. "I am dressed, you know that."

Harry's dark brows rose slightly. "Sorry, I couldn't tell." He sighed.

Selena turned away from the door. "Come in, I just need to put on my boots and earrings."

Harry's eyes were still on Selena's outfit. Though it was in his nature to tease her mercilessly, he had to admit that she was a knockout. The white retro short-suit was long-sleeved with a gold zip-front bodice. A wide gold belt surrounded her tiny waist. The shorts offered an admirer just a glimpse of the swell of her bottom.

"You tryin' to reel him in, aren'cha?" Harry asked, taking a seat on the sofa.

"Who?" Selena called from the bathroom.

"Darius McClellan."

Selena walked back out to the living room, a fierce scowl darkening her face. "Don't mention him to me."

"Ouch. Y'all still haven't talked?"

"Nope. And we're not going to."

"Selena—"

"Harry, please . . ." she said, pressing her fingers to the bridge of her nose. "This really isn't the time."

"All right, all right," he said, not about to make her miserable all over again. Instead, he whisked her away to the party that was already in progress.

"You know, I was in a good mood before you mentioned Darius," Selena grumbled as she and Harry entered the lounge.

"Girl, I'm sorry," he cooed, already jumping to the beat of the music.

"Mmm-hmm," Selena drawled, with a smirk coming to her

face. "I wasn't going to drink much, but I think I'll have a little something before tackling the dance floor!"

"Well, the bar's got everything you need, so have fun and I'll see you later!" Harry called over the music, kissing Selena's cheek before he walked away.

Selena had no problems attracting dance partners once she made it to the floor. The pumping bass worked with the power of the drinks she'd downed and she lost herself in the music. It had been a long time since she let herself go and really had fun. Suddenly, her hips were drawn into an unbreakable hold and she whirled around.

"Darius," she breathed, though it was impossible to hear her own voice.

A delicious smile crossed his handsome face and he leaned forward. "I'm sorry. I was wrong. Forgive me?" He spoke into her ear, the deep bass of his voice rivaling that which pulsed from the speakers.

Selena pulled away and stared up at him. Her strong buzz didn't enable her to misunderstand what was said. Her spirits lifted even higher and brought a smile to her lovely face. She knew Darius had a lot more explaining to do, but for the moment she decided to let the sweet apology suffice.

"We'll talk later?" she asked, her expectant stare prompting a response.

Darius shrugged and pulled her closer. "You got it."

Their argument forgotten for the moment, Darius and Selena surrendered to the suggestive lyrics and pumping bass of the music. Just about everyone in the place appeared to be locked in sensual embraces, but Darius's and Selena's movements seemed even more erotic.

"You've done this before?" Selena asked, as she draped her arms around Darius's neck.

"Once or twice," he murmured, gripping her hips tightly and holding her in place across his thigh.

"I wouldn't peg you for a Miami Bass lover," Selena noted, trying to ignore how the closeness was affecting her.

Darius's warm stare narrowed a bit more. "What'd you have me pegged for?"

Selena pulled her arms from his neck and rested her hands lightly against his chest. "Hmm . . . lemme see . . . more of a jazz or maybe R and B, with a bit of hip-hop thrown in—the good stuff, not that crap they're puttin' out today."

"Good guess," Darius said, his sleek brows rising in an impressed gesture. "But this music does have its rewards."

"Really? Such as?" she asked, trying to sound completely innocent.

"Like getting a fine, sexy woman dressed—or undressed— to grind on your thigh," he smoothly replied.

Selena's laughter was music to Darius's ears, before it was drowned by another song. The twosome remained on the dance floor another fifteen minutes. Then, they parted company and went to mingle a bit more.

"Vodka and cranberry juice please," Selena told the bartender, returning the man's pleasant smile.

"Gettin' your drink on tonight, I see."

Selena turned to find Darius a few feet away. "I need to tonight," she confided.

Darius took his gin from the bartender and waited for Selena to receive hers. "Why tonight?" he asked.

Selena took a sip of her drink and trailed her light gaze over his well-built, devastating form. Goodness, she thought, he was a gorgeous thing standing there in his sagging blue jeans and a lightweight designer sweatshirt coordinated with a fantastic pair of tan suede hiking boots.

"I want to have an excuse for doing what I'm doing tonight," she finally admitted.

Darius tossed back the remainder of his drink, then looked out over the balcony where the bar was partially located. "You plan on getting *that* wild?" he asked.

"I wouldn't mind if I did," she replied, waiting for his reaction.

Darius watched her for a moment, before hauling her tiny form against his huge one. His head dipped and he thrust his tongue past her lips. Selena gasped, allowing him to deepen the kiss. Her glass slipped from her weakened hand, but no one noticed. Darius cupped her bottom and pulled her closer, as his fingers teased the exposed swell of her buttocks beneath the shorts. Selena was an eager participant in the kiss. Her long nails grazed the muscular dark expanse of his back when they ventured beneath his shirt.

Though their actions were being mimicked all over the hotel, Darius wanted a more private arena. Cupping her face, he pulled away to whisper into her ear, "Let's get out of here."

Selena had no thoughts of refusal and soon they were heading to her suite.

The instant the polished oak door closed behind them, Selena led Darius to a high-backed armchair in the living room. He took a seat and pulled her down to straddle his lap. A purely wolfish smile tugged at the curve of his mouth when he buried his face in her full chest. She cried out and watched as his strong teeth tugged at the gold zipper. Her breasts spilled over the tops of the wispy black bra she wore. Darius simply pulled it away and cupped one of the full caramel-colored mounds in his palm.

Selena threw her head back and moaned once his lips covered the tip of her breast. He pressed one hand to the small of her back and brought her closer to his mouth.

"Darius . . ." she breathed, setting herself more snuggly against his powerful length.

Darius switched to the other breast and his persuasive fingers began to tease the moist nipple he'd abandoned. Selena felt helpless to do anything other than cup the back of his head and massage his soft hair.

"Mmm . . ." she moaned, when his damp kisses trailed her neck as he pulled the suit from her shoulders.

Suddenly, Darius set her away, making her stand before him. He finished removing the outfit, raining kisses down her body.

"Take these off," he grumbled, tapping one of his shoes against her boots. He leaned back in the chair and watched her.

Selena did as he asked. When the white boots were discarded, the outfit pooled around her ankles. She stood there almost nude with the exception of the black lace panties.

For a moment, Darius simply enjoyed the sight of her. His brown eyes paid homage to every inch of her small, voluptuous form. After what seemed like an eternity, he pushed himself from the chair and towered over her.

A tiny scream escaped her lips when he caught her by the waist and hoisted her against his hard body. She instinctively locked her shapely legs around his lean waist and slid her fingers through his soft, close-cut hair.

Darius cupped her derriere in his hands and gently squeezed. He kissed Selena with an intensity that would have frightened her had she not been as starved for him.

As they kissed, Darius took them into the bedroom. Selena snuggled into the cushiony fabric of the comforter. Her hazel eyes narrowed as she watched him take off his clothes. Never one for being passive in the bedroom, Selena assisted in the removal of his jeans. When that was done, and he was completely nude, she began to lavish his chest and abdomen with kisses. Her laughter filled the room when he flexed the chiseled pectorals in his massive chest.

"Very nice," she complimented, before teasing his navel with her tongue.

The look on Darius's dark, handsome face was serious. *"How* nice?"

In response, Selena pressed a few more kisses to the defined muscles in his abdomen. Then, her mouth trailed lower until she reached the rigid length of his masculinity.

"Mmm, damn, Selena . . ." he breathed, appreciating the intimate caress. Her mouth worked over him and she moaned when he pressed her head more closely to his body.

Before he reached total fulfillment, Darius pushed her away. He put protection in place, then his heavy frame covered her body and he immediately buried the startling extent of his arousal into the heart of her. Selena gasped each time she felt one of his rough, heated thrusts. When he pulled one of her legs across his shoulder, her gasps became breathless cries of delight in response to the increased penetration.

They were in paradise and their passionate whispers could be heard throughout the suite. Before they could reach total satisfaction, Darius withdrew and took Selena with him. Facing the head of the bed, she grasped the huge brass headboard as Darius took her from behind.

His thrusts were even more heated than before as he buried his head against the crook of her neck and cupped her breasts in his large hands.

He breathed her name again and again as he cherished the feel of the beautiful woman in his arms. Afterward, they both collapsed onto the bed, satiated yet exhausted. Sleep arrived quickly.

"Selena! Selena! Girl, come on and get up! Selenaaa!"

"Harry?" Selena groaned, hearing her friend's faint yet familiar voice. Thinking it was a dream, she dropped her face back into the pillow.

"Selena! Get up! I know you're in there!"

The heavy rapping on the door and Harry's repeated calls finally woke Selena. Still groggy, she made her way out of the soft, warm bed. Grimacing, she pressed one hand to her pounding head and noticed that Darius was nowhere in sight. A cynical smirk lifted one corner of her mouth, before she left the room.

"Damn it girl, are you all right?" Harry bellowed, pushing his way inside the suite when Selena opened the door.

"I was, until you started yelling and banging on my door

like a fool," she chastised, pulling her blanket a little tighter around her otherwise nude body.

"Sweetie, there's a fire—"

"What? Where?"

"Here in the hotel on the other end," Harry quickly explained as he ushered her into the bedroom. "Now they almost have it contained, but they want everybody out, so put some clothes on."

Selena didn't argue. She hurried around, getting herself together. In less than three minutes, she was dressed in a comfortable sweatsuit and sneakers.

Once Harry had escorted her through the crowded lobby and outside, Selena was shocked to see how much damage had been done. The fire-torn end of the hotel was destroyed as far as she could tell. Selena prayed no one had been hurt, but her thoughts were almost totally centered on Darius.

Meanwhile, the object of Selena's thoughts was near the fire trucks speaking with one of the chiefs.

"Can you tell what started it yet?" Darius asked, wincing as he took in the demolished wing of the hotel.

Chief Gene Reynolds removed his hat and wiped a blackened handkerchief across his forehead. "We haven't really had a chance to investigate this yet."

Darius nodded in understanding. After leaving Selena's room, his plan was to check in with his team and then go back to her . . . maybe. News of the fire, however, changed all that. Instead, he sent Harry back to get her to safety. "I don't see how you could investigate anything in all this mess," he grumbled.

Chief Reynolds chuckled. "You'd be surprised, my friend," the older, white-haired gentleman stated. "I'll tell ya one thing though, this is gonna be one hell of a bill to pay," he added.

Darius chuckled. "Hmph, you got that right." Then, his sleek dark brows drew close as the man's words settled in. The thought that entered his mind was so far-fetched that he had to shake his head to clear it.

* * *

"That guy's gone too far this time," Darius commented, as he watched Velma pace behind her desk.

Because the fire had been contained and had occured so far away, the fire crew had allowed only hotel staff back inside. Darius had gone to comfort Velma, but, of course, it wasn't working.

"I'm sorry, Darius. Did you say something?" she asked, her eyes worry-filled.

Darius cleared his throat and rested his head back against the wall. "I said, Charles went too far this time. I hope you called the police already?"

Velma offered a nervous laugh and waved off the comment. "Please, a guest probably left a cigarette burning or something."

"Velma—"

"Plus, the insurance will cover it."

Darius's probing, mellow gaze focused solely on Velma. His conversation with the chief, earlier that evening, came roaring to the forefront of his mind.

"Um, Velma, listen, I'll see you later. There's somethin' I need to do."

Velma was so preoccupied she didn't notice him leaving.

Darius headed through the crowded hotel lobby, until he spotted Max on a pay phone. His first assistant had just finished the call when he approached him.

"Man, this was some night, huh?" Max asked, running one hand across his bald head.

"Hmph," Darius cynically replied, nodding his agreement. "Listen, I need to get a number from you."

Max frowned. "Who?"

"Velma Morris's ex-husband, Charles Herbert."

All business concerning *Reigning Queens*-Miami could finally be handled by Selena's staff. Although she loved the weather and sights, she was more than ready to get away from the city, and Darius McClellan especially.

"I still don't see why you have to leave so soon," Harry complained, as he and Selena shared an early breakfast. "You're starting to act as wierd as Velma."

Selena rolled her eyes and concentrated on spreading jam on her toast. "I *do* have another business in New York and Velma *did* just have her hotel catch fire. Cut us some slack, will you?"

Harry leaned back in his chair and watched her. "You sure this don't have anything to do with—"

"Don't say it, Harry."

"Darius McClellan?"

Selena shrugged, her gaze downcast. "We were on . . . good terms the last time I saw him."

"Mmm-hmm, but he hasn't called you since, right?"

"Harry, damn, it was only last night," Selena snapped, bringing her palm to the table.

"I know it was only last night and he didn't even call or come check on you after the fire."

Selena finally raised her eyes to Harry's face. He could tell that he'd hit a nerve—an extremely sensitive one.

"Honey, I'm sorry." he whispered, patting her hand. "I shouldn't have said that anyway. After all, he did send me to make sure you got out of the hotel alright—told me not to do another thing until I made sure you were out of there."

"Will you please drop it now?" she pleaded, watching him nod. The rest of the breakfast passed in silence.

Harry and Selena made plans to get together once he returned to New York. Selena cleared up a few things at the front desk, before leaving. When she walked outside, there was a sleek beige limo waiting for her. Just as she took the chauffeur's hand, she glanced up in time to see Darius headed for his own car.

Before he settled into the driver's side of the Infiniti, his gorgeous brown eyes caught sight of her. Their gazes held as though they were memorizing each other. Selena took a deep breath and shook her head. Then she disappeared inside the limo.

Darius's eyes followed the car down the long, wide, curving driveway until it was out of sight. An unexpected surge of anger welled inside him and he banged his fist against the roof of the car.

Harry rapped his knuckles against the polished mahogany end table and sighed. He'd decided to spend a few hours with Velma before heading out of town. Though he'd chastised Selena for leaving early, he realized that the city's charm had worn thin on him as well. That, plus the fact that his cousin was about as much fun as a bag of nails. They'd been in her office close to an hour and she'd barely spoken two words.

"Maybe you should think about coming back with me."

Velma's head turned quickly in her cousin's direction. "Come where? To New York?"

"Hell yeah, you need to get away from this mess for a while," Harry decided.

"I'll never get away from this," Velma solemnly replied.

Harry stood. "Honey, I know what this must be doin' to you. All the trouble you went through to make sure nothing negative would happen . . . but it's not your fault and once all the repairs are made, you'll forget all this crap ever happened."

"Ha!"

Harry shook his head. "Girl, what is it—"

"Harry! Listen to me. You wouldn't get it if I told you. I don't want to get into this with you!"

Harry said nothing more. He simply tossed his hands in the air and walked back to the sofa. The moment he took his seat, the office door flew open and Darius stormed inside.

"Velma, we need to talk," he said, stopping a few feet in front of her.

"Darius, what—what's wrong?" Velma whispered, unable to hide the nervous undertone to her voice.

Darius looked back at Harry and tilted his head upward in greeting. Then, he turned back to Velma. "I paid a visit to Charles today."

Velma frowned. "Charles?"

"Charles Herbert. Your ex-husband."

Velma closed her eyes and nodded. "Yes, yes, I know. Why?"

Darius pushed one hand into the deep pockets of his light-weight gray trousers and bowed his head. "Something he said got me to thinking."

Velma remained silent, though her eyes were filled with concern.

"That comment he made about you having so many bills to pay. Remember that?"

"What are you trying to say, Darius?"

"I think you know. How could you afford to keep this place going when you're filing for bankruptcy?"

Velma's gaze grew murderous. "How did you—are you accusing me?"

"Would I be wrong if I did?"

Velma ran one hand through her hair. "I don't believe this," she breathed. "I call *you* down here to help me and you try to make *me* out to be the bad guy?"

Darius's temper had been growing more heated since he'd left Charles's Herbert's office earlier that afternoon. He had always prided himself on being able to control his emotions. This, however, had him enraged. The one thing he hated was to be made a fool of.

"I should've gotten the cops down here to help me," Velma muttered, feigning exasperation. "I would have expected this from them, but you—"

"Velma, be quiet!" Darius finally roared, surprising himself as well as everyone else in the room. "Just admit it," he ordered, bringing his deep voice to a fierce whisper. His brown eyes were even more narrowed and guarded.

Velma watched Darius for a moment, before she rolled her eyes. "Get out."

Darius shook his head. "Why'd you do this?"

Velma ordered herself not to lose control, but she couldn't continue to lie with Darius watching her so intently. At last, she bowed her head and squeezed her eyes shut. "Didn't Charles tell you that?"

"There wasn't much he could tell me. That's why I'm here and, baby, I don't have much patience left," he warned her.

Velma sighed and leaned against her desk. "I was going to file for bankruptcy," she admitted, rubbing her hand across her watery eyes. "But, I wasn't about to lose this place because of it. I knew some people in the . . . lending business and I gave them a call."

Darius's brows drew close. "Loan sharks?"

"Hmph, much worse."

Harry, who had remained quiet until then, finally broke his silence. "Girl, why didn't you come to me?"

Velma smiled at her cousin. "Honey, you couldn't have done a thing for me then."

"Why'd you call me?"

Velma looked back at Darius. It killed her to see him watching her so coldly, but she realized he would probably never look at her any other way ever again. "I needed someone on my side. It seemed like the perfect plan. Everyone knew how bad things were between me and Charles. I hated him so much . . . I guess I thought I could ruin him and cover my own butt at the same time."

A short, quiet laugh escaped Darius and he turned away from Velma. "So, what about the fire?"

"My 'friends' who loaned me the money were becoming impatient. I had to do something, quick. I had to get the money fast," she snapped, moving to pace the room again.

Suddenly, Darius had enough. "I need to get out of here," he muttered, heading for the door.

"Darius, I—"

"What!"

Velma sniffed and tried to gather her courage. "I—I never meant to—"

"To what, Velma? To bring me all the way down here and have me waste my time on some damned wild-goose chase?"

Velma realized there was nothing she could say and pressed her fingers to her mouth as she watched Darius continue toward the door. Just as his hand touched the gleaming gold knob, he turned back to her.

"As your, uh . . . 'security,' I suggest you speak with a lawyer," he advised, before leaving the room.

Eight

"Nooo! Stop it, that can't be right."

"I swear it is. I was there to see the whole thing."

Selena uttered a sound of pure shock as she flopped back in her seat. Harry had called her in New York and updated her on the news about his cousin. In Miami, it was already big news.

"Is she going to jail?" Selena asked, still in awe of the situation.

Harry sighed. "Nothing's definite yet. The police want her cooperation, so maybe she'll wise up and make a deal with them. They may show her some mercy if she gives up the people who loaned her the money."

"Hmph, Harry, we could be talking about the Mafia here. Do you really think she'd do that?"

"Well . . . you're probably right. Damn! Why'd she have to go and do somethin' like this!"

"Hearing you this upset, Harry, I can imagine how Darius must've taken it."

"Honey, it wasn't pretty."

"I'll bet." Selena sighed. "I know it tore him apart to discover Velma had been lying to him all that time."

"You're right. The man went off so bad, his voice could've been heard clear across the hotel."

"I don't think I've ever seen him quite that angry," she noted.

"Believe me, you don't ever want to," Harry assured her. "He did ask about you, though."

"What?"

"Mmm-hmm, before he left town."

"What'd you tell him?" Selena probed, trying to hide the frantic sound from her voice.

"What's there to tell?"

"I mean, you didn't give him my address or phone number or anything like that, did you?"

Harry chuckled. "Love, he could find that out on his own."

"Harry . . ."

"No, no, I swear I didn't tell him a thing about you."

"Good," she whispered, not wanting to own up to the mild disappointment she felt.

"Listen," Harry said, before clearing his throat, "I'm getting out of here today, so I'll call before I drop by your house or anything."

Selena frowned. "Why?"

"You know, in case you have, um . . . male company or anything."

"Harry . . ."

"Bye. . . ."

Selena stared at the phone for a second or two before she replaced the receiver. She placed her fingertips against her temples and massaged the slight ache she felt there. The dull pain was beginning to subside when the phone buzzed again.

"Yeah, Mary?"

"Selena, you've got a call."

"Who?" Selena asked the woman who had been working in Anna Edwards's place while she was out on maternity leave.

"Sweetie, I don't know. He wouldn't give his name. If I were you, though, I wouldn't keep him waiting."

Selena felt her heart somersault to her throat. Could it be Darius? she thought. She'd already resigned herself to accepting that their "aquaintance" would go no further than Miami. Maybe she was wrong.

"How'd he sound, Mary?"

"Well . . . his voice is clear and deep . . . very sexy. But why ask me, when you could be talking to him yourself?"

"You're right. Put him through," Selena decided. "Hello, Darius," she greeted once the connection was made.

Brief silence met the greeting before there was a response. "How'd you know it was me?" Darius asked.

"A feeling."

"I see," he said after a brief laugh.

"I . . . I heard about Velma."

"Mmm . . ."

"I'm sorry."

"Stuff happens, as they say."

"Hmph, you got that right."

"I was surprised to see you leaving the other day."

Selena's breath caught in her throat before she managed to voice a reply. "Why didn't you walk over to say good-bye?"

"Why didn't *you?*"

"Excuse me?"

"You heard me."

"Well, I wasn't the one who left after we—left that night without saying good-bye or 'It was good' or 'See ya' or anything. I didn't know where your head was," she snapped.

"Wait a minute, you thought I'd just up and leave you like that?" Darius queried, his deep voice barely above a whisper.

"Well, what was I supposed to think?"

"So I guess treatment like that is something you expect from men, huh?"

"It's usually the way things go," she solemnly acknowledged.

"And you slept with me anyway?"

"I had too much to drink."

"Bull."

"Darius—"

"Selena, stop it. That's a crock of crap and you know it."

"Wait a minute—"

"No, *you* wait," he ordered, his voice still deep and calm. "Now, you wanted what happened as much as I did. Yes, I left you, but I was coming back there when all hell broke loose."

"Mmm-hmm."

Darius sighed. "I care about you, Sel."

She gasped at the soft admission and the way he'd shortened her name. Refusing to let herself be overwhelmed by it, she steeled herself against it. "You care about me, hmmm? Yeah, I could tell how much you cared by the way you rushed to find me and make sure I was all right after the fire."

"Baby, do you realize how busy I was after that mess?" he asked in a fierce whisper.

"Not busy enough to track down Velma."

"I was working for her."

"Mmm, and look where that got you," she sniped, silently berating herself for the words. She hated fighting over something so petty, but a few days alone had forced her to face many things. A relationship with Darius McClellan would be far too complicated. In spite of how very close she felt toward him, it was best to push him away and let the association end.

"I didn't call to fight with you," Darius whispered, strain and aggravation finally touching his voice.

Selena would not allow herself to soften. "So why did you call?"

"You know, Selena, I have no idea," he countered, before slamming down the phone.

Selena mimicked the action after a moment or two. "And that's my cue to go home for the day," she decided, leaning back in her cream suede chair.

Lord, I made such a mistake becoming involved with that man, she told herself. It was best to stick to her vow to forget relationships. She had everything she needed: a lovely home, car, money, family, and friends . . .

"Not to mention my booming business," she added, admiring her lovely office with its cream and mocha color scheme. A polished oak desk sat on a plush champagne-colored carpet. Thick cream-colored armchairs filled every corner. An impressive entertainment center and a huge glass bookshelf completed the chic environment.

"Yeah, I have everything I need," she assured herself, unwilling to admit how untrue that statement was.

Meanwhile, in his own posh Brooklyn office, Darius was raging. He wanted to kick himself for calling Selena, but knew he would have done the same thing all over again. As much as he hated to admit it, he was finding it next to impossible to get the woman out of his mind. He found himself wanting more of what they'd shared in Miami.

Miami. Ha! What a disaster, he thought. Had it not been for the case, he and Selena could have spent more time together. Perhaps they wouldn't be fighting. Darius admitted his fault in many of the misunderstandings that had occurred. More than anything, he wanted to apologize and make her understand. Why he felt such a strong need to do so was a question he hadn't found an answer to.

Judging from the disastrous phone call, however, Selena obviously wanted nothing more to do with him. Maybe it was a good thing that she didn't. Unfortunately for him, forgetting her was a feat he felt powerless to accomplish.

"Goodness, that wind is pickin' up out there!" Synthia Witherspoon told her cousin when they met outside the Corner Rib Shack.

"I know, I hope Warren has some fresh coffee brewed," Selena said, rubbing her hands across the long sleeves of her fitted denim jacket.

As usual, the establishment was crowded and noisy. Still,

it possessed a coziness and personality that appealed to scores of Brooklynites.

"Well, well, if it ain't my two favorite curly-haired light-skinned-ed sistas!"

The two petite beauties laughed at the boisterous, stocky dark man behind the bar.

"Why do we take your abuse, Shawn?" Selena groaned as she and Synthia chose two stools at the long cherry-wood bar.

"'Cause I mix in just enough flattery with my abuse," Shawn Bevins replied.

Synthia eyed the restaurant's proprietor with playful suspicion. "So you give this treatment to all your other customers, huh? I think I'm jealous."

Shawn pretended to look over his shoulder as though he expected to find an eavesdropper. "Now, how many *natural* curly haired black women do y'all think I come across in this city?" he asked, joining the cousins when they burst into laughter.

"Shawn, please tell us a fresh pot of Warren's coffee is on the stove," Selena begged.

"Two cups with plenty of cream and sugar comin' right up," Shawn obliged.

"Gosh, I'd forgotten how busy this place could get," Selena said, her eyes taking in the rushing waitresses and loud patrons as they located a quiet back table.

"I know," Synthia agreed. "If I'd remembered I would've suggested us going someplace else."

Selena turned in her seat and looked around the bar. "Well, you couldn't force me out of here now. It's getting real cool out there," she said, nodding toward the bay window at the front of the restaurant.

Synthia smirked, taking in the overcast view as well. "Nothing like Miami, huh?" she asked, watching Selena's easy expression grow guarded. "Have you talked with Darius since we got back?" she inquired.

"Thanks, Sarah," Selena said to the waitress who'd just

arrived with the coffees. "He called me once. We argued about the way he just up and left after we . . . you know."

Synthia squeezed her cousin's hand. "I'm sorry, honey."

Shaking her head, Selena pulled away and focused on her coffee. "I'm not. It's for the best."

"I can't believe that."

"You know Synth, maybe this whole thing with Darius happened for a reason—to make me appreciate what I have," she declared, her light eyes taking on a defiant glean. "I have everything I need and then some. Darius was a fling—a very enjoyable fling, but that was it."

Synthia studied her coffee as she stirred it. "And you're very mistaken if you think I believe that."

Selena cleared her throat and decided not to reply. "Where is that girl? I'm ready to order," she grumbled, looking around for their waitress. "I feel the need coming on for a stiff drink," she pointedly announced, while glaring at her cousin.

"Order me one, too," Synthia called, when Selena stood.

"Hey, Warren," Selena greeted, when she caught the eye of the Corner Rib Shack's head bartender.

"Mmm, Selena, Selena. Long time no see, girl," Warren Gandy drawled, as he leaned across the counter to kiss her cheek.

"Been out of town awhile," she explained, smoothing both hands across her fitted denim zipper-back pants. "Could I get two Long Island iced teas?"

"For you, anything," Warren said, already turning away to prepare the order.

"Selena?"

Glancing in the direction of the deep voice, Selena was shocked to find herself staring into Max Richardson's handsome dark face. "What are you doin' up in here?" she cried, as they hugged. A gasp caught in her throat when she saw Darius at the bar also.

"Best food in town," Max said. "Synthia here with you?"

"Mmm-hmm," Selena absently remarked, before waving her hand in the general direction of their table.

Max wasted no time heading over, leaving Darius and Selena with an awkward silence between them.

He finally broke the quiet. "How are you?"

Selena only nodded, preparing to move farther down the bar.

Darius stood. "Selena, wait—"

"I'm fine, Darius. I'm just fine," she snapped, cursing herself for the sudden loss of control.

Darius raised one hand a few inches above the counter. "I'm sorry I asked."

"Well, what'd you think?" she countered, not wanting to be affected by his soft apology. "Did you think I'd fall apart over some stupid phone conversation?"

"I'm sorry about that."

"Me too."

"Selena, girl, you want these drinks delivered?"

"Nah, Warren, I'll take 'em. Thanks." She sighed, reaching for the two tall coolers.

"War, put those on my tab," Darius instructed, while handing the man his usual tip.

"Thank you," Selena whispered. For a moment, she allowed her eyes to linger on his gorgeous chocolate-toned face before she walked away.

"I wanted to ask Max and Darius to join us, but . . ."

"Thanks, I'm glad you didn't," Selena told her cousin in a nonchalant tone.

"Damn it, Sel," Synthia snapped, watching her sip the pungent mixed drink, "when are you just gonna admit that what happened between you and that man was more than some fling and that the way things turned out is bothering you?"

"Jeez, why is everybody on my back about Darius Mc-Clellan?"

"Because it's obvious *you're* emotional about it and doin' a bad job of hiding it," Synthia threw back, her wide almond-brown gaze gleaming with a fire of its own. "It's not like you to react this way over a man. You enjoy him, you're elated, it ends, and you're *still* elated."

"And I haven't been in a relationship like that in years," Selena reminded her cousin.

"So?"

"So maybe this thing with Darius—the way I'm reacting or underreacting—is just my way of being cautious about getting my feet wet again."

Synthia shrugged. "If it works for you." She sighed, toying with a lock of brown hair that lay outside the French roll she wore.

"Mmm," Selena grunted, setting aside her drink in order to massage her temples.

"Selena? This just arrived for you."

Selena and Synthia looked up to see the hostess extending a small white envelope. Selena seemed hesitant to take it and her cousin noticed.

"What is it, girl?" Synthia asked.

"Not—nothing," Selena assured her. "Thanks, Ronnie," She told the young woman and accepted the note.

Selena tore into the note, all the while reminding herself that there hadn't been a message in weeks. *Lie down with dogs, get up with fleas.*

The note slipped through her fingers and landed in her salad plate.

"Selena?" Synthia called, hearing her cousin's gasp. "What does it mean?" she asked, after snatching up the note and reading it.

"I—I don't know," Selena stammered, unable to mask her unease.

Synthia gave the note a tiny shake. "Is this connected to the notes you were getting down in Miami?"

Selena ran both hands through her hair and closed her eyes. "I don't want to believe there's a connection, but now . . ."

"You know better?"

Selena opened her eyes and gazed around the dining room

with a pensive stare. "I think there could be someone out there with a score to settle."

"Who?"

"I'd be talkin' to the cops if I knew who."

"Shouldn't you be talking to them anyway?"

Selena braced both her elbows on the table. "I don't think my mystery writer is through with me."

"And you're gonna wait till they are before you go to the cops!" Synthia cried, unmindful of the stares she received.

Selena covered her face and spoke through her hands. "I don't want a big stink to set this person off," she said, laying her hands flat on the table. "I'll handle it quietly. I'll find someone who can help me privately."

Synthia nodded, fiddling with the oversized collar of her clinging coral dress. "What about Max?" she finally suggested.

"What *about* Max?" Selena asked, obviously confused.

Synthia rolled her eyes and leaned forward. "Go to Max for help. I'll even talk to him for you. He *is* in the investigating business, you know?"

"I don't think so," Selena decided as she reached for her drink.

"But, you just said—"

"Synth, the last thing I need or want is for Darius to hear about this. Max does work for him, remember?"

Synthia understood her cousin's reluctance. "Just promise to consider it, if things get too hairy. I don't want you tryin' to handle this on your own or goin' someplace that won't be as discreet as McClellan Securities. At least you know them."

Selena's eyes grew brighter and when she began to applaud, Synthia waved her off. "Quite a fantastic pitch, Miss Witherspoon. Tell me, how well do *you* know McClellan Securities? Or should I say Max Richardson?" she teased.

Synthia couldn't hide the smile from her face. "We've been seeing each other since Miami."

"Ah, Synth, that's wonderful," Selena breathed, smiling as she reached across the table to take her cousin by the hands. "I'm glad things are working out for you."

"Well, we're just trying to take things slowly," Synthia explained, a small shrug following her words.

Selena responded with a knowing smile. "I always admired you for your ability to do that. Maybe my own love life would've been more stable, secure, had I practiced more patience."

Synthia tensed. "Now you stop it," she ordered, shaking her cousin's hands. "Stop tearing yourself down. I won't listen to it."

Selena pressed a kiss to the back of Synthia's hand. "Thanks, girl," she whispered and decided to enjoy what remained of the lunch date.

"Am I healthy?"

"As a horse. I wish you'd eat a little more though."

Selena grimaced at her gynecologist and sighed. "Eat more? Why? So you can get on me about gaining too much weight?"

Dr. Dennis Davis ran one hand through his wavy Afro and grinned. "I don't want you to raid your refrigerator every night. Just put a few more rolls on your plate."

"I just haven't had a big appetite, Denny," Selena complained, as she tied the shoestrings on her Nikes.

"Well, at least you know you're not pregnant," Denny joked.

Selena, however, swallowed past the lump in her throat when she heard the word. "You know, I ate quite a bit when I was in Miami," she went on to say.

Denny pushed the cap closed on his pen and raised his soulful dark eyes to her face. "Well, keep up the good work. For me, please."

Selena almost laughed at the look on his handsome face. "All right. For you."

Great friends, Dennis and Selena always took time to chat after her exam. They would spent almost another entire hour talking about everything and nothing.

"Well, sweetie, I need to hit the road. I got a lot of personal stuff to do today," Selena said.

Denny hugged her close. "I have a lunch date with my brother too, so make an appointment with Glenda and we'll be in touch."

Selena hurried out to speak with Glenda Harris, the receptionist for the eight doctors in Denny's practice. After scheduling her next appointment, she headed for the elevators. The wide mahogany doors opened with a quiet swoosh and she was about to step inside, when her way was blocked by a solid wall of muscle.

Looking way up, she almost gasped when she found Darius staring down at her. No words were spoken, one just as surprised to see the other. Selena's gaze was the first to waver as she looked down. Darius didn't respond and simply walked past her.

Selena watched him head over to Glenda's desk. Her hazel eyes held an unmistakable longing as they glided over his devastating length.

"My brother around, Glenda?" Darius was asking, while ordering himself not to turn his head back in the direction of the elevators.

Glenda nodded, smiling at the handsome man leaning against her desk. "Yeah, he just finished up with a patient, but let me see if he's ready," she said, reaching for the phone. "Darius is here to see you, Denny. . . . Okay, go on in, hon."

Darius favored Glenda with a sexy wink and strolled on into his brother's office. Meanwhile, Selena remained near the elevators. Her mouth fell open when she heard Darius asking for her doctor.

* * *

"You ready, man?" Darius asked the moment he stepped into Denny's office.

A smile brightened the younger man's face as he looked over at his half brother. "Yeah, I was wrapping up a few things. I just finished with a patient."

Darius nodded, perching his tall, muscular form against his brother's desk. "Mmm-hmm, Glenda told me. . . . Her name wouldn't be Selena Witherspoon, would it?"

Denny's head snapped up and he frowned. "How'd you know that?"

Toying with a crystal paperweight from Denny's desk, Darius shrugged. "I saw her leaving."

Denny shook his head as he placed a few files in his cabinet. "Damn, I didn't know you knew Selena. I guess you *are* the ladies' man they say you are."

The dimples in Darius's cheeks appeared as he chuckled. "Well, I met her down in Miami."

"Oh yeah . . . I heard about that, man. Sorry it turned out like it did."

Darius waved his hand. "Forget that. I have. The only thing I hate is not getting Selena's address."

Denny's onyx gaze narrowed as he watched Darius suspiciously. "No," he finally answered.

"No what?"

"I can't tell you that, man."

"Why not?"

Denny removed his white jacket and walked around the desk. "It's privileged."

"Hell, Denny, I'm not asking you to give me her medical history. I only want to know where she lives."

"Darius . . ."

"Denny, you owe me, *a lot.* Don't forget that. I've never cashed in on it before, but I am now."

Denny watched his brother for a while. "Selena's not only my patient, man, she's a friend. If you don't know where she lives, I'm sure there a good reason."

"Denny—"

"She lives in Brooklyn. That's all I'll say."

"Hell, I already know that."

"Then that should get you started," Denny stubbornly replied. "You're the detective, figure out the rest," he added, noticing the frustration clouding the man's face. "Damn, D, I know she's fine, but fine enough to have you flippin' this way? You're losing your edge, man."

Darius couldn't help smiling. "Yeah, but what scares me is that I don't seem to mind."

"I never would've known."

Denny laughed at Selena's amazement. "Well, he *is* my half brother. We don't have the same last names and besides, I never would've known the two of you knew each other."

Selena sighed. "Yeah, well, my knowing Darius McClellan is something I'm starting to regret."

"Why?"

"Well . . . don't get me wrong. Any woman would love to have your brother in her life. But sometimes, he's just so . . ."

"Cold?"

"Exactly."

Again, Denny laughed. "Selena, there's something you should realize. Darius has had quite a few relationships in his time. One, in particular, messed him up. Bad. It's very hard for him to trust. More than it ever was before, if that's possible. And that mess with Velma Morris . . . he's probably even more untrusting now."

Selena rolled her eyes toward the ceiling as she leaned back on her sofa. "I haven't given him any reason not to trust me."

"Maybe you don't think you have. But, with D, the least little thing can set him off."

"Well, what got him like this?"

"That's something you should ask him," Denny suggested.

"Would he tell me?"

"Probably not."

"Thanks."

Denny smiled at Selena's sour tone. "Seriously though, girl, I think D is more caught up over you than I've ever seen him about any woman."

Selena didn't want her heart to beat faster when she heard that. Of course, the reaction was inevitable. "You think so?" she heard herself asking.

"Hell yes. My brother has a reputation for being a real ladies' man. He rarely gets taken in by one in particular."

"Denny, I know you're his brother but how do you know he feels this way about me? Did he say something when he came to your office?"

"Well . . . he—"

"Damn," Selena said.

"What?"

"Doorbell's ringing. Look, I'm gonna call you back, all right? I wanna finish this."

"No problem. Call me at home."

"Bye, Denny. . . . Now, who could this be?" Selena asked herself, the instant she clicked off the phone.

In the cozy comfort of her lovely brownstone, she'd changed from her sweatsuit into a T-shirt and a pair of tattered denim shorts. Shrugging off her attire, she answered the door.

Darius was leaning against the doorjamb. He was always devastating in whatever he decided to wear, and that evening was no exception. The cream trousers hung just right over his long legs and a navy blue linen shirt lay outside the pants. Matching navy suede boots completed the sexy ensemble.

"Your doctor gave me an idea of where to find you," he unnecessarily informed her.

"Mmm . . . why am I not surprised?" she softly replied, her hazel stare traveling over his tall, powerful frame.

Darius traced his neat mustache and pushed himself away from the doorjamb. "May I come in?"

"After going to all this trouble to find me? Sure you can come in." She stepped away from the door.

As soon as Darius was inside, his sleek brows rose and his sweet chocolate stare held an unmistakably impressed look. "Very nice," he said, walking farther inside.

"Thanks."

Darius glanced back at Selena and shook his head. "No, I mean it, Sel. I didn't expect your place to look this way."

A frown crossed Selena's lovely features. "Well, how'd you expect it to look?"

Rich, deep laughter escaped his throat, and his dimples were fully visible. "What I mean is, I didn't expect your home to be so, uh . . . dark, mellow."

Understanding finally crept into Selena's eyes and she nodded. "Oh, okay. Well, I hate sunlight coming through in the mornings and when I come home, I like to feel that this is my own private world—away from everything."

Darius nodded. "Very impressive," he complimented, looking around the spacious living room with its mixture of browns, burgundys, greens, and other warm colors. "You always surprise me."

Selena pushed her hands through her thick, bouncy locks and sighed. "Yeah, well, that's me."

"I regret the way that phone call turned out," he said, getting right to the point.

"Don't worry about it."

"That's not my style," Darius softly informed her, massaging one hand across the back of his neck.

Selena propped her hands on her hips. "What? Not worrying about it or not hanging up?"

"Both. You didn't deserve that."

Selena could see the sincerity in his eyes and she smiled. "We just had a misunderstanding, that's all."

"I never meant for you to think I left you."

"I know."

"That night was just so damned crazy and then on top of everything else, Velma lied to me. . . ."

Darius had made himself comfortable on the sofa and Selena decided to join him. "I still can't believe that," she said.

"Hmph," Darius said, propping the side of his face against his palm. "Almost four weeks wasted screwin' around down there."

Selena cleared her throat and shifted uneasily on the sofa. "Sorry," she whispered.

Darius slid his gaze over her legs and thighs, before settling on her face. "The best thing about it all was meeting you."

"Don't lie," she warned.

"I'm not."

"We argued half the time."

"I enjoyed every minute of it."

Selena rolled her eyes. "Please."

"Just tell me how."

Suddenly, she laughed. Darius, however, appeared completely serious as he uttered his suave one-liners.

"Boy, you are too much!" she raved, wiping tears of laughter from her eyes. "Do you know how you sound?" She turned to face him more fully.

Darius's intense stare never faltered. "I think I sound like a man using everything he knows to keep seeing a woman he enjoys spending time with."

Selena's soft chuckling was curbed by a sharp gasp at the firm, sincere statement. "You want to see more of me?" she asked.

Long, dark lashes closed over his eyes. "Very much," he confirmed.

"When?"

A wicked smirk lifted the corners of his mouth and he pulled her close. "Right now," he told her, his lips slanting across hers.

Selena voiced a low moan as she returned the kiss. Darius's large hands disappeared beneath her top and he favored her back with teasing strokes. It felt like heaven and she hoped it would never end.

They made love well into the night. As Selena enjoyed the ecstasy, though, she realized that sex always seemed to be there to smooth over the unpopular areas of a relationship. She prayed that it would not become the foundation of her relationship with Darius. Especially when she wanted them to be so much more.

Selena woke the next morning to find herself alone in the four-poster canopy bed. Stretching herself across the smooth satin sheets, she found a note folded on a pillow. *Early meeting. HATED to leave! I'll call. D.*

Selena smiled and touched the note to her lips. She buried her head in Darius's pillow, inhaling the scent of his cologne. Before she could drift back to sleep, the phone rang.

The loud clamors succeeded in keeping her somewhat lucid. "Yes?" she grumbled into the receiver.

"Selena? What are you still doing in bed?"

"Anna?"

The woman sighed on the other end. "Yes, it's me. Did you forget your appointment with Sabrina?"

Selena pulled one hand through her tousled hair. "Sabrina?"

"Sabrina Little, your head photographer? You have a meeting—"

"Oh, damn!"

"You want me to cancel?"

"No, I'm getting up right now. Just tell her to hold on. I'll be there in two shakes." Hanging up, Selena flopped back onto the bed. Then she flipped the covers away and headed for the shower.

The meeting with Sabrina was as productive as it was interesting. Since Selena never tired of going over pictures, it was approaching the lunch hour when she finally left the photo department. When she left the elevator, Anna Edwards looked up from behind her desk.

"You had a delivery," she called.

"What?" Selena asked, tapping her long nails on the desk.

Anna shook her head, which bobbed with short black curls. "Damn, if I knew you were going to ask me that, I would've opened it."

Selena rolled her eyes. "Hush up. Shouldn't you be at home with the baby, anyway?"

A dreamy gleam crept into Anna's brown eyes. "Ha! Don't tempt me."

"I'll open this in my office," she retorted.

Behind closed doors, Selena's easy expression faded. Lately, unexpected packages weren't tops on her list. Still, her curiosity was piqued as she opened the cardboard box to find an elegantly wrapped package. She tore into the silvery box and, in seconds, was extracting a long, seductive caramel-colored negligee.

With a shriek of delight—and relief—she shook the silk creation. A real lingerie horse, she couldn't wait to try on the garment. Before doing so, however, she searched the box and wrappings for a card. After a few moments, she gave up and went to try on the gorgeous piece.

The gown flattered her tiny, voluptuous form as did the color of the material. The slip-style bodice hugged her full breasts, while the lace covering the cups offered tantalizing peeks at the lush mounds. Selena was so in love with the beautiful gift, she didn't hear her office door open and someone walking inside.

"Selena, you in here?"

Jumping at the deep voice vibrating in the room, Selena realized it was Darius. Of course, that did nothing to calm her. *Goodness, does he always have to catch me undressed?* she wondered.

Darius had made himself comfortable against her desk. He

spied the cardboard box and familiar wrapping from the gift he'd sent. A knowing smirk crossed his handsome face as he looked around the office. "Selena?" he called again.

"Just a minute," she replied. Pressing one hand against her nervous stomach, she peeked around the corner. There was Darius, looking as though he owned the place, and she could feel her heart race at the sight of him.

Of course, the case of nerves didn't last long. Selena knew she'd have to come out to retrieve her clothes. She really didn't mind about her appearance, though. She looked forward to modeling the piece of eye candy for the man in the next room.

When Darius saw her walk out into the office, he pulled his bottom lip between his perfect teeth to keep his mouth from dropping open. His brown eyes took in every inch of her in the revealing gown. Though he loved the way the split offered glimpses of her shapely legs and thighs, his eyes kept returning to the gown's bodice.

"My God . . ." he breathed.

Selena's eyes seemed to sparkle with delight. "Thank you."

"You're welcome," Darius replied, as he bowed his head. "I wasn't sure of the size, but I'd say I guessed right."

Selena's eyes were wide as she stared at him. "You? You sent this?"

Darius pretended to be hurt. "Who else?"

Selena uttered a quick laugh and raked one hand through her hair. "It's just that I order so much on-line, I lose track sometimes . . . I never thought you'd do something like— never mind." she stammered.

Darius understood. "Listen, I just wanted to do this for you. Don't get the wrong idea—"

"Oh no!" she said, not wanting to hear the rest of what he had to say. "You don't have to explain to me. Believe me, I have no crazy ideas about us. I know what this is."

They both wanted it to be more. Still, Darius felt it best not to voice that feeling and Selena agreed. Aside from the tremendous pull they felt toward each other, their vows never to be hurt again took precedence.

Darius's gorgeous cocoa eyes settled on Selena's attire once more and he shook his head. "So how do you like it?"

"Are you serious?" she cried, twirling around the room in the sleek negligee. "I love it. I usually don't wear these things, but I guess I should start."

Darius uttered a low sound, his probing gaze growing a bit more narrowed. "Damn right," he agreed.

Selena's own eyes narrowed and she began to take small steps toward her desk. Close enough to touch, she traced the strong cords of muscle in Darius's forearms visible beneath the rolled sleeves of his gray shirt. She inched closer, and began to favor the side of his neck with soft kisses. She busied herself removing his tie, and once it was discarded she went to work on the shirt buttons. Darius groaned in response to the soft kisses and she smiled, her lips pressing against the pulse at the base of his throat.

Once his shirt and coat were removed, Darius pushed the negligee down and it pooled around her bare feet. He lifted her and carried her across the office. Depositing her on the cream sofa, he finished removing his clothes. Selena's eyes followed every movement of his fingers, and soon his sleek, dark form was covering hers.

She could feel her thighs tremble just slightly when he pulled them apart to settle himself. He practically smothered her tiny form beneath his, but she didn't mind. Her body melted into the sofa cushions, which felt heavenly against her bare skin.

A soft moan passed her lips when Darius lowered his lips to hers and invaded her mouth with his tongue. He stroked the darkened cavern slowly and deliberately as one hand rose to cup her breast. In response, Selena locked her legs around his lean waist, her long nails stroking his back.

A wicked smirk tugged at Darius's lips as his mouth eased down the smooth column of her neck. His tongue circled the hard peak of her breast, his eyes snapping to her face, when he heard her gasp.

Selena pushed her head farther into the cushions, her body arching in response to his teasing. She pulled his head closer to her chest, moaning when he tugged the nipple between his lips and gently suckled. Doubling the steamy caress, he trailed his forefinger along the satiny folds of her womanhood.

"Yes . . ." she breathed in anticipation of the intimate caress.

Darius teased her with a few more strokes, so light she barely felt them. Then, he thrust two fingers inside, grunting when he felt the creamy moisture touch his skin. He added two more fingers to the caress, loving the soft sounds she uttered near his ear. He put protection in place, then he buried himself in her wet center.

Selena arched off the sofa when Darius's heavy, throbbing length entered her. For a long while, he simply allowed himself to enjoy the intense pleasure of her inner walls sheathing his arousal. Selena wasn't used to playing such a passive role during lovemaking. With Darius, however, she admitted the role felt surprisingly wonderful.

Bracing himself on arms taut with cords of muscle, Darius increased the force of his thrusts.

Selena gripped his arms and met the forward motions of his hips. As they neared satisfaction, pleasure-filled cries gained volume. Faintly, Selena remembered her staff, who were surely aware of what was going on in her office. At that moment, her only concern was the desire that threatened to consume her.

A long while later, Darius raised his head from the crook of Selena's neck and smiled down. Her gaze roamed the handsome dark face above her. She traced the neat mustache and dimples with unforgettable intensity.

"Have dinner with me tonight?" he asked.

"What time?" she purred.

"Seven-thirty."

"You got it."

Mentally pleased and physically satisfied, Darius nodded and reluctantly pulled away. An easy silence filled the office. Selena was content, watching as he headed to her private bath to wash up. As she lay there thinking how sexy and incredible he was, Darius was thinking the same about her.

His clothes in place, Darius leaned down to place a kiss to her mouth. Selena was so exhausted, she didn't bother leaving the sofa. Snuggling beneath the comfortable, dark afghan, which lay across the back of the sofa, she drifted off to sleep.

Around three o'clock, Selena forced her eyes open when she felt a constant nudging at her shoulder. Standing above her was a tall, lovely dark woman with a chic short hairstyle and striking black eyes.

"Nelia?" Selena groggily inquired, clearing her throat as she pushed herself into a sitting position.

Nelia Cannon gave her friend a knowing smile, though her words held a tone of surprise. "Girl, what the hell are you doin' conked out in the middle of the day?"

"I haven't been sleeping well and there's been a lot goin' on," Selena promptly replied, knowing Nelia would not be readily convinced.

"Like what?" the woman challenged.

Shaking her head, Selena wrapped the afghan around her shoulders and proceeded to gather her clothes. As she freshened up and dressed, she told her friend about Miami—never mentioning the strange notes she'd been receiving. Nelia, however, was more interested in hearing about the man Selena mentioned.

Nelia's dark eyes were filled with curiosity. She stood with her arms folded across her chest—a message to Selena that more details were necessary.

"I met him in Miami," Selena called from the washroom as she quickly showered and donned her things.

"Ha!" Nelia cried as she began to nod. "I know you, Sel. I'm sure you two did more than just *meet,*" she drawled, hearing her friend's laughter.

"Well, we got very close, but there's really not that much more to it."

Nelia took a seat behind Selena's desk. "That can't be true. I mean, I'm assuming from your . . . disheveled appearance that something interesting just happened in here. Should I also assume that this mystery man just came all the way up here from Miami to see you?"

Selena left the washroom, checking the posts on her hoop earrings. "No, he lives in New York, owns a security firm in Brooklyn . . ."

Nelia's long silky brows drew closed. "A security firm in Brooklyn . . . Who is he?"

"Mmm, I don't think you know him," Selena absently remarked as she folded the afghan and replaced it on the back of the sofa.

"Well, what's his name?" Nelia persisted.

"Darius McClellan."

Nelia's mouth fell open and she leaned forward, her palms flat on Selena's desk. "I don't believe this! You're jokin', right?"

Selena turned and fixed Nelia with a strange look. "What? You know him?"

"Know him? He's one of Stephan's best friends," she revealed, referring to her husband.

"Get out."

"I'm serious," Nelia insisted, standing behind the desk. "They've been friends for years."

"And y'all never introduced me?" Selena asked, slightly aggravated by the fact.

Nelia only shrugged. "I didn't think he'd be your type."

"What?"

"What I mean is, Darius is . . . well . . . he's not a *one*-woman kind of man, get it?"

"Mmm . . ." Selena murmured. She got it all too well. "I figured as much," she finally admitted.

"Hmph, maybe he's trying to turn over a new leaf," Nelia decided. "I haven't seen him in a while."

"I doubt it. I mean, how successful a ladies' man was he?"

Nelia shot her friend a stunned look. "Girl, just look at him!"

Selena's smile was one of pure sensuality. "I have," she purred, sending her girlfriend into peals of laughter. Still, Selena tried to shrug off the news of Darius's well-known lady-killer image. She told herself that it really didn't matter, since their relationship had no hope of going beyond what it was. Of course as much as she hated to admit it, the statement didn't quite ring true.

Nelia and Selena had a great visit, and gradually the subject shifted to other matters. By the time they made it out of the parking lot, they were still chatting away.

Whenever the two friends got together, they always lost track of time. The twosome had a late lunch and spent the remainder of the afternoon catching up. Selena didn't even realize how much time had passed until she was on her way home.

She remembered Darius's invitation to dinner and rushed into her home, stripping out of her clothes. She prepared a bath and was about to settle into the foamy bubbles, when the doorbell rang. She hesitated, looking from the tub to the bathroom door. Finally, she decided to answer the door.

A scowl darkened Darius's features as he leaned against the stoop. When he saw Selena wrapped in a short green towel, the scowl transformed into an expression of sensual shock.

"What took you so long?" he asked, running one hand across his hair-roughened cheek. "Didn't I say I'd be here at seven-thirty?" he continued, hoping mock aggravation would help him keep his hands off her.

Selena closed the door and hurried back toward the stairs. "I'm sorry, I got caught up with a friend and lost track of time. I won't be long," she promised, reaching the top of the staircase where she pulled away the towel.

She had just eased into the tub when she felt creamy bubbles being smoothed across her back. Darius had removed his brown linen shirt and was kneeling on the floor beside the tub.

"A backrub?" she whispered.

"Do you mind?"

"No . . ." she sighed, feeling his lips caressing the nape of her neck. "But, um . . . didn't you make reservations?"

Darius pulled his hands out of the water and stood. Selena's eyes were helplessly drawn to his waist as he removed his jeans, boxers, and boots.

"No need for reservations," he finally began to explain. "I had a feeling we might be late."

Later, Selena watched Darius sleeping. She thought about what Nelia had told her about him and couldn't help wondering . . . Selena knew her own feelings were becoming more complex and she was helpless to stop them. Of course, the last thing she needed just then was an in-depth relationship. Unfortunately, she'd always been highly optimistic and with everything going so well . . .

Laughing softly, she tried to put things in perspective. An in-depth relationship? Please! She and Darius were far from having anything like that. Though she'd had no qualms about their sex life, it still concerned her. Would that attraction ruin their ability for something more solid? She couldn't help wondering if his feelings for her might run deeper.

"What's wrong?"

Selena jerked herself from her thoughtful state when she heard Darius calling to her. His warm, gorgeous stare was intent as he watched her.

"I'm hungry," she teased, hoping to hide her unease as she tapped one finger to his mustache.

Darius smiled and pushed himself up in bed. "Say no more."

"Uh-uh," she argued, grabbing his wrist when he made a

move to leave. "Where are you going?" she scolded, beckoning him back beneath the covers.

"You know, I love what you have on, but I wish you hadn't worn it."

Selena pulled her eyes up from the menu to pin Darius with a stare. "Excuse me?" she queried, completely innocent.

"You heard me."

"What's the matter with what I'm wearing?" she asked, glancing at the gold silk jumpsuit she sported.

"Every man in here has made a point of speaking to you," he noted simply, though his gaze was hard.

Selena brushed off the comment. "Sweetie, that has nothing to do with what I'm wearing. I just know a lot of people."

"Mmm-hmm."

"Anyway," she began, returning her attention to the menu, "I could say the same thing about most of the women in here."

Surprise registered on Darius's handsome dark face. "Don't even try it," he ordered.

"What? It's true," she replied, still focusing on the menu.

"Selena—"

"Darius," she said, raising her eyes to his, "since we stepped out of the car, a slew of women have been up in your face."

Darius waved his hand. "Whatever," he mumbled.

Selena's lilting laughter turned a few heads. "Don't try to deny it. I mean, I know what a ladies' man you are."

"Where'd you hear that?" he asked, his tone dripping with interest.

Selena took a deep breath and decided to bite the bullet. "Nelia Cannon is a good friend of mine."

"Nel? You know Stephan's wife?" he asked, becoming silent as he digested the information.

"Mmm-hmm."

"What'd she tell you?"

"Why? You have something to hide?"

"Hell no!"

Selena enjoyed the power she felt at her ability to shake the man's usually cool demeanor. "Actually, she flattered you. Told me how, uh, successful you are with the ladies."

Darius tapped one finger to his mustache and regarded her thoughtfully. "I'm surprised. She never fails to tell me how much she disapproves of the way I lead my private life."

Selena shrugged, pretending not to be too interested in the choice bits of information she was coaxing from him. "Well, I think she *was* sort of surprised to find out that we, uh, knew each other in Miami and were still . . . 'seeing' each other now."

"Hmph, I would've liked to see the look on her face when she discovered that," he proudly admitted.

Though he seemed pleased by the fact, Selena was still a bit confused. If only she could be certain that his feelings went beyond . . . sexual. Brushing off the thought, she decided it was for the best.

Once the waiter had taken their orders, Darius tapped one finger to the pearl-white tablecloth to draw Selena's attention.

"I think we'll eat in the next time I ask you *out* to dinner," he decided, nodding when she laughed.

Though the words were delivered lightly, Selena caught the underlying hostility lacing them.

Nine

"I'd like to take you to the Entrepreneur's Ball, unless you already have plans to go with someone else."

Selena stared across the table at Darius. Her fork was poised over the mouthwatering vegetarian lasagne she'd prepared for their lunch date at her home. His invitation left her more than a little surprised.

"I, um . . ."

Darius smirked, causing his mustache to twitch adoringly. "It's all right if you already have a date."

"No, no, I—I don't," she hurriedly replied with a quick shake of her head. "But how'd you know I'd been invited?"

Darius set his fork aside and fixed her with a probing look. "Well, you, like me, are a minority and an entrepreneur."

"Now I see why you're such a success at what you do."

Darius tilted his head at the teasing remark. "It wasn't too hard to guess. So? Do we have a date?"

Though the offer was very appealing, Selena felt reluctant to accept. "There's been so much going on lately, I just don't know if I'm in much of a party mood," she confessed, her thoughts turning to the mysterious letters.

"This I can't believe," Darius admitted, in a playful, lazy tone. He rested his hand across the Grambling State logo on his sweatshirt and leaned back in his chair. "You know, I really don't want to take no for an answer."

"You don't *want* to, does that mean you would?" Selena asked, her voice sounding small.

Darius grinned at her cunning. "I see I'll have to speak frankly with you."

"Please."

"I don't like the word no since it usually prevents me from getting what I want."

"I see." She sighed, folding her arms across the snug front of her V-neck blouse. "Well . . . I *am* up for an award."

"Then what are you hedging for?" he cried, raising his hands in the air.

"It does sound like fun," she admitted, smiling at the soft look that had crept into his gorgeous browns.

"So we got a date?"

Selena replied with a decisive nod, "We do," just as the distinct ring of a cell phone pierced the air.

Darius grimaced and pulled the pocket-sized object from his sagging jeans. "Darius," he answered.

Selena stood and began to clear away the lunch dishes. She went into the kitchen for about five minutes. When she returned, Darius was at the front door.

"Gotta go?" she called, strolling toward him.

"Unfortunately," he confirmed, easing his arms about her waist. "This was nice," he said, glancing around the cozy, dim living room.

"Mmmm . . . no male or *female* acquaintances approaching our table to say hello . . ." she noted softly, feeling his rumbling of laughter against her cheek.

"Amen."

Selena fixed him with a soft, lingering stare and pressed her lips together when he toyed with a lock of her curly hair.

"See you soon," he whispered, then turned to the door.

Selena shook her head, watching him go. A second or two passed before the phone demanded her attention. "Selena Witherspoon," she greeted.

"Have you checked your e-mail today?"

The computer generated voice filled her ears, rendering her speechless and motionless. When the connection was broken, she hesitated awhile longer before resigning herself to head to her home office. Once there, she took slow, unsteady steps toward the PC on the corner of the desk.

"Come on, Sel," she prompted herself, determinedly logging on and entering her mail program.

Only one message grabbed her attention. The subject line read *Ooo La La*. There was no identification regarding the sender. There was also no typed message, only a blinking icon that indicated sound. One click brought the unmistakable sound of a woman's passionate moans into the room. A man's voice, or perhaps several men's voices, was added to the melee. The woman's moans gained volume as she gasped.

A pained cry escaped Selena's throat and she closed down the page. She moved away from the desk, casting frightened looks across her shoulder as she reached for the phone.

"Synth? It's me. I think I'd like to take that meeting with Max Richardson now."

"Thanks for coming. Did Synth fill you in?"

Max rubbed Selena's back reassuringly when she led him into her home two hours later. "She told me what she knew and you know I'm happy to offer whatever help I can."

"Mmm . . . but you want to know why I didn't call Darius?" she asked, hearing the unspoken question in his voice.

"He *is* the top man," Max teased.

"I just don't want to worry him with this," she explained, while leading the way through her living room. "The nature of the . . . communications has me suspicious."

"Suspicious?" Max blurted. "Of what?"

"My past . . . a past incident I haven't thought about in years," she clarified, watching some of the confusion leave his face. "Someone's threatening me again and it scares me out of my mind to think of how far they may go with this. This way," she urged, taking him into her home office.

Displayed on the desk was every note she'd received since

Miami. The pieces of evidence were arranged in clear plastic bags next to the PC.

"Efficient," Max complimented, smoothing one hand across his shaved head.

"I spent a few hours scouring them myself," she admitted, rubbing her arms to soothe the sudden chill she felt.

Max sat behind the desk and began to study the brief notes. After a moment or two, he looked up at Selena. His confusion had returned.

"The e-mail message may help you to draw your own conclusions," she advised, waving toward the computer. "Just click on the blinking icon."

Max followed her instructions, then reclined in the chair and waited. He massaged his jaw as the sound began to roll. Then, noticing Selena's reaction, he shut it off.

"Is that you?" he asked.

"I don't think so. At first, I thought maybe . . . but then I heard the voices of more than one man and I knew I never . . ."

Max nodded. "Any thoughts on who would do this?" he asked.

Selena turned away, tucking her hands into the flowing sleeves of her sky-blue knit sweater.

"Selena?"

"Max, anyone could be responsible for this. It could be any number of people. I *am* in the public eye to a certain extent, and there's always someone out there hoping to ruin your credibility and, subsequently, your business."

"I really can't see you having one enemy," Max said, soft laughter following his words.

Selena shrugged and perched against the arm of the chair before her desk. "You'd rethink that statement if we were in business together. I can be pretty shrewd."

"Kind of rough on yourself."

"Not as hard as I should be. My past doesn't read like a fairy tale," she said, needing him to understand.

"That still doesn't give anyone the right to send you crap like this," Max argued, waving toward the desktop.

Selena's laughter was brief and bitter. "I hope that's *all* they have in store."

"And you wouldn't feel better if we brought Darius in on this?"

"I said no!" she snapped, shoving her hands through her hair. "I'm sorry, Max, but I can't have him knowing about this," she whispered, turning to face him. "A long time ago, I went through a lot of mudslinging over crap like this. I can't drag Darius in, knowing it may turn out like that again. If this puts you in an awkward position, I can find someone else to—"

"I won't say a thing," Max vowed, standing and raising his right hand as though he were taking an oath. "Just promise me you'll consider talking to him if this mystery person goes any further?"

Selena couldn't mask her concern. "I'll do it then. You'll have no argument from me. I promise."

Max's dark, deep-set eyes narrowed a bit. "You care a lot about my boy, don't you?"

"Mmm-hmm," she admitted, tears beginning to glisten in her light eyes. "I don't want him to know anything about this. Our relationship has enough dramatics without me adding any more to the pot."

"Well, for the record, I think you're pretty incredible and D knows that too," Max said, pulling Selena's arm through the crook of his.

Selena looked down and smiled. "Thanks, Max."

"All right, enough of this sappy mess," he decided, squeezing her hand before he turned back toward the desk. "I'm gonna carry this with me." He collected the messages, leaving his card in their place. "My e-mail address is there. Forward me that message."

"I will," she promised, following with a curt nod.

Max waved his hand toward the door. "Show me out?"

Selena secured all her locks following Max's departure. She muttered an exasperated curse, while surveying the line of dead bolts and chains, suddenly realizing how strongly the situation had affected her. Struggling to find something else to focus on, she remembered her date that evening.

"I'm almost positive they'll have some of that at the banquet," Selena teased when she opened her front door around 7:00 P.M.

Darius occupied his now familiar leaning stance against the doorjamb. He looked impossibly gorgeous in a stylish black tux. The casually sexy look of his attire was enhanced, not only by the fact that the jacket required no tie, but also by the few unfastened buttons on the crisp white shirt.

"I agree," he said, raising the bottle of wine and two glasses he carried. "But we have a while before things get started and . . . at lunch, I got the distinct impression that you needed to relax."

Selena tucked her hands in the oversized pockets of her robe. "You're beginning to know me pretty well, Mr. McClellan." She sighed. "What?" she queried, noticing the way his gaze grew more narrowed.

"Later," he decided, rising to his full height. "Will you let me come inside?"

Selena smiled at the softly suggestive undertone of the question and moved aside.

Darius's slanting eyes raked her ankle-length pink and blue patchwork robe.

"I didn't expect you quite so early," she explained, noticing his dimples appearing.

"I'm not complaining," he whispered, the neat mustache twitching a bit more.

Selena pushed the door closed, then let her hands slap her thighs. "Well, since you seem to like it so, maybe I don't need to change?"

Darius shook his head and strolled into the living room. "Nothing I'd like better than to watch you in that robe all night. *But* I don't think the awards folk would appreciate it too much."

Selena sighed. "I don't know . . ." she drawled, spreading her arms about her small frame. "I just may win all the awards in this getup."

"I don't doubt that," he admitted, uncorking the bottle and pouring two glasses of the fragrant Chianti.

"Thanks," Selena said, accepting the glass and fixing him with a soft look. "Really, Darius, thank you for this," she said, taking a seat in one of the deep-wine armchairs flanking her sofa.

Darius took his place right before her on the edge of the coffee table. "Wanna talk about it?" he asked, tapping the stem of his glass against her knee.

Selena shook her head. "No."

"So there *is* something wrong?"

Selena closed her eyes. "Let it go," she pleaded.

Darius shrugged, but abided by her request.

"So are you gonna tell me why you looked at me so funny earlier?" she asked, leaning back to sip her wine.

"When you said I knew you pretty well."

Selena looked down into her glass and grinned. "No . . . I said you were *beginning* to know me pretty well."

"Exactly my point."

"What?"

"I want to get to know you better."

A teasing light twinkled in Selena's gaze. "I don't think you could know me *any* better."

Darius braced his elbows against his knees and studied the plush navy carpeting beneath his wing tips. "I'd like to get to know you *outside* the bedroom."

He'd said it. Her question regarding how he viewed their relationship had been answered. "Why?" she blurted anyway, instantly regretting the slip.

"You can't tell me a man has never said that to you before," he softly delved, intrigued by her response to his simple admission.

"Hmph," Selena grunted, swirling the remnants of wine in her glass. "I might've run scared if he had."

"Why?"

"My . . . success with men has managed to flounder as it relates to 'getting to know you.' I seem to be a miserable failure when it comes to that."

"Yeah," Darius agreed, helping himself to the rest of his wine, "my track record isn't much better there either." He set the glass aside. "Maybe we could change that."

Selena fidgeted in the chair, tucking her legs beneath her.

"And what would you have in mind?" she asked, her eyes probing his own.

Darius spread his hands. "Nothing over the top like Miami. Simple, but enjoyable."

"Such as?"

"Such as every Saturday I jog in Prospect Park." He fixed her with a challenging stare. "If you're up for it, perhaps you'll join me?"

"If I'm up for it?" Selena parroted, on the verge of a laughing fit. "I don't know how long it's been since I've been out for a jog. It may be over before it begins," she warned.

"Should I take that as a yes?"

Selena chewed her bottom lip, never noticing how intently Darius followed the action. "What time should I meet you?" she finally replied.

"So, is this just an exercise in health or do you have something else in mind?" she was asking once they'd discussed the particulars.

Darius shrugged. "We could do anything—talk . . . maybe I could find out how your family reacted when you told them about the magazine."

Selena laughed, but the sadness still crept into her eyes.

"Bad memories?" Darius guessed.

"Most of my family." She sighed, looking out across the living room. "My parents. They practically disowned me, but that was way before I started the magazine." She cleared her throat amidst the swell of emotion rising in her throat. "My grandmother and Synthia are the only ones I consider family. They've always supported me."

Darius watched her strangely. "I can't believe someone like you would have those kinds of problems."

"Someone like me?" she asked, eager to hear his explanation.

"Sweet, caring—especially toward friends and family. I can tell those relationships are important to you."

Selena stood from the chair and inched past Darius. "The person you see before you now has changed a lot over the years. I know the things—the people that are important. I don't think I realized it then as much as I do now."

"But still, for your family to close you out like that," he went on, watching her from his place on the coffee table. "I can't see you doing anything to warrant that," he said, watching as she forced a smile to her face. He glanced down at his wristwatch and made a face. "We better bounce soon."

Selena snapped her fingers and made a move for the stairway. Suddenly, she stopped and turned to him. "Thank you," she called, her smile genuine. "This was very nice of you."

"No problem," he said, his stare growing more intent as he watched her leave the room.

Darius had hoped he could remain faithful to his decision to practice self-control. When he helped Selena out of her coat and saw the dress she'd chosen for the banquet, he feared self-control was a hopeless expectation.

The stunning creation hugged her curvaceous form like a second skin. White satin, sensual to the touch, it had a draping halter neckline—leaving her back bare to the dip of her spine. The ankle-length skirt molded to her full bottom while the deep front split enticed an admirer with the view of her legs and thighs.

"Darius McClellan!"

Selena and Darius were about to take their seats when they heard the call.

"What's goin' on, kid?" a handsome, muscular man greeted, while extending his hand.

"Cory," Darius replied, accepting the handshake as he hugged the fifty-something gentleman.

"Congratulations, man," Cory Scotts said, hearty laughter filtering the words.

"'Preciate it, man. 'Preciate it."

"Congratulations?" Selena softly interjected, watching the two tall gentlemen with a raised brow.

Darius turned and set his hand on the small of her back. "Selena Witherspoon, this is Cory Scotts—a colleague or, should I say, competitor?" he teased.

"Either is appropriate," Cory agreed as he stepped closer to envelope Selena's small hand in both of his. "Pleasure to meet you, Ms. Witherspoon," he said, his dark eyes raking her form in a way that was flattering and in no way lecherous.

Selena returned his smile. "Same here."

Cory nodded and turned back to Darius. "I was congratulating this man on his nomination tonight."

Selena slapped her hand against Darius's elbow. "You didn't tell me you were up for an award too," she playfully scolded, watching him shrug.

Cory was chuckling. "Well, good luck to you both," he said, squeezing Selena's hand and hugging Darius again before he moved on.

"Will this be your first win?" she asked, as they claimed their seats.

"First nomination. I don't know about first win yet."

"Modest," she accused.

"And what about you?" he asked, leaning back in his chair to study her profile.

"I won the first year *Reigning Queens* was published," she said, turning to see his reaction.

Darius's dimples instantly appeared. "A success right off the bat," he raved.

"It keeps me warm at night," she remarked, being intentionally glib.

Darius made a face. "It sounds cozy."

Selena laughed. "I could say the same about your lifestyle."

"How so?" he asked, propping his elbow along the edge of the table.

One bare shoulder rose slowly as she shrugged. "Well, you're a successful ladies' man," she drawled, "respected, intelligent, gorgeous, no-nonsense. Perfect husband material," she admitted, without averting her gaze. "You haven't been snared yet, so obviously your success has been a cozy bed partner as well."

Darius looked down as he chuckled. "That lifestyle does offer less drama and make for a more restful night's sleep."

"See?" she teased, her smile radiant.

"Still," Darius cautioned, as he stood, "every once in a while, I pine for the companionship of a partner more, um . . . lively."

"Ah . . ." she acknowledged with an airy wave.

"Shall we?" he requested, extending his hand.

The stunning, stylishly dressed couple strolled to the dance floor. The music had taken on a slower, more seductive tempo.

"I think this is going to be pretty interesting."

"What?" Selena almost purred, loving the way his arms encircled her waist.

"Us. Getting to know each other."

Selena toyed with the gray-and-black-checkered handkerchief peeking from his breast pocket. "How so?" she added.

"My fascination with a woman usually ends once she's been in my bed."

Selena nodded, wondering if he could feel the gooseflesh where his fingers stroked her spine. "So I suppose you take most women to bed before getting to know them?"

"I don't care about getting to know them."

"I see . . . so this is, um, a first for you?" she asked, watching him closely.

Darius's expression hardened so briefly, it could have been imagined. "Somethin' like that," he said, after a silent second or two.

Selena's lips parted to probe him with more questions, but she was jostled from behind. She and Darius pulled apart and turned to find another banquet attendee standing next to them.

"So sorry, Selena," Francine Johns apologized, her words as phony as the smile she offered. Her astute green gaze surveyed Selena with unmasked dislike, and then she turned adoring eyes toward Darius. "How are you, sweetie?" she greeted, leaning close to press her cheek against his.

"Frankie," Darius cooly replied.

Francine's attention was already refocused on the woman at his side. "That dress makes you look very healthy, Selena."

Disregarding Francine's snide remark and smug grin, Selena looked down at her dress. "Thanks, Frankie, I think so too," she sang.

Her dig not producing the desired affect, Francine rolled her eyes and smiled at Darius. "I'm surprised to see *you* here."

Darius responded with a lopsided grin. "Yeah, I hardly come to this stuff, but this year I just had a desire to be here," he told her, but was looking down at Selena.

Francine read the look on his face and fought to smother her grimace. "Well, I only came over to congratulate you on your nomination."

"Thank you. Selena's up for an award as well," Darius announced, his gaze sharpening.

Francine allowed her dislike to shine through. "Well . . . trash always appeals to someone," she sneered, giving her plum chiffon scarf a decisive tug before she strolled away.

"Bitch," Darius whispered, bitter laughter following the word. Then, remembering the woman at his side, he closed his eyes. "I'm sorry, Selena. I shouldn't have said that and I apologize for Frankie too."

Selena responded with a flippant wave. "I'm used to it," she drawled.

"Known her long?" he asked, leaning back and pushing a fist into his trousers pocket.

"We went to college together," she said, when her expression turned guarded. She followed Francine's departing figure with a curious, horrified gaze. "We went to college together," she repeated in a softer, absent tone.

Darius tilted his head. "You all right?" he whispered, trailing his finger along her forearm.

Selena stared off a moment longer, then shook her head as if to clear it. "I'm fine," she insisted.

"May I have your attention!" the emcee announced over the microphone behind the head banquet table. "If everyone would take their seats, we're ready to begin our awards presentation!"

"And in our final publishing category—Women's Magazine of the Year . . . *Reigning Queens* magazine! Selena Witherspoon, publisher!"

Applause and cheers filled the hall while Selena remained seated. Her hand covered her mouth as happy tears pooled her eyes.

Darius pressed a lingering kiss to her cheek. "Get up there," he ordered, squeezing her elbow.

Amid the fervent cheers, Selena stood and made her way toward the front of the elegant room. There, she made a brief but lovely speech. Another round of applause followed her words and she headed back toward her table with both hands clutching the stout, gold-toned statue engraved with her name.

"Congratulations," Darius whispered, kissing her cheek again, while the next award was being announced.

"I never expected to win again," she admitted, turning to nod and wave toward those who congratulated her from afar.

"Glad you came?" Darius asked as he stepped over to hold her chair.

Selena waited to take her seat. "Very glad," she assured him, her expression soft.

"Excuse me, Ms. Witherspoon?"

"Yes?" Selena was all smiles as she acknowledged the waiter at the table.

"Congratulations on your win, ma'am," the young Asian man said as he leaned closer to the table. "There's a phone call for you. You can take it at the bar."

"Thanks," she said, resting her hand against Darius's chest. "I'll be right back." She hurried toward the bar, shaking hands with everyone who congratulated her.

"Selena Witherspoon," she sang into the receiver of the bar phone.

"Congratulations."

The voice on the line sounded heavy and distorted. It said nothing further, but shortly afterward another sound rolled. Selena's heart dashed from her chest to her stomach to her throat as she recognized the message from the earlier e-mail. Slamming down the phone, her heart still racing, she dashed toward the nearest exit. She was halfway out the door when a hand clamped over her wrist.

"What's the matter?" Darius demanded, frowning fiercely as his intense stare searched her apprehensive gaze.

Selena's lashes fluttered as a combination of fear and nervousness threatened to overwhelm her. "I'm—it's—I need to handle business. It's my business," she tried to explain.

"Let me take you," he offered, already searching his pockets for keys.

"No!" she cried, wrenching her wrist from his grasp. "It's okay, Darius, really. You should stay anyway. They haven't even gotten to your award yet."

Darius could tell she was desperate for reasons to discourage him from leaving with her. "Lemme get you a cab," he offered instead, ushering her through the lobby.

"I'll call you at home later," he told her once a car had been hailed.

Selena couldn't look him in the face. "Mmm-hmm . . ." she mumbled.

"Are you sure?"

Selena wrapped the patchwork quilt more tightly around her body and nodded. She'd dialed Max and Synthia on her cell phone the moment her cab left the banquet hall. The couple had been on their way out, but canceled their plans once they received her call.

"God . . ." she moaned, her voice as shaky as the rest of her body.

"Oh, sweetie . . ." Synthia soothed, pressing a dozen kisses to her cousin's temple.

"Someone has to be following me," Selena breathed, turning her red watery eyes toward Max.

"And you didn't recognize the voice?" he asked, resting his elbows against his jean-clad thighs.

Selena bowed her head. "It sounded all distorted, like some monster or something." She shuddered.

"This don't make a damn bit of sense," Max snapped, the situation eating away at his usually impenetrable demeanor. "Your past is no real secret. It's obvious this whole mess is a pack of lies. You said you'd been bothered by rumors like this before, right?"

"Mmm-hmm . . . remember, Synth?" Selena asked, watching her cousin nod.

"So why would someone wanna blackmail you with it now?" Max pointed out.

"What—what are you saying?" Selena whispered, uncertain she wanted to hear his theory.

"This could be about revenge," he voiced, massaging his neck as he leaned back on the sofa. "You said it yourself that you've stepped on a lot of toes."

"Hmph. Yeah, but for someone to go to all this trouble . . ." she said, managing to chuckle in spite of the coldness riddling her bones. "Oh . . . oh my God . . ."

Synthia began to rub her cousin's knee. "What, honey?" she whispered.

"Francine Johns," she said, recalling the run-in at the banquet.

"When'd you see her?" Synthia asked, her voice dripping with distaste.

"The ball," Selena said, wrapping the quilt even more tightly about the dress she had not bothered to change. "She couldn't resist walkin' over and giving me one of her nasty looks and remarks once she saw me."

"Is this Francine Johns someone that would or could do somethin' like this?" Max asked.

"In a heartbeat," Selena confirmed without hesitation, as she stepped over to the windows offering their view of Brooklyn.

Max looked to Synthia for answers. His dark gaze was steady and expectant.

"Sel dated Francine's boyfriend in college before they got together, but during the relationship, he tried to get back with Selena and then again once he and Francine divorced." She rubbed suddenly damp palms across the skirt of her denim jumper.

Max nodded, needing no further clarification. "Selena?" he called, watching her turn to face him with an expressionless gaze. "What else can you tell me about this woman?" He questioned, hoping she would snap out of her daze.

"She, uh . . . she owns a bookstore," Selena began, leaving the windows to stroll back to her chair. "Actually it's been in her family for generations. A very revered place, dating back to the renaissance period in Harlem. The bookstore is what brought us together." She swallowed past a sudden lump lodged in her throat. "It's how we became friends. I loved publishing and books and everything that encompassed. I worked in the store the summer before college. Our friendship was on the rocks by our second-semester sophomore year," she recalled. "The only emotion between us now is utter dislike, maybe even hatred on her part. She has no problem showing others how she feels about me. She couldn't wait to show Darius."

Max's long brows drew closer. "How'd you explain running out on him?"

"Told him it was business," she said, remembering the persistent ache in her chest when she had had to lie to Darius.

"You still sure about keeping him out of this?"

"Absolutely sure."

Max sighed, sending Synthia a concerned look. "I'm still going to have a background check done on Francine Johns," he was telling Selena, when the doorbell rang.

"I'll get it," Synthia called, already heading toward the foyer.

Darius waited outside the door. Sudden surprise registered in his gaze when Selena's cousin answered his ring. "Hey, Synthia," he said.

"Darius," she gasped, just as surprised by his appearance. "Come in," she urged.

"Everything all right?" he asked, while she closed and locked the door.

Synthia frowned as though confused. "Just fine, why?"

"Selena left before the banquet was over. Said there was some problem with the magazine."

"Sel always overreacts," Synthia drawled, waving her hands in the air. "Smallest thing about that magazine sets her off. Sel! Max! Darius is here!" she called, hoping to give them a second to wrap up their conversation before she and Darius entered the living room.

"What's up, man?" Darius greeted, shaking hands with Max. The curiosity in his expression was difficult to miss.

"What's going on, D?" Max remained cool, all too aware of his friend's extraordinary perception. "I was goin' out with Synth, when she got Selena's call."

"Just tagged along, huh?" Darius noted softly, expertly masking the intensity of his voice.

"Well, I know you two must be hungry," Selena interjected, leaving her spot by the sofa. "I think we got it all under control now."

Synthia slapped her hands to her sides. "I guess that's our cue?" she said to Max.

Max leaned over to press a kiss to Selena's cheek. "I'll call you," he whispered against her ear. "All right, man," he said to Darius, shaking hands once more before walking out.

"Everything okay?" Darius found himself asking again, once he and Selena were alone.

"Yeah, why?" she asked, conjuring a light voice and breathless laughter.

Darius only shrugged. He perched his tall frame against the corner of the message desk near the arched doorway.

"So, what are you doin' here?" Selena asked, as she folded the quilt. She could feel his eyes on her and she shivered briefly. "I thought you were going to call," she added.

"I would have," he explained, reaching back when he moved off the desk. "I thought you might like to have this tonight."

Selena turned, seeing her award in his hand. In an instant, the light returned to her eyes.

"Darius, thank you," she breathed, taking the statue and standing on her toes to kiss his mouth.

Darius pulled the trophy from her fingers and set it aside. He kept Selena close, his expression intensifying as he studied her face. "I want you to call me. Call me if you need anything, do you understand?"

"I will," she vowed, nodding like a small girl promising to be good.

"So, should I expect you for our run in the morning?"

Selena closed her eyes, recalling the jogging date she had completely forgotten. "Would you mind if I took a rain check? I'm just—just in no mood to—"

"It's fine. Selena, it's fine," he softly assured her, amused by her unease over turning him down. "So long as you promise to reschedule with me later?"

"Sounds good," she accepted, her luminous gaze trailing across his neat mustache and incredible mouth. "Maybe we could have dinner or something?"

"I promise to call first," he saw fit to add.

Selena's laughter bubbled forth in a ticklish wave. "Thanks, and thank you for being so great about this."

Nodding, Darius pressed a kiss to her temple before he moved past her.

"Damn," Selena whispered, when she heard the front door close behind him.

Ten

The following morning, Selena's nose was in the air as she followed it to the kitchen. The unmistakable aroma of breakfast had roused her from bed. She found Harry at the stove, adding a few more pancakes to an already towering mound.

Selena closed her eyes and smiled. Then, strolling over to the stove, she eased her arms about Harry's waist. "Oooh, how'd you know I needed this?" she whispered, pressing her cheek against his back.

Harry's chuckling shook his entire body. "I take that to mean you don't mind that I used my key?"

"I'm glad you did. After yesterday, I could use a whole day of pampering."

"Synth told me what's been going on," Harry said, handing Selena a mug of creamy mocha.

"I didn't want you to be worried," she said, inhaling the scent of the fragrant brew. *"But,* I know I need the support of my friends."

"Mmm," Harry grunted, setting the stack of pancakes on a porcelain platter. "The support of your friends, but not your lover, right?"

"Harry—"

"Girl, this mess sounds serious. Why the hell wouldn't you want him involved? This is his field of expertise, isn't it?"

Selena leaned against the white double-sided refrigerator. "If Synth told you what's been going on, you should know why I don't want him involved in this," she said, staring down into the mug of coffee.

"Don't you ever get tired of handling things on your own?" Harry asked, for the first time his take-charge tone of voice adopting a concerned tone. "In a situation like this, I'd think you'd want all the support you can gather. Remember the last time—"

"Harry, I could never forget the *last* time," Selena snapped, shoving the spoon into her mug.

Harry closed his eyes, regretting his choice of words. "Sweetie—"

"Harry, my parents disowned me. They actually said they didn't want to *know* me—and I didn't even do anything! But because of my . . . personality I was outgoing and liked by a lot of people . . . especially men. They accepted the fact that the person in those photos was me. I've never felt as close to anyone as I did with my parents. Not my grandmother, not Synthia, not even you," she admitted, smiling when he took the hand she extended. "But with Darius . . ." She sighed, conjuring the man's image in her head. "I feel some part of me, I don't know, coming alive, I think. Like I could experience that kind of indescribable closeness again. But it's an even more powerful kind of closeness than with my parents. It's the kind that you can only experience with that one person, one special person. I don't know . . ." she groaned, shaking her head as though the notion were silly.

Harry leaned forward, pressing a soft kiss to her cheek as he pulled her into a close embrace. "Look atcha," he scolded, pushing a lock of hair behind her ear, "no makeup, ugly ponytail, and is that crust in your eye?" he cried, chuckling when she slapped his chest. "Baby, you know, in spite of everything you've been through, I've never known you to let it get you down. People concoct rumors and gossip all the time. You know this."

"But now Darius is in the picture, at least, I want him to be. I just don't want to—"

"Do anything to scare him away?" Harry guessed, noticing the guilty look in her eyes. "Listen to me, you take care of yourself first of all, you understand?" he argued, brushing his thumbs across her cheeks. "You've done a lot of toughening up over the years. Don't start beating yourself up now over whatever mess went down in the past."

Selena rolled her eyes. "I just don't think he'd be able to look past it."

"And if this mystery person takes it further than notes and e-mails?"

"I'll go to Darius if things get too crazy," she said, spotting the disapproval in Harry's dark gaze. "I don't expect you to completely understand," she muttered.

"Aw, shush," he ordered, hugging her tightly. "I didn't mean to push." He kissed her cheek. "Now come eat."

"They got any leads?" Harry was asking when they were halfway through breakfast.

"Aside from Francine, there's no one," Selena groaned, helping herself to more of the delicious scrambled eggs with cheese.

"Frankie should be over that mess by now."

"Harry, it doesn't have to be her, you know? There're plenty of fools out there. Some of them don't even need a reason." She shuddered at the thought.

Harry added more cream to his coffee. "You think this person will follow up with more than that e-mail?" he asked, looking up at her.

Selena's initial confusion over the question cleared. "I remember all that mess that was stirred up years ago. I mean, the girl who did all that stuff could easily have been me, so who knows what else she did—what else may be out there to be revealed?"

"Well, just try not to dwell on it, all right?" Harry ordered, heaping more sour cream over his hash browns.

Unfortunately, Selena's worries weren't so easily assuaged. "This is almost all I can think of," she confessed.

"You know, there *is* a bright side to all this."

"And if you can tell me what that is, you're on a level I could never even hope to reach."

Harry laughed, though a serious light came to his eyes. "Girl, you've at least got your health and friends who know you well enough not to believe anything or anyone out there who says you're somethin' you're not."

Selena buried her face in her hands. "I'm all too aware of that," she whispered. "I know how blessed I am."

"So, besides Francine, you got any other ideas on who it might be? Maybe some disgruntled business associate?"

Selena shook her head at the idea. "At first, I thought that could be a possibility. Now . . . I don't think so. I mean, wouldn't they choose a more sensational way to destroy my rep than with mysterious messages and secret e-mails?" she asked, watching Harry shrug. "Anyway, I'm more inclined to believe it's personal—a woman."

Harry watched as Selena poured blueberry syrup over her pancakes. "And Francine Johns is the only woman you could come up with?"

"She's the only suspect we have," Selena said, her voice shaking a bit. "I pray she's the one; then I can put this mess behind me," she decided, as a tear glided down her cheek.

"Hey, hey . . ." Harry soothed, reaching across the table to grasp her hand.

Selena hurried in to the office the following Monday. Aside from all the work she imagined had accumulated on her desk, she hoped the constant hustle at the magazine would lift her spirits.

The remainder of the weekend had been thankfully un-eventful. She'd missed not speaking with Darius, but was glad he'd realized that she needed her space. Moreover, she thought it best they not see each other with things as they were. Sourly, she acknowledged that would be difficult since Darius's right-hand man was handling her case.

"Hmph. A case with no new leads," she grumbled, flopping into her wine-suede desk chair. Leaning back against the cushiony headrest, she fiddled with the frayed neckline of the curve-hugging cobalt-blue dress she wore. Her eyes were focused on the computer and, a moment later, she was pulling up the lewd e-mail she'd received the week before.

"Sounds interesting."

Selena bolted up in her seat, hitting several keys in her haste to shut down the message. "Just some trashy e-mail Carla forwarded me," she lied, watching Darius move from his leaning stance against her office door. Her stare lingered on him, admiring his tall, muscular form as he strolled around the room. The quiet power he possessed seemed to follow him like a living thing. His mannerisms, unhurried and deliberate, made him all the more irresistible. The sandstone trousers and matching jacket had a casual fit that drew attention to his well-defined physique and flawless chocolate-chip complexion. The crisp eggshell shirt was worn with no tie—the collar unbuttoned to reveal the strong prominent line of his neck. He stopped next to her desk, slipping one hand into his trousers' deep pockets as he studied the case that housed her awards.

"So, what brings you by?" Selena inquired, hoping to dismiss the butterflies in the pit of her stomach.

"I was very worried about you," he said, turning away from the trophy wall when he heard her surprised response to his admission. "What? Hell, Selena, what kind of men have you been seeing?"

"Well, believe it or not, no man has ever admitted to being worried about me before," she slowly confided.

Darius massaged his neck and fixed her with a doubtful glare. "I *do* find that hard to believe."

Selena stood behind her desk, missing his brown eyes rake

her body several times. "Thanks for your concern, but I'm fine. I promise."

"You were pretty out of it the other night when you left the banquet," he recalled, focusing on the carpet as he closed the distance between them.

Selena perched on the edge of her desk. "Sometimes I let my business get the best of me. All I wanna do, once it's handled, is hide out."

"Hmph. I can relate to that."

"So I've eased your mind?" she asked, tilting her head to watch him with curious eyes.

"You did." He briefly raised an index finger in her direction. "Now I can get to the real purpose of my visit."

"There's more?"

"Oh yeah."

"Let's have it then."

"Well . . . after you chickened out of the jogging—"

"Hey!" Selena called, her wounded tone matching the look in her eyes.

"I decided to show you what you missed out on," he continued with a grin.

Selena appeared skeptical. "So we're going jogging now?" she asked, moving off the desk.

"Not quite," he said, taking the spot she'd just vacated. "I'm gonna show you what you missed out on aside from the jogging."

"How?"

"Breakfast. Here in your office. I already ordered it."

"And I'm always ready to eat," she said, smiling and clapping her hands like an adoring child. "Thank you for being so sweet. You know, I'm beginning to think you're serious about really wanting to know me."

"You still doubted it?" he asked, his eyes settling on her mouth before rising to meet her gaze.

Selena rested her hip against the desk and pondered his question. "I did, but I don't know why I should've had any doubts—you've already had me several times," she remarked, noticing his jaw clench in response to the way she phrased the statement.

Darius brushed his thumb across the curve of her chin. "You think I'm playing a game?" he asked.

Selena's lashes shielded her eyes as she responded, "I hope not. I don't think I could handle that right now."

Darius's seductive stare was still trained on her mouth. Selena didn't retreat when he leaned forward to kiss her. Their lips were only a breath apart when the phone buzzed. Breakfast had arrived.

Over a spread of hard-scrambled eggs, salmon croquets, toast, muffins, and juice, Darius remarked on the impressive manner in which Selena handled her business. He was quite interested in knowing how difficult it must have been to get it off the ground.

"You won't believe how many people—how many *black* people—told me black women wouldn't buy a magazine like *Reigning Queens*. I told them they were crazy," she reminisced, leaning back as she sipped her juice. "I said, 'Not only would black women *buy* the magazine, but they'd be on edge for the next month's issue.' "

Darius buttered a huge apple cinnamon muffin. "What'd they say to that?" he asked.

"They still weren't havin' it. So . . . I tried to sell them on how untapped the black market still was—especially the black female market. "There aren't a host of publications that really speak to a black woman's concerns on politics—how they affect our jobs and families. There certainly aren't enough magazine's that talk about our sexuality and our format is designed to voice an opinion which will inevitably draw response."

Darius shook his head. "Quite a pioneer, aren't you? But I agree, and there does seem to be a lack of original ideas especially in today's market."

"Well, speaking of the *black* market, I know it must've been just as difficult for you. Starting a security firm consisting of an all-black staff?"

"The hardest, longest struggle of my life," Darius admitted, popping a moist muffin morsel into his mouth. "But it's been worth it," he added, amidst his chewing.

Selena eyed the juice in her glass. "Except when it comes to the effect it's had on your personal life, right?"

Darius shrugged. "I told you how I felt about that and it has *all* been worth it."

The silence resumed, only pierced by the soft clattering of utensils against china. In a short while, however, Darius's deep chocolate stare had refocused on Selena.

"What's the story between you and Francine Johns?"

Selena looked as though she were choking. "Why would you want to know about her?" she asked, finding it difficult to swallow all her food.

"Seems interesting," Darius remarked, turning back to his plate.

"It's not a story I like to share. Suffice it to say, she doesn't like me and that's putting it mildly."

"Mmm, and how do you feel about her?"

"Excuse me?"

"I got the feeling the dislike was mostly on her part."

"How?"

Darius shrugged in a lazy manner. "I think you were hoping she'd be polite. I could tell by your reaction when she first approached us."

Selena wasn't put off by his astute observations, and tilted her juice glass toward him. "How'd you get to be so good at reading . . . reactions?" she asked.

"Comes with the job."

"So if I were to say that we were old college rivals, you would say . . ."

"That explains it. More juice?" he asked, holding the pitcher, then joining in when she laughed.

The office door had been left ajar, but Joni still applied a tentative knock before entering.

"What'd you do this time?" Selena asked Darius when she noticed the long gold flower box Joni brought into the room.

"I had nothing to do with it," he said, with one wave of his hand.

"Mmm . . ." Selena muttered and strolled over to her desk. "Thanks, Joni," she called.

Greeted by at least a dozen long-stemmed red roses, Selena smiled and lifted one of the fragrant flowers to her nose. A card was attached to the inside of the top cover. *Does someone like you even bother to use these?*

Selena groaned, realizing what was going on. The rose she held slipped from her hand and back into the box. Then, Selena noticed what else had been delivered. Dozens upon dozens of unpackaged condoms were strewn throughout the thorny rose stems. Her gasp and brief cry interrupted Darius and Joni's light conversation.

"You okay, Selena?" Joni called.

Darius walked toward the desk when she didn't answer. "Selena?" he called.

Slipping the cover back over the box, Selena managed a shaky nod.

"What is this?" Darius asked, already reaching for the gold box. His expression sharpened with suspicion when she clutched it and moved it out of his grasp.

"Joni, can you give us a minute?" he called.

"No problem," she said, her eyes narrowing out of concern.

"This is where you tell me what's going on," Darius told Selena when they'd stood alone in the office for several seconds.

"It's noth—"

"The truth this time."

"I can't do this now." She sighed, bowing her head.

Darius reached out for the box again and again she pushed it aside. "I don't have a lot of patience left here, Selena," he whispered close to her ear.

Selena swallowed as though it pained her to do so. "It's nothing for you to concern yourself with."

Darius hesitated only a second longer, before taking Selena's arm in a firm hold. He pulled her away from the desk, leading her toward one of the chairs that flanked the sofa.

"Darius . . ." she protested, her gaze riveted on the box. She inched to the edge of the seat, watching as he strolled back to the desk. She waited, closing her eyes when he uttered a low curse.

"What the hell? What the hell is this, Selena?" he called, still staring down into the box. "Who would send you somethin' like this?" he asked, turning to look her way. "Is this why you rushed out of the banquet Friday night?"

"I told you why I had to leave," she retorted, leaving the chair. "That had absolutely nothing to do with this."

Darius leaned against the desk, folding his arms across his chest as he watched her pace the room.

"Besides, my staff is always pullin' this kind of stuff," she rambled, unaware of how shaky her voice sounded. "They pull the craziest pranks. I don't even know why I'm getting so uptight about it," she added with a nervous laugh.

Darius shook his head and looked back into the flower box. He closed it none too gently, then stood with it in hand. "Get your things. I'm taking you home."

"Oh, Darius, you don't have to—"

"And I'm going to have someone stationed outside your door."

"Darius, wait," she called, forcing firmness into her voice. "Please listen to me. Now, I'm sure this is nothing to get crazy over."

Darius blinked, his lips parting in surprise. "You did see what was in that box, right?"

Selena walked toward him, her hands extended in a pleading manner. "Just don't worry yourself with this. At least not until I've had a chance to speak to my staff."

Darius shrugged. Clearly he disapproved. "I'll wait," he decided, watching her expectantly.

Selena massaged her arms to ward off the sudden chill she felt. "I can't just—Carla and the others aren't in right now. I—I'll have to call them and explain and I just don't feel like doing that right now."

Darius nodded, then headed toward the office door. "Let's go then," he called.

"I'll expect you to call me in four or five hours. I don't hear from you, I'll be back."

Selena nodded. "I'm sure it's just a stupid prank."

"Mmm-hmm. We'll see."

Selena folded her arms across her chest. "So what are you gonna do with the, um, flowers?" she asked, glancing past him.

"Don't worry about it."

"Darius—"

"And I don't have to tell you to be careful who you open this door to?"

"No, no, you don't." She sighed, shaking her head.

Darius pressed a kiss to her forehead, then closed the door and checked it once she'd clicked the locks into place. Alone, she let her mind race. She was definitely afraid. Afraid of what else would happen and afraid of the way Darius would react to all that was sure to follow.

"You have to tell him something, Sel."

"Your cousin's right," Max was saying. He and Synthia had stopped by the magazine that afternoon to check on Selena, and Joni told them how upset she seemed over a delivery. "D's too smart to be kept out of the loop and he'll be even more pissed to know that you—and me especially—kept it from him *this* long."

"That delivery was the worst of it," Selena confided,

propping her elbows on her knees and sliding both hands through her deep brown locks. "Maybe it's over," she reasoned.

Max and Synthia exchanged glances.

"Didn't you say he was expecting you to call?" Synthia asked.

"Damn," Selena muttered, having completely forgotten. "Maybe I can catch him before he comes back over here." She reached for the phone on the coffee table.

"What are you gonna tell him?"

"I won't know till I start talkin', Synth," Selena sarcastically replied.

"Sel—"

"No, Synth," she argued, the receiver poised in her hand. "You can't understand this and I don't expect you to. You've always been the perfect girl."

Synthia took offense. "What's that supposed to mean?" she snapped, hooking her thumbs through the belt loops of her hip huggers.

"Sweetie, I don't mean anything by it," Selena consoled, replacing the receiver. "Any man would be proud to have you on his arm and you have to know that."

Synthia bowed her head. "Honey, it's true for you too. More than you know."

Selena wouldn't believe it. "I don't know a lot about Darius and his past lovers, but I know they were dramatic enough to give him a real cold attitude toward his need for a solid relationship with a woman. He finds out about this and he'll just chalk it up to another stressful involvement that he doesn't need or want."

"Over something that's not even your fault?"

"It doesn't matter."

"How can you say that?"

"Because I've gone through it before, remember?"

Synthia massaged her neck, inhaling deeply before she responded. "Honey, if I could change the past, I would. I'd certainly start with erasing that scandal you had nothing to do with, and as for your parents—"

"Sweetie, it's not your fault. Anyway . . . I can't involve Darius in this any more than he already is. I'll find some way to make him stop worrying about this."

"And what will you do when something else happens and he's here?"

Max's question multiplied Selena's anxieties tenfold. Losing the last of her resolve, she turned and allowed him to see how lost she was. The doorbell rang then and she appeared even more wilted.

Synthia went to the door. Selena followed, coming to a halt in the foyer's entrance.

Synthia's smile was grim as she greeted the deliveryman on the stoop.

"Package for Ms. Selena Witherspoon," he announced.

Synthia looked back at her cousin, who responded with a slow nod. "I'll sign for it," she said.

Selena had returned to the living room, watching Synthia approach her with the delivery as though it were a poisoned apple.

"Sel—"

"Thanks," she said, taking the eight-by-twelve tanned envelope from her cousin.

"Sel, you don't have to."

"It's okay," she decided, already tearing into the package.

The noxious bile rose with a vengeance, making her feel queasy and faint. Her low moan brought Max to his feet and Synthia rushing over. Selena lost consciousness just as they reached her. There was a card lying at her side. *A picture is worth a thousand words. These are worth much more.*

When Selena opened her eyes, she didn't recognize her surroundings. Frowning, she blinked several times in hopes of getting her bearings. She realized she was in her own bedroom, just as memories of the lurid photos flashed in her mind. The gasp she uttered caught on a sharp cry and she bolted up in bed.

"Shh . . . Sweetie, it's okay," Synthia called, already there to stroke her cousin's hair.

Selena was a mass of nerves. Synthia's soft words and gentle touch only agitated her more. "I need to get out of here," she muttered, kicking away the covers.

"Sel, wait—"

"You and Max can go on and leave. I'll be fine."

"Sel—"

"Synth, I'm just going down—"

"Darius is down there."

"Oh . . ." she moaned, pressing her fingers to her temples. "You didn't tell him anything? Where are the pictures? Synthia, who's doing this? Why—what—what are they gonna do next?"

"Sweetie . . ." Synthia whispered, rushing toward the bed and hugging Selena as though that would ward off all the badness. "Honey, it's gonna be all right," she vowed, though she scarcely believed it herself.

"Where are the pictures?" Selena asked, her voice a monotone.

"Under the message board on the desk in the living room."

Selena pulled away. "I better get down there," she decided, heading to the private bath at the rear of her bedroom. "Tell Darius I'll be down as soon as I take a quick shower."

"What are you gonna tell him?"

"I'll know when I get down there," she decided, but stopped before stepping into the bathroom. "I'd appreciate it if you and Max would leave so I can talk to him alone."

Synthia nodded, her hand already on the doorknob. "No problem, sweetie," she said, blowing a kiss before leaving the room.

Under the steamy, invigorating water, Selena pondered all that had occurred, from her affair with Darius to the threat hanging over her head. She couldn't stop herself from wondering why Darius had to come into her life then. Perhaps it had nothing to do with romantic reasons, but instead, to help her through the strange turn of events that were scaring her out of her mind.

"I don't think it's the best idea, man."

Darius's sleek brows drew closed at Max's opinion. "You don't think it's a good idea to put security on this woman when there's someone out there sending her crap like this?"

"I only meant that we may be givin' it more attention than we should. Some fools live for this stuff—the publicity, the sick glamour of it—and we need to remember that Selena's a public figure."

"The stuff looks serious, Max," Darius argued, leaning back in his armchair. "I'm willin' to bet it's been goin' on far longer than today with that delivery," he said, his gaze narrowing further. "I'm also willin' to bet you know much more than you're tellin' me."

Max tensed visibly, his dark eyes sending Synthia a meaningful look. "Told you," he said.

Darius watched them both. "I'm right, aren't I?"

Max extended his hand. "D, man—"

"Hey, Darius."

Everyone stood when Selena called out. They all watched as she descended the stairs.

"How you doin', Sel?" Synthia asked.

Selena only nodded, hiding her hands in the pockets of the ankle-length olive lounging shirt.

"We should get out of here, Max," Synthia decided, already grabbing her purse off the end table.

Max needed no further coaxing. Soon, he and Synthia had left the house.

* * *

"Somethin' you need to tell me?"

Darius's question, voiced after several moments of heavy silence, sent a now familiar shiver up Selena's spine.

"Why are you keeping this from me?" he asked, strolling toward her. "On top of that, you're having my right hand and best friend lie to me."

"Darius . . ," she shuddered, rubbing her arms to ease the chill.

Darius slipped one hand into the pocket of his saggy black sweats and massaged his neck with the other. "I'm listening," he prodded.

"Since Miami," she began, pacing the room as she spoke, "I've been getting weird notes and . . . other things. Max has all of it—he can show you."

"What's it all about?"

"My past. More specifically, someone else's past. Some white girl, with a real good tan. She did some pretty wild stuff and it was caught on camera and who knows where else? It wasn't me, but I've been paying for it for years."

"And you felt you had to hide this from me?" he probed, his voice soothing and nonthreatening.

It made Selena even more nervous. "Believe me, if you knew all that I've been through because of this, you'd understand why."

"Mmm-hmm, so you just took it upon yourself to assume this?"

"Darius—"

"You want us to get to know each other, but you hide the fact that you're being threatened?"

"You wouldn't understand."

"Well, it would be impossible for me *to* understand, now, wouldn't it, Selena? You've virtually been hidin' this crap since we met."

Selena stood before the message desk. "I couldn't tell you in Miami. I mean, I didn't even think there was anything to it. Besides, you were involved with Velma and all that—"

"Don't even try it. You should've come to me."

Selena stared down at the message pad, her fingers grazing its edge. Then, she was pulling the pictures from underneath and turning toward him. "Maybe these will help you to see where I'm coming from."

Darius clutched the photos she shoved against his chest. He shuffled them into a neat stack, his eyes narrowed, his head bowed in concentration.

Selena watched his face—she didn't want to, but had to see his reaction. As she feared and expected, the shadow of disgust contorted his handsome features. His reaction was brief, but blatant.

"I think you get the idea," she said, watching him pace the room as he studied the pictures. She walked over, snatched them, and tossed them to the sofa.

"When did they get here?"

"Over an hour ago."

"Who delivered them?"

"I don't—"

"Who are the men in the photos?"

"Darius, stop it! Just stop, all right!"

"Hell, Selena, after that damned delivery at your office today and now this mess . . . Don't you see how serious this is?"

Selena shook her head. "How can you ask me that?"

"Then you should understand how important it is for us to get the names of all those guys, because any one of 'em could've sent those pictures. We need names, where they might be living—"

"Darius, please!" she raged, clutching fistfuls of curly locks between her fingers. "You're so smart, but you can't seem to figure this out. I kept this from you for a reason," she said, her hands clasped before her chest. "I don't want you involved. I'll work with Max or anyone else on your staff, but not you."

Fearing his temper would get the best of him again, Darius

put more space between them. "You care to tell me why?" he asked.

Selena hesitated, her hazel gaze resting on the photos strewn across the burgundy sofa. "You've seen those pictures . . . and I know you're disgusted. There's no way you couldn't be."

"That was a long time ago."

"But you're just seeing them today," Selena countered, dragging her eyes back to his face. "For me, it doesn't make it seem like so long ago. Would you please go now?" she asked.

"I don't want to leave you. Not after this."

"But, I want you to. Besides, you won't be able to stand the sight of me much longer."

"Selena—"

"You know, you just asked if I knew who the guys were in the pictures. You never asked if I knew who the woman was. You just assumed it was me."

"No, you'd already told me it wasn't."

"Can you honestly say you believed it wasn't when you saw for yourself?"

Darius closed his eyes and nodded, realizing her point. He wanted to tell her she was wrong, but he couldn't. The images caught on film were almost branded on his brain, and his fists clenched in response.

"Just go."

Instead, Darius moved closer, wanting to offer her some consolation.

"Would you just go!" she whispered, pressing her lips together as tears pooled her eyes.

When he made no move to do so, she stomped to the front door and whipped it open. She waited until he decided there was nothing more to be said. She let the door close with little more than a click of the lock, before she slid down the length of the cool wood and cried.

Eleven

Selena stayed home for three days, her only contact with the world via computer or phone. The knock on her door was startling, but went unanswered. This visitor, however, would not be ignored and the steady knocking soon turned thunderous. At last, she looked out the peephole.

"What is it?" she snapped, after pulling the door open for Harry.

"I was about to use my key. I go out of town for a week and come back to a crap-load of messages on my machine from Synthia," he explained.

Selena rolled her eyes away from his dark gaze. "I'm in no mood to talk."

"Mmm-hmm," Harry grunted, completely ignoring her request and stepping inside. "Look at you," He criticized, taking in her disheveled hair, wrinkled sleep pants, and T-shirt. "Synthia begged me to try and get through to you."

"Harry, damn!" she raged, kicking the door shut. "I just don't want to talk right now!"

"Fine. I'll do the talking," he happily decided, tossing his keys to the cherry-wood desk. "So how are things going with you and Darius?"

Harry's simple attempt at conversation was Selena's undoing. He watched her impenetrable facade crumble as she dissolved into a fit of sobs.

"God," he whispered, rushing over to pull her close. "Honey, I've never seen you this way," he breathed, pressing kisses to the top of her head. "You're really in love with him, aren't you?"

Selena couldn't answer. Her sobs only gained volume.

Darius met with his executive staff regarding Selena's dilemma. The group, which included Max Richardson, Kevin Amos, Hamilton Adams, and Maurice Starkes, scoured every piece of evidence linked to the case.

"So what do we have in the line of suspects?"

"Right now, this Francine Johns is our only lead," Kevin told Darius.

"Frankie Johns . . . and the only reason she's even a suspect is some tension between her and Selena," Max added.

"Well, we still don't know who this woman is. Not to mention who these guys are," Maurice mentioned. "Any one of 'em could be Ms. Johns's man."

"That may be true," Darius corrected, though there was an air of disbelief in his voice, "but something doesn't set right with me that she'd choose *now* to avenge Selena for stealing an old college boyfriend."

No one could argue the point. Unfortunately, accepting it as fact put them even further away from discovering the identity of the harasser.

"You think we should strike her as a suspect, D?"

Darius tapped his index finger along his mustache. "Nah, Ham, I think we should try diggin' a little deeper and find a more solid motive for Ms. Johns."

"You think there could be somebody else pullin' the strings behind this, man?"

Darius allowed Max to see his despair over the possibility. "I feel much better about it being a woman scorned. At least we know what we're dealing with. But, not knowing if this person is crazy or murderous is a hundred times worse," he said, unbuttoning his shirt a bit more as a wave of heat washed over him. "She's been getting these anonymous messages for months and this mystery person has yet to approach her with his terms."

"So, what are you thinkin'?" Kevin asked, watching his boss closely.

"It doesn't make sense for it to be about money with Francine," he pointed out. "If revenge was on her mind, why not just leak the photos to a competitor and ruin Selena that way?"

Max followed Darius across the room when he turned away from the table. "Y'all, we're gonna call it a day here. Go on and take off," he instructed, watching the guys collect their things and head out. "How you holdin' up, man?" he asked, clapping a hand to Darius's shoulder when they were alone in the office.

"She won't talk to me. Won't see me . . . I don't know . . ." he responded, his voice unusually hollow.

"You tried seeing *her?*" Max asked, watching his friend shake his head.

"I don't want to push her," Darius replied, with a short, humorless laugh. "Anyway, *you* probably know more than I do."

Max grimaced and offered an uncertain shrug. "Synthia tells me her cousin ain't in the best shape. She's made herself a prisoner in her house, shutting everybody out—"

"Damn it!" Darius thundered, pounding his fist against the window. "We gotta find out who's doin' this and why."

Selena waved toward Nelia as the host escorted her to the table. She'd awakened that morning feeling strangely rejuvenated and confident. It excited her so that her stomach rumbled from joyful anticipation. She'd awakened remembering something she'd forgotten: she'd never been a victim and it had been a long time since she cared about what anyone thought of her. Now was certainly not the time to start. Still, she couldn't forget that there was one person whose respect she wanted to gain.

Selena . . . she quickly chastised herself, forcing herself to cast Darius McClellan out of her mind. *He's gonna help me find whoever is threatening me. That's all.* There was no hope for romance, let alone a meaningful relationship, she told herself.

"Hey, girl," Selena whispered, greeting Nelia Cannon with a hug and kiss.

"Hey, listen, just skip all the small talk and tell me what the hell is going on with you."

Stunned by the request, Selena uttered a short laugh. "Okay," she said, smoothing the medium blue trouser skirt beneath her as she took a seat. By the second round of drinks, she'd relayed the entire story and how Darius fit right into the middle of it.

" . . . So I'll just have to see him as a professional acquaintance and nothing more."

"Do you really want to do that, girl? I mean, I saw the glow on your face that day when I came to your office," she smoothly acknowledged, and popped a cube of ice into her mouth. "If you weren't in love with him then, you certainly are now," she added, while crunching.

Selena fixed her friend with a scathing look.

"Besides," Nelia continued, her dark eyes narrowing in their familiar, knowing way, "after everything you've shared with him, there's no way he'd stand for you working with his team and he not be involved. Plus, you know you couldn't resist him if he came within ten feet of you right now."

"I agree. That's why I want to keep him out of this. Completely out of this," Selena vowed, her hand curling into a fist for emphasis. "I want him out of it and if I do have to see him at some point, I want it to be strictly business. I'll show him I'm not who he probably thinks I am."

"Would you stop saying that? Your reputation suffered because of some woman who couldn't or wouldn't come out of the woodwork and own up to what she did," Nelia reminded her friend, leaning forward when Selena rolled her eyes. "Sweetie, Darius is a fair and understanding man. If you told him that woman isn't you, I know he believes that."

"My own mother and father knew me since before I could talk and they were quick to believe all those lies. How could I not think Darius would feel any differently? Those pictures were so terrible, so damning."

"Hell, Selena, can you imagine some of the sick stuff he must come across in his line of work?"

Selena fiddled with a glossy curl dangling from her ponytail. "When that 'sick stuff' involves someone you're romantically interested in, all that fairness and understanding flies right out the window."

Nelia sucked her teeth, while tugging at the lapels of her lavender pantsuit. "I can't talk to you when you're like this. I don't know why I even try," she grumbled, waving her hands around her head.

"I'm sorry it's not what you want to hear. I'm sorry I got involved with Darius even more."

"And you don't *even* believe that."

"From the moment we met, it was intense," Selena recalled, envisioning her and Darius alone in Velma Morris's office in Miami. "From the very moment," she stressed. "I should've run the moment he shook my hand. I got no place in my life for intensity like that. Now, something uncomplicated with a person who's fun-loving? *That's* what *I'm* used to."

"Mmm-hmm . . . someone like Ramon Harmon, huh?"

"Bite your tongue, Nel!" Selena urged, looking as though she'd just been doused with a bucket of ice cold water. "Whenever you mention that fool's name, he always shows up."

The two friends stared each other down for a couple of silent moments. Then, laughter bubbled forth and lightness set in.

* * *

"So how's my cousin doin'? You get to see her more than I do," Selena teased the next evening when she opened her front door.

Max grinned, though he was obviously a bit embarrassed by the observation.

The light, animated mood Selena had been enjoying since early that morning faded when she saw that Max had not arrived alone.

"Hey, Darius," she whispered, sounding uneasy as she recalled memories of their last conversation.

Darius only nodded, his gorgeous coffee stare settling briefly on her face before it raked her casual lounging gown.

"So, what's up?" she asked, hoping to sound refreshed when the silence grew thick.

"We apologize for stopping by out of the blue, Selena," Max said, perching on the back of the sofa. "We wanted you to know that there'll be two guys parked outside your door in the morning."

Selena's light eyes shifted between the two men in her living room. "Is that a good idea?"

"They're two of our best guys," Max assured her.

"What I mean is, don't you think you're being a little too overprotective for an old jealous college roommate?" she clarified, hoping the question didn't sound as edgy as she felt.

Max cleared his throat, but offered no reply. Darius was silent and observant as usual, but something in his demeanor concerned Selena more than normal.

"What's really going on here?" she asked, posing the question toward him. "Darius?" she called, when he remained noncommunicative.

"Something about it all doesn't set right with me," he finally shared, hiding both hands in the front pocket of his Tuskeegee sweatshirt.

"*What* about it?" Selena probed, slowly taking a seat on the edge of the message desk.

Darius massaged the back of his neck. "Frankie's gone

through a lot of trouble just to get back at you for stealing her man in college," he noted, pacing the dim living room. "Too much trouble. Now, either there's more motivating the woman or there's someone else responsible for this mess."

"Well, I better go," Max said, the silence prompting him to leave. "Selena, we only came by to tell you about the guys. Try and get some sleep, all right?"

"Thanks, Max," Selena said, squeezing the hand he extended. "I'll treat you and Synth to dinner some time next week."

"Sounds good," he replied with a smile, before nodding toward his associate. "All right, D," he called.

Selena's unease intensified once Max left. "Was there something else?" she asked Darius when he kept staring.

"How are you? With all this stuff going on?" he asked.

Selena shrugged. "As well as I can be, considering . . ."

Darius nodded, folding his arms across his chest as he stepped closer. "Have you talked to your staff about what was going on?"

"And tell them what?" she snapped, her expression a cross between surprise and aggravation. "Tell 'em what, Darius? That once again, I'm paying for something another woman did that mostly everyone I know will probably believe is true."

"Damn, why do you put yourself down like that?" he whispered as though her words pained him.

Selena wouldn't look at him. "It beats everyone else to the punch."

"Everyone doesn't think that way."

"Oh, Darius, please! We both know that's not true, don't we?" she asked, turning away to hide her tears.

Darius felt his frustration causing his temper to heat. There was something eating away at her and it went beyond a few lurid pictures and e-mails. Of course, the last thing she needed was to have him pestering her for details. Without another word, he left the house.

The next two weeks were relatively quiet. Selena eased back into work, and within days she was back up to speed to the delight of her colleagues and employees. Her contact during that time was mainly through Max or the others from McClellan Securities who had been assigned to her case. Darius distanced himself, as she'd asked. Selena wasn't sure if his cooperation relieved or disappointed her, but she knew the relationship that had bloomed so sweetly had no chance of surviving.

"Good to see her out, huh?" Max was asking once he'd followed the line of his friend's gaze across the conversation-filled dining room.

Selena was there, having lunch with her assistant. Darius responded to Max with a barely audible comment before returning his attention to his menu.

"You talked to her lately?" Max asked, hoping to spark some discussion that would soothe his partner's moody demeanor. The sour expression he received in response, however, forced him to let it go.

Darius looked at the tanned leather menu. His eyes stared unseeingly at the list of delectables offered by the Chinese restaurant. Max's well-meaning attempts to discuss his now "business only" relationship with Selena Witherspoon caused him to silently acknowledge how much he missed her. How or when it had happened, he wasn't sure. Still, he'd come to like having her in his life.

The woman in those pictures . . . He had instantly assumed that it was her and she'd been hurt by his assumption. Only to himself could he admit that his feelings would not have changed even if she had been the woman in the photos.

He sighed and massaged the bridge of his nose as the snapshots flashed in his mind. He knew he should have been eager to leave the situation alone, but he couldn't. True, the drama of another high-maintenance relationship was something he had no desire for—no place for in his life. His involvement with Selena had proven to be that and then some. If only he could shut down his feelings when he was around her and when she looked at him with those eyes . . .

"D? D, man, you with me?" Max was calling, waving his hand before his friend's face and grinning when the man blinked.

When Darius snapped to, he looked past Max and saw that Selena was preparing to leave.

"'Scuse me, man," he absently remarked, as he pushed his chair back and left the table.

"You're crazy! I think I should be payin' you more for psychiatric help," Selena teased Joni, who had just made an outrageous comment.

Joni's smile widened when she noticed the man approaching their table.

"How you doin', Joni?" Darius asked, while his hand closed around Selena's elbow. "We need to talk," he said, without waiting for a reply.

"Darius? Darius, what is it?" Selena questioned, her heart racing frantically, as he led her away from the dining room toward a remote corridor off from the rest rooms.

"Darius—" she began, only to have him take full advantage of the moment to kiss her. His tongue thrust deeply and repeatedly, stroking every inch of her mouth. The act was lusty, wet, and hot as pent-up emotions were released in a savage onslaught.

Darius simply held on to her arms as he bruised her soft mouth beneath the passionate possession of his own.

Selena squeezed her eyes shut when the persistent tingle of arousal positioned itself at her most sensitive area. Wantonly, she responded, moaning his name as her fingers curved weakly around the lapels of his rich, almond suit coat.

Darius forced her deeper into the recesses of the corridor,

until he left no space for her to retreat. Not that she wanted to; having been denied the pleasure of his touch had her praying now that he would never stop.

Darius began to tease her lips with soft wet pecks that made her whimper in anticipation of more. "I want you to stop shutting me out," he groaned in a ragged whisper, before his tongue delved deeply, briefly.

Selena knew what he meant. "It's easier this way," she whispered, when he broke the kiss again. Tears began to pressure her eyes.

"Easier? Why?"

Because I'm in love with you, she silently admitted. "Because you're disgusted by all this. I know you're finding it hard to believe me when I say that woman isn't me," she told him instead.

Darius pulled away then. His fingers bit into her arms, bared by the capped sleeves of her simple curve-hugging copper cotton dress.

"That's not true and you know it. You have to know that, Selena," he insisted, his gaze searching her eyes as he waited for some confirmation. "Baby, I admit that it threw me, but I believe everything you've told me in spite of my distrusting nature," he added with a smile. "I like the woman I'm getting to know and I want to keep on knowing you."

"Darius—"

"Just say you'll let me," he whispered.

Knowing it could only lead to more heartache, but unable to resist what he was offering any longer, Selena nodded. Her eyes settled on his mouth, her fingers tracing his mustache and the delicious curve of his mouth as she pulled him into another kiss.

Selena and Darius's relationship continued to strengthen. They saw each other almost every day, but every night they spent together. It wasn't long before Selena knew she loved and was *in* love with Darius. Though she tried to deny it, each time they made love a part of her ached a little because she knew his feelings couldn't possibly be as deep as hers. There had been no more threatening messages, but that in no way diminished the fiercely protective streak Darius had developed where she was concerned. If his mood toward the men she knew was frigid before, now it was positively frostbitten. Still, aside from his concern for her well-being, Selena had her doubts about any other feelings he may have had for her.

In spite of how far the relationship had advanced, Darius refused to allow himself to completely let down his defenses. Of course, he knew he loved Selena, but it scared him a little to discover that he was still capable of the emotion. It had become something alien to him. He had allowed it into his life once and it had badly burned his heart and soul. He wasn't about to let it happen again.

"You gotta be kidding me," Selena breathed, stepping back from her office door.

"Long time no see, girl."

Selena squeezed her eyes closed briefly, before looking up again. Damn you, Nelia. She silently shuddered. The tall man standing in her office doorway had not changed a bit.

"Ramon," she slowly stated.

"In person," Ramon Harmon bellowed. Bending a little, he picked her up and twirled her around the room.

"Ramon, put me down!" she ordered, propping her hands on her hips when he granted her request. "What the hell are you doin' here?"

Ramon pretended to be shocked. "Well, I expected a much friendlier greeting."

"Don't lie. What are you doing here?" Selena repeated, her hazel eyes narrowed in suspicion.

"Damn," he breathed, pulling the brown Kangol away from

his head and running a hand through his short dreads. "I guess you changed your mind about us being friends, huh?"

Selena threw her quarter-length leather coat on a chair and walked over to her desk. Ramon Harmon, with his loud personality, loud mouth, and wild sense of humor, had been a huge part of her life a few years ago.

Ramon was a well-known photographer. He was extremely skilled in his craft and could pull a smile from anyone. Including Selena, who had fallen in love with him right away.

Unfortunately, Ramon "loved" everyone. So much so that he once told Selena that there was simply "too much of him for one woman." Even though he'd led her to believe he wanted to be with only her, she soon realized he was incapable of committing to such a thing. Selena had lost count of the times she'd heard about or seen him with other women. She had definitely grown wiser since then.

"We are 'friends,' Ramon, and the farther we stay away from each other, the friendlier we can be," she finally retorted, a grim smile playing about her lips.

Ramon winced. "Ouch, who ruined your day?"

"Ramon, what the hell are you doing here!" she snapped, tiring of his cheery attitude.

"Okay, okay, calm down," he said. "I haven't seen you in a long time and I wanted to touch base."

"Uh-huh," Selena grunted, her light eyes still suspicion-filled.

"Maybe we could go out for lunch or something?" he asked in a hopeful tone, his dark eyes gazing at her expectantly.

"Uh-uh, sorry. I don't have that kind of time today," she hurriedly replied, remembering that she was on her way out to meet her accounting department.

Ramon wasn't put off. "Well, maybe sometime this week or next. It's been a while since we caught up."

"Mmm-hmm. . . ." Selena continued to watch Ramon guardedly. Though they had parted on unfriendly terms, his personality made it difficult to remain hostile. Selena found that things went a lot better by choosing to be friends instead of enemies. Even if it wasn't the closest of friendships.

Ramon, who hated serious discussions, or confrontations as he liked to call them, rarely paid visits to her on a whim. He knew how badly he'd hurt her and hoped they could really get past it one day. Thankfully, Selena had a sixth sense where the man was concerned. Suspicion was a given emotion when she was around him. Yes, Ramon Harmon was up to something . . . but what?

"Listen, just set up something with my secretary. She knows when I'm free," Selena decided, heading toward her office washroom to freshen up.

"That's cold, Selly," Ramon chided.

"That's life!" Selena merrily called from the washroom. From there, she heard her phone ringing. Before she could rush out to answer it, however, Ramon had taken charge.

A fierce scowl began to form on Darius's face when he heard the comfortable male voice on the other end. His sleek pitch-black brows drew close and he clutched the receiver a bit more tightly. "Is Selena Witherspoon there?" he asked.

"Yeah, she's here but she's, um, freshening up right now," Ramon explained, his voice alive with the laughter that was always just beneath the surface.

Darius ground his teeth, hating the man's cheery tone. He realized the man could have been a business associate, answering for Selena while she was away. Unfortunately, he didn't believe that for a second. "Would you tell her she has a call?" he asked, unable to mask the authority in his tone.

It was rare for Darius McClellan to lose his temper. That was one of the things he'd prided himself on. However, when he heard Selena's soft voice on the other end of the line, his temper quickly reached its breaking point.

"Hello?" Selena repeated when there was no response to her initial greeting.

"Too busy to answer your phone?" he finally asked, his mellow baritone brogue sounding unnervingly calm.

"Darius . . ." she breathed.

"Who answered your phone?" he asked, dismissing the pleasure he received from the way she sighed his name.

Selena cleared her throat. "Just a friend of mine."

"So I guess it's not business?"

"No . . ." She trailed away, clearly able to see where the conversation was leading.

"So, who is he?" Darius rephrased, disliking the stiff tone in his voice but unable to mask it.

Selena was quickly losing patience. "Darius, he's just an old friend who stopped by to pay me a visit," she angrily whispered. Silence greeted her on the other end. "Is this why you called? To grill me about a man answering my phone?"

"I don't know why I called," he threw back, before slamming down the receiver.

Darius knew he'd been wrong and felt like a heel the moment he hung up the phone. How had he let that woman into his heart? He had sworn that it would never happen again. Selena Witherspoon, though, had managed to change his adversity to a serious relationship without him ever being aware of it.

As badly as he felt about the call, however, his suspicions were still raised about the man who had answered the phone. His voice and the way he spoke to Selena sounded a bit too familiar for Darius's comfort.

Leaning back in the black suede chair behind his desk, he decided to pay Selena a visit and find out a bit more about her mysterious old friend.

Selena curled her freshly polished toes into the sofa's thick cushions and sighed. She'd been relaxing there for the past three hours while talking on the phone with her grandmother.

"Grammy, hold on a second, somebody's at the door."

"Well, look out first, before you open it," Secelia Rogers hurriedly cautioned.

Selena smiled and shook her head. "I will."

The fierce expression on Darius's face alone was enough reason for Selena not to let him in. After their heated phone conversation earlier that day, he should be lucky if she ever spoke to him again. Not relishing the idea of another argument, Selena knew they'd have to talk some time. Taking a deep breath, she gathered her strength, opened the door, and walked away.

"Grammy? Yeah, I . . . I'll call you later, all right?"

"Is everything okay?"

Selena glanced back at Darius, her hazel eyes gliding over his tall, athletic body. "Mmm-hmm, everything's fine."

"Is it that young man you were telling me about?" Secelia asked, the humor apparent in her lilting voice.

"Good-*bye,* Grandma," Selena said, laughing before she hung up.

The scowl Darius wore had slowly disappeared when he realized whom Selena was speaking with.

"You sound close to your grandmother," he noted, walking farther into the living room.

Selena waved her arms around her body, then hugged herself. "I love my grammy," she sang.

"So do I," Darius revealed. "I'm very close to mine too. She practically raised me."

Selena's light brown brows arched impressively at the information. "Mine too. Sess Rogers is an unbelievable woman."

A soft smirk caused Darius's mustache to twitch a little. "Sess?"

"Hush," Selena warned. "It's short for Secelia."

"I see," he replied, before they both shared a laugh. The mood, somewhat lightened by talk of grandmothers, made more important words flow more freely.

"I'm . . . I'm sorry about before."

"Darius, Ramon Harmon is who answered the phone. He's a friend now. He used to be more, but that'll never happen again."

Darius nodded. "You don't have to explain to me."

"Obviously I do or you wouldn't have hung up on me today."

"I'm sorry about that. I was out of line and I'm sorry. I guess with everything going on with you—the case and . . . my own issues—it's just getting the best of me."

Selena could see the sincerity in Darius's warm brown eyes. When she began to chuckle, his stare grew questioning.

"You know, I only tolerate Ramon because it's easier to be friends."

Darius scratched the tiny laugh line near his left eye. "Sounds like the situation was messy."

"Messy?" Selena drawled. "Messy is a good start in describing my relationship with Ramon."

Darius unbuttoned his heavy Adidas jacket and hung it on the brass coatrack near the doorway. "What happened?" he asked.

Selena curled up on one of the cushiony armchairs and pulled the extra-large T-shirt across her legs. "Everything. Everything negative. You know, you and he have something in common."

The gorgeous, chiseled features of Darius's face registered shock. "Excuse me?"

"Well, you're both ladies' men, *but,*" she emphasized when he looked ready to interrupt, "Ramon is far too self-centered to think about anyone's feelings but his own."

Darius seemed pleased by the comment. "I take it you didn't like being one of his . . . women?"

"Hmph, to let him tell it, I was *the* woman. He was always lying to me about wanting to settle down, but his actions said just the opposite. I can't count the times I caught him with other women and he didn't seem to care."

Darius was intrigued. "I can't believe you'd stay with a man like that."

"You do a lot of things when the possibility of love is in the air. Not to mention when you're younger and more starry-eyed."

"Ha! *You* starry-eyed?"

Selena smiled in spite of herself. "I don't have to tell you how it is. . . ."

"But you're still friends with this guy?" Darius asked, propping the side of his face against his palm.

Selena ran both hands through her luxurious dark brown tresses and sighed. "Ramon makes a far better friend than boyfriend. He was always able to make me laugh."

Darius's easy expression faded at the sweet, innocent remark. Selena noticed and decided to turn the conversation away from her past. "So, tell me about yours?"

Darius's gaze narrowed and he tilted his head just slightly. "Come again?" he asked.

"I told you about my bad-luck romance, now you tell me about yours?" she persisted, leaving her chair to adjust the heat.

"I always get angry when I talk about it. You may not want me to go into it," he warned.

Selena stood beneath the vent, enjoying the warmth of the air that washed over her. *"You* angry? Well, that's something I don't get to see very often. . . . Spill it."

Darius took a moment to respond. His gorgeous eyes feasted on Selena's tiny form encased in the oversized T-shirt. With her standing there with her hair curling and bouncing around her shoulders and her bare feet disappearing into the thick carpet, he couldn't get past how truly lovely and special she was. Sighing, he decided to share as much of his story as possible.

"Tenike Harris," he began, "was my girlfriend in college. I thought she was it. I mean, 'the one.'"

"Did you mess it up?" Selena whispered.

"Believe it or not, no, I didn't."

"She messed it up?" Selena blurted, unable to believe that any woman would jeopardize a relationship with him.

"Surprise," Darius confirmed.

"What happened?" Selena breathed, sounding as though she were receiving the scoop on a piece of juicy gossip. "Did she cheat on you?"

"She did."

Selena's mouth dropped open. By now, she was seated opposite Darius on the sofa. "No . . . I don't believe it."

Darius stood from the sofa. "Tenike hated being second best to anything. I knew I wanted to have my own business before I graduated. I worked day and night to build that security firm. Most of the guys you met in Miami are friends from school."

"She couldn't handle the time it took away from her?" Selena figured.

"I guess not. Like you, Tenike knew a lot of guys. She never wanted for male company, in bed or out."

Selena winced. "Ouch. Is that what you think of me?" she slowly inquired.

Darius smoothed one hand over his thick dark hair. "Not as much as I used to," he admitted.

"But enough to make you question my actions whenever I'm around another man, right?"

"Selena—"

"Darius," she interrupted, deciding to bite the bullet, "listen, I'm gonna say this now because I'll go crazy if I don't. I love you. I've known that for a while now. But, you've got to work on this suspicion of yours. I know that's difficult, considering everything that's going on right now. But if you don't get a handle on this, what happened today on the phone will only be the tip of a nasty iceberg."

Darius's eyes held a look of unmistakable admiration. Selena appeared so exquisite at that moment, he couldn't look away. "I love you too," was his only response, as he reached out to her.

For Selena, it was more than enough. She took his hand and curled onto his lap. He forced countless moans from her when he kissed her deeply and nuzzled her neck. Selena was about to surrender to the persuasiveness of his mouth and hands, when she managed to push him away. Darius's handsome face was a picture of disappointment and confusion as his long, jet-black brows drew close.

"What are you doing?" he asked, his hold loosening a bit.

"We know each other so well, physically," she began, choosing her words carefully, "maybe we should get back to getting to know each other beyond the physical for a while."

"Are you serious?" he asked, laughter lurking just below the words.

Selena could see his humor and grimaced. "Very," she assured him.

Darius tapped his fingers along the smoothness of her bare thigh and studied her lovely face. "How long are we supposed to practice this . . . abstinence?"

"Not long," she promised, "but long enough."

"Baby doll, a day is too long!" Darius bellowed uncharacteristically. Selena had no idea what she was asking.

"Sweetie, even you have to admit to how sexually charged this relationship is."

Darius gave a quick nod. "Damn right. That's the way I like it," he retorted, not even smiling when Selena laughed.

"Well, I need to know if there's more to it than that . . . so, we abstain."

Darius glared at the voluptuous beauty on his lap and groaned. "Whatever you want," he finally agreed.

Selena tapped one mauve-colored nail to his mustache and smiled. "Good. Now get comfortable, 'cause I want you to stay the night."

"Without . . ." Darius couldn't even complete the thought, he was in such a state of disbelief.

Selena, however, had already eased off his lap and he looked at her helplessly. He honestly didn't know if he had the strength to remain there an entire night and not touch her.

He knew he wasn't about to disappoint her, though, and surprised himself by tamping down the desire that drove him.

Little did Selena Witherspoon know that she had just ventured into another realm of Darius McClellan's heart. The place that held his highest respect.

Twelve

A satisfied smile played around the seductive curve of Selena's mouth. Darius had awakened her with a soft kiss that had left her tingling.

"Meet me at my office for lunch?" he asked, grinning when she gave him a sleepy smile and nodded.

Darius had already donned his clothes from the night before. He was about to leave, when his curiosity took over. He glanced back at Selena's sleeping form beneath the crisp burgundy linens and decided to investigate her closet. The large walk-in room was filled with enough pieces to stock a small boutique. The cut and style of the provocative wardrobe aroused him so that he was tempted to crawl right back into bed with her.

"And that won't do a bit of good," he mumured, remembering Selena's ban on sex. Darius laughed shortly, thinking about the request that seemed completely out of character. Holding off on sex was the last thing he ever thought she'd say. Still, knowing that she loved him, and seeing how committed she was to making things work, knocked down so much of the wall he'd hidden behind.

The phone rang, pulling him from his thoughtful state. He went to answer it, not wanting to awaken Selena. He had the receiver off its hook before it rang a second time.

"Hello?"

The person on the other end hesitated momentarily, obviously taken aback by the clear, deep male voice that answered briskly. "Is Selena there?" the caller finally asked.

Darius frowned upon hearing the vaguely familiar male voice. "She's in bed. Asleep."

"Could you tell her Ramon called?" the man asked, unshaken.

Instead of confirming that the messaged would be delivered, Darius simply set the receiver on its cradle. Keeping his temper in check, he closed his eyes for a moment. Then, he grabbed his jacket and keys before walking out.

Selena was finding it difficult to hide the smile that tugged at her shapely lips. When she stepped into the elevator at the gorgeous glass high-rise that housed McClellan Securities, a small male group had already formed. Each man offered his assistance in helping her locate the office she needed.

"Guys, please, thanks so much for your help, but I don't need it," she assured them, smiling at the disappointed looks on their faces.

"Well, where are you going? I could point you in the right direction," someone in the crowd offered.

Selena fiddled with the oversized tan button on the bodice of her snugly fitted low-cut top. She nodded, slightly assessing the crowd before speaking. "I'm headed to the top floor to have lunch with Darius McClellan. Do any of you know him?"

The elevator doors opened and Selena almost burst into laughter when everyone made grand excuses. Suddenly, they all remembered other obligations that would prevent them from escorting her to the boss's office. Selena stepped off the elevator alone.

"Hey, Melissa," Selena greeted Darius's executive assistant.

"Hey, Selena, Darius said he was expecting you."

Selena ran one hand through her thick curls. "Is he in a meeting or can I just go in?"

Melissa frowned. "Nah, he said to send you right in, but I warn you, he's not in the best mood."

* * *

"Not in the best mood" seemed to be an understatement, Selena thought when she stepped into the office. Darius was in the midst of what appeared to be a heated argument. Since she'd had the unpleasant experience of fighting with him on more than one occasion, Selena didn't envy the person.

Darius's sharp ears picked up on the sound of the door closing and he looked up. He tilted his head back in acknowledgment of Selena's presence before returning his attention to the call.

"Listen, Gerald, since it's apparent that we won't get anything solved by phone, I'll be saying good-bye. . . . No, I'll call you. . . . Mmm-hmm."

Selena winced a little when Darius slammed down the phone. Choosing to ignore his foul mood, she sauntered around the large mahogany desk. Darius's sexy eyes were focused on her, narrowing a bit when she deposited herself into his lap.

"I guess I shouldn't ask how your day is going," she whispered, while pressing a soft lingering kiss to the smooth spot just below his earlobe.

Darius tapped his strong fingers against Selena's thigh encased in form-fitting tan pants. The expression on his face was guarded. "How much do you know about Ramon Harmon?"

Selena pulled away and stared at him in disbelief. "Ramon?"

When Darius only stared at her, she shook her head. "Didn't we just have this conversation last night?"

"We did."

"So why are you asking me again today?"

Darius cleared his throat, his fingers continuing their methodic tapping along her thigh. "He called you this morning. You were asleep."

"So?" Selena asked, then shook her head. "Never mind. I can't get into this with you again," she decided, starting to move away.

The fingers that had been coolly caressing her leg suddenly stopped. One hand clasped tightly over her thigh and held her in place. "Why the hell is he callin' you at home?"

"Darius . . ."

"I'm listening."

"That's hard to believe, since I thought you were *listening* to me last night," she remarked, glaring at him. "I don't know how many times I have to tell you that we're just friends."

"I don't like that either," Darius grumbled.

"Well, you know what? I don't give a damn. Excuse me!" she snapped, pushing herself off his lap and storming toward the door.

"I'm gonna have him checked out. It's already in the works."

Selena turned to face him. "Checked out?" she asked, her hazel stare sharpening. "For what?"

Darius fixed her with a pointed look that answered the question.

"You can't be serious?" Selena breathed, taking a few steps back into the room. "You actually think he's a part of this madness?"

"Everyone's a suspect."

"Everyone, Darius? Or just every man who looks at me for more than two seconds?"

"I'll let you know what I find out," Darius said, coolly dismissing her gibe.

Selena rolled her eyes. "Don't bother," she threw across her shoulder as she bolted out of the office.

Darius remained calm until the door slammed shut behind her. "Damn!" he thundered, slapping his palm flat against the desk as he cursed his suspicious mind.

Selena was so furious when she left Darius's office that it took a while before she realized she'd gone without eating. Luckily, Nelia had caught up with her in time for them to have a late lunch.

"You know, Nel, after that mess with Ramon I said I would

never get caught up over another man," Selena confided as she and her friend enjoyed fried chicken in Central Park.

"Yeah, but this is Darius McClellan we're talkin' about here," Nelia pointed out, giving Selena a knowing smile.

"So? It's still not worth it. The crap I've had to take off that jerk is just not worth it."

"Honey, he's been through a lot—"

"So have I!"

Nelia chewed on a crunchy piece of chicken skin before she spoke. "It's different for men though. You know, having a woman cheat on them."

"Nelia! I hope you don't believe that?" Selena asked, shocked by the woman's point of view.

"Aw, Selena, you know what I mean. Their egos are so fragile. It's probably gonna take Darius a long time to *really* trust."

Selena threw a clean bone into the chicken bucket and leaned back on the bench. "It's hard for me too. I want more than a fling with him and that scares me. I really think Darius wants the same thing. He says he loves me, but that doesn't mean a thing if he can't get past these insecurities."

Nelia patted her hand reassuringly. "Maybe he just needs some more time."

"I hope that's all it is, Nel. 'Cause if he can't trust me in this thing, then we'll have nothing."

While his wife, Nelia, and her best friend were talking in the park, Stephan Cannon made his way to Darius's office. What the laid-back thirty-year-old lacked in the way of height, he more than made up for in looks and personality.

"What's up, man?" Stephan called to Darius as he walked inside the office.

"I don't believe it," Darius breathed, "you actually walked out of that store before closing time?" he marveled.

Stephan blew off his friend's comment, rolling his midnight

eyes toward the ceiling. "I don't spend half as much time there as you think I do," he informed the man.

A devious smile tugged at Darius's mouth. "You must be sick."

"No, opening another store."

Darius began to laugh and shake his head. "Damn, man, you got a death wish or somethin'? The five stores you have now worry the hell out of you."

Stephan ran one hand through the mass of dark curls that formed his short Afro. "I wouldn't trade 'em for a damn thing. I just needed a change."

"Well, congratulations."

"Save it for the party," Stephan replied. "That's what I came here for, to invite you."

"I don't think so." Darius sighed, spreading his hands across his desk.

"From the looks of you, you need one."

"Thanks."

"Anytime. Hell, bring Selena with you," Stephan added.

Darius's head snapped up at the light request. His brown eyes narrowed in suspicion. "What do you know about that?"

"Man, are you forgetting that Nelia's my wife?"

"Say no more."

"So, how's that going?" Stephan asked, lounging back on the black suede sofa in the far corner of the office.

"It's not." Darius sighed.

"'Scuse me?"

"Man, all we do is fight. Most of the time it's my fault, but I can't seem to do anything about it," he admitted.

Stephan chuckled and leaned his head back on the sofa. "Hmph, well, Selena's somethin' else."

"Damn right," Darius agreed. "She's nothin' like Tenike was, but that keeps me from trusting her."

Stephan looked over in surprise. "Tenike? Man, how many years ago was all that mess?"

The neat mustache twitched above Darius's mouth. "You know, I don't even remember."

"And how many woman have you been with since her?"

"None that I wanted to spend the rest of my life with."

The quiet admission shocked Stephan but he quickly recovered. "It's *that* serious?"

Darius could only shrug.

Stephan sighed and pushed himself up off the sofa. "Well, my man, all I can do is tell you to let go of that mess. It hasn't bothered you before, so don't let it bother you now."

Darius smiled and nodded. Of course, Stephan was right, but unfortunately letting go had been easier said than done.

Selena angled her black BMW into a reserved parking space outside her brownstone. She remained inside the plush interior of the car humming the last few bars of an early Faith Evans song, before stepping out onto the pavement. Just then, Darius rolled up in his gray 4Runner.

In an attempt to calm herself, Selena smoothed her hands over her pants. As she waited for him to approach her, she grimaced, aggravated by the way the blue three-piece suit flattered his athletic form.

"Just getting in?" Darius asked, once he'd approached her. His slanting gaze traveled across her face and outfit, stopping at the low-cut bodice of her blouse.

"Mmm-hmm, I was out with Nelia. You have her number so you can call and check it out if you want to," she smartly replied.

Darius rolled his eyes. "Selena . . ."

"Yes?"

"I didn't come here to argue."

"Oh?"

"No, I came to invite you to a party Stephan is having for a new store."

Selena watched him in disbelief. "A party? That's all you came to see me about?"

"That's right," Darius said, sounding quite pleased with himself.

"What about today in your office?"

"What about it?"

Selena folded one hand over her hip. "Your accusations about Ramon Harmon, remember that?"

Darius bowed his head and turned away from her. "Just let it go," he muttered.

"Let it go? Until when, Darius? Until you get upset again?"

"Can you drop it?" he coolly requested, though the tone in the deep of his voice brooked no argument.

Selena, however, wasn't fazed. "Uh-uh. If you think you can just come over here and invite me to a party without explaining yourself for coming down on me today for nothing, then you're about to be very disappointed."

The muscle in Darius's jaw jumped wickedly. He walked over to Selena until he practically towered over her. "You know, for someone so tiny you've got a very big mouth."

Selena's smile was purely seductive. Her expression only aggravated Darius more.

He clenched his fists and fought the urge to shake her then. Before losing all control over his restraint, he headed back to his truck. "I'll pick you up Friday at seven!" he called, while storming to the driver's side.

Selena kicked her tire, then turned and stomped all the way to her front door.

"Darius!" she cried, whirling around to see if he had gone. "Darius!"

He was about to shove the key into the ignition, when he heard her cry. "What now?" he groaned, knowing his temper could withstand no further annoyance from her. Tapping his key against the steering wheel, he grimaced and turned to look at her. Even from the distance, he could tell that something was very wrong. A second later, he was leaving the SUV.

Selena had already reached the door. She stooped to collect the thin eleven-by-fourteen cardboard box labeled with her name and address. The postmark read New York, New York, but offered no information regarding its sender. Hearing Darius's heavy steps behind her, she turned and thrust the package toward him as though it burned her fingers.

"Let's go inside," he decided, nodding at the door as he studied the front of the box.

Selena responded dazedly, her hands shaking so terribly the key tapped the lock several times before she was able to insert it. Once again, her mind was racing with all she'd managed to forget during the last several weeks. *What a fool I've been,* she thought. Weeks and weeks of no contact had weakened her defenses. The delivery had taken her completely off guard. She knew there could be nothing good inside the ominous-looking brown box.

"May I?" Darius asked, once he'd carefully inspected the outside of the box. He didn't wait for Selena's permission, which she gave with a flip of her hand.

Inside was a thin piece of black cardboard, slightly smaller than the box it'd arrived in. Darius took a seat on the sofa. Slowly, he extracted the board, muttering a vicious curse as it came into full view.

"What?" Selena whispered, as she pushed the front door shut. His silence sent a foreboding shiver beneath the flaring sleeves of her light knit top.

A response, however, proved to be unnecessary. Selena watched Darius closely—his expression changed from confusion to anger, then disappointment. She couldn't tell which emotion she saw more of.

"Looks like they forgot to include these pictures with the others. I guess I'm safe in asking who the guy is. I think I already know the woman."

Of course, Selena had no desire to look, but felt her feet inch forward of their own accord. At last, she was looking

down at the coffee table. Nothing prepared her for the faces
she saw in the photos.

"Oh my God." She groaned, horrific realization creeping
into her light eyes when she saw her face.

"Who is he?" Darius asked again. He watched her hands
settle onto her stomach as they shook noticebly. He stood
when she moved to sit down.

"James Johns," she answered. "Francine Johns's husband,"
she added, figuring he needed more clarification. The man
had been at the center of her thoughts ever since Darius and
Max announced they were giving her protection. In light of
everything else that had happened, how could she have
thought that particular batch of lies would never resurface?

Darius didn't want to know, but he had to. "Was he her husband when these were taken?" he asked, waving toward the
photos.

"They were divorced. During the marriage, he tried but . . .
nothing happened."

Darius massaged the back of his neck and began to pace
the living room. "Why didn't you tell me about this?" he
questioned, the softness of his deep voice in no way masking
his frustration.

Selena braced her elbows on her knees as she studied the
thick, dark carpeting. "Because nothing ever happened between us, Darius. Nothing but a few reassuring hugs and a
kiss on the cheek. Frankie's hated me ever since she discovered James was attracted to me. Something like an innocent
hug and kiss could easily have been misconstrued. She
must've been having him followed when those pictures were
taken."

Darius asked no more questions. Selena watched him walk
over to the phone and punch in several digits. Did he believe
her? She wondered. No one else ever had. One lie simply
crouched on top of another, painting her into an even darker
corner.

" . . . Yeah, it's me. Listen, find Max or Ham and tell 'em

to get started on a tap for Ms. Witherspoon's home and office. . . . Mmm-hmm . . . yeah. Thanks, Melissa."

"Darius, is that really necessary now?" Selena asked, once he'd ended the call. "Obviously Francine's behind this."

"Yeah, but we still don't have anything solid against her," he explained, already preparing to make another call. "We need to actually catch her in the act. We'll tap your phone, wait for contact," he said, while dialing a new number, "and hopefully Frankie'll call and state her terms, or better yet, threaten you, and we'll be there to get it on tape," he said, turning his back toward her once the connection was made. "Yeah, Stiney, it's me. . . ."

Selena studied Darius while he handled the call. He was so businesslike. The set of his broad shoulders beneath the gray jacket made her wonder if he was just too angry to let himself focus on anything else.

"All right, that's done," he was saying as he reset the receiver on its cradle. "Now—"

"Darius, stop a minute. Please," she urged, watching as he fixed her with an expectant look. "Are we back to feeling awkward around each other?"

Though Darius maintained eye contact, he was asking himself that same question. He wanted to ask if there were any other secrets she needed to reveal. Silently, he acknowledged that he was afraid to know. He knew Selena wasn't who this mystery mailer was making her out to be, but the truths that were being revealed were beginning to rattle him just as much as the lies.

"Darius?" Selena called, still waiting on a response to her question.

His soft, bedroom gaze focused on her face. "I need to get everything in place for this tap," he said, rushing toward her. "I'll call," he promised, squeezing her shoulder when he passed the sofa.

Selena watched him go. Her lashes fluttered closed when she heard the front door slam.

* * *

The pumping sounds of Redman filled the interior of Darius's truck. He hoped the pulsing rhythm of the music and the powerful rhyming style would take his mind off his trials with Selena. The speakers were vibrating and producing sounds so clear, he almost didn't hear his cell phone ring.

"Baby, what the hell are you doing?"

"Hey, Granny," he greeted, delighted by the sound of Loretta McClellan's boisterous voice.

"Honey, I'm not sayin' another word until you turn that stuff down!"

Darius shook his head and hit the volume button on the sound panel. "Better?" he asked.

Loretta chuckled, humored by her young grandson. "What are you trying to do, go deaf?" she asked.

"Hmph. No, just tryin' to forget my problems," he admitted.

"You're just a baby, ain't old enough to have problems yet."

"I wish." Darius sighed. "So, what's goin' on? How are things in Jersey?"

"Well, they were fine when I left."

"Left? Where are you?"

"In your office."

Darius was thoroughly surprised. "I don't believe it. You actually drove that Jag all the way to Brooklyn?"

"I did," Loretta replied, sounding pleased with herself. "Is this a bad time?"

"Nah, I'm glad you're there. I need a *real* woman to talk to for a change."

"Ooooh . . . now, what young lady has your jock in a bunch this time?"

A humorous grin crossed Darius's dark, handsome features. "I'll tell you about it when I get there."

* * *

"I think I just got caught up in the sex. I should face it."

Loretta McClellan's round face was full of humor as she shook her head at her grandson. "You don't believe that."

Darius pulled his suit coat away from his wide shoulders as he stood. "If I were smart, I would," he argued. "I keep messin' up with her. I love her . . . I think. But if that were the truth, I would trust her, right?"

Loretta only shrugged her response. Her huge brown eyes were glued to Darius. She was intrigued by this new vulnerable side to his strong, brooding demeanor.

Darius paced his office. "Every time I see her with another man, I flip and I hate it. I've never been caught up like this over a woman. Not even Tenike. What's wrong with me?"

Loretta closed her eyes as her shoulders rose in another lazy shrug. "Baby, you're a man with a very large ego. You got hurt by that girl and it still bothers you. I can understand you not being full of trust right now, but that happened a long time ago. Sooner or later you will have to forget it."

"She owns a magazine," Darius said, changing the subject as he lounged in his desk chair.

Loretta's perfectly arched brows rose appreciatively. "You think she'd give me a free subscription?" she asked in a sneaky tone.

Darius laughed. "It could be arranged."

"She sounds like a lovely person," Loretta decided, clasping her hands together.

"You don't even know her."

"Well, you do," Loretta argued. "So, is she?"

A heavy sigh escaped Darius as he rolled his eyes. "I love her."

"Well, honey, if that's the case you need to start trusting her."

"I'm trying, but I don't know what's wrong with me. I

wanna know if she's worth it," Darius admitted, running his large hands across his head.

Loretta lounged back on the sofa and studied her brightly polished, perfectly manicured nails. "Sweetie, I think you already know that she is, so I suggest you act on it. I'd hate to see you wind up alone because you can't get over being betrayed by a woman who cared nothing about you."

Darius had no response to his grandmother's words, he was too busy praying he could take her advice.

Thirteen

Darius decided to swallow his tension and give Selena another call. Stephan Cannon's party was that evening, and he decided to use that as reason to phone her. He knew she probably wouldn't be any more responsive to him and he couldn't blame her. Still, he had to admit to himself that if they were ever going to work, he would have to make the first move.

"Hello?" Selena answered after the second ring.

"Hey, it's me."

"Me?"

"Darius," he said after clearing his throat.

"Oh, and what can I do for you?" she asked in a tired tone of voice.

"Stephan's party is tonight and I was calling to see if you'd still go with me."

"Hmph, this is quite a change."

Darius's sleek dark brows drew close. "What's that supposed to mean?"

Selena couldn't believe what she was hearing. "Do you recall the way we left things the other day? You could barely look me in the face."

"Selena—"

"I tried to get you to tell me how you felt and you just clammed up. Do you know what that did to me?"

"Selena, listen, I'm sorry about that. Very sorry and I very much want you to go with me to this thing."

Selena wanted to give in to the soft tone of his voice. He

sounded sweet and sincere. Still, she knew it wouldn't be long before her past would become a nasty intrusion.

"Look, Darius, Nel already invited me, so I'll be there. No need for us to go together, all right? I'll talk to you later," she quickly promised before slamming down the phone.

"What are you doing here?"

Darius moved away from the doorjamb, rising to his full height to look down at her. "I already asked you to go with me and I'd feel better if you did," he grimly replied.

Selena ground her teeth. "For my safety?" she sneered, irritated by his arrogance.

"Of course."

"Are you so desperate that you have to hound me for a date?"

"You knew I'd be here. I didn't want to disappoint you." He uttered the cool barb as he stepped inside.

Knowing that she was in no mood to argue, Selena slammed her front door and went to collect her wrap. Though her decision added even more confidence to his smug demeanor, she decided not to acknowledge the part she played in heightening his self-assurance.

The party was held at Stephan Cannon's new store in Manhattan. The building had been designed so that the establishment covered the spacious lower level while the upstairs was a plush studio apartment/office. The gathering was just getting started when Darius and Selena arrived. Several male acqaintances of Darius's complimented him on his taste in women. They all told him how this time he had outdone himself.

"Hey, D, you gonna introduce us, man?" a man's voice rose behind them.

Selena had just accepted a coat-check ticket from a young man behind the counter. When she turned to Darius's side, she saw the small group of men standing around him. It was impossible to ignore the murderous expression on his face and she prayed they would get out of the party with their moods intact.

"Selena, lemme introduce you," Darius was saying as he eased one arm around her waist and pulled her close. "James Newark, Matt Hampton, and Larry Stone, this is Selena Witherspoon."

"Nice to meet you all," Selena greeted, smiling as she shook hands with each man.

"Likewise," Matt said as his dark eyes appraised the alluring navy blue Calvin Klein slip-style dress she wore.

The three men were quite nice and Selena enjoyed the attention. Still, she kept her gaze glued to Darius for any signs that he may have been becoming too agitated by the situation. Surprisingly, he seemed just fine.

When they eventually parted company to mingle, Darius met up with tons of old friends he hadn't seen in a while. They were all interested in his much talked about relationship with the beautiful magazine publisher.

Meanwhile, Selena had been mingling and catching up with just as many old friends. Like Darius, she had heard just as many compliments regarding her date. After a while, the need to get away for a few moments became her top priority. She decided to take the opportunity to enjoy the cool breeze from the terrace in the upstairs apartment.

Selena wasn't sure how long she'd been there before she had company. Darius had followed her upstairs and tossed his Boss suit coat across her shoulders when he found her outside.

"Cold?" he asked.

Thick, glossy curls bobbed along Selena's neck from her high ponytail. "Nah, I'm fine, thanks. You can keep your coat," she assured him.

"It's no problem, believe me," he firmly replied.

Selena's head bowed in a defeated gesture. "Darius, is there a problem with my dress?" she asked, knowing she was a fool for approaching the subject.

"Uh-uh," Darius quickly denied. "The dress is fine. Leaves nothin' to the imagination," he grumbled.

Selena smiled as she turned to face him. "Well, that's easy for you to say. You've seen what's beneath the dress," she reminded him, her voice low and seductive.

Darius grimaced as his chocolate stare drifted out over the fantastic view of Manhattan. "Yeah, and every jackass at the party is tryin' to figure it out."

Selena could sense his tension. Before an argument could arise, she threw herself against his wide hard chest and kissed him. Darius smoothed his hands over her waist and cupped her bottom as the kiss deepened. When he finally allowed her to pull back, she pressed her hands against his chest and looked up at him.

"The dress was worn with you in mind," she softly informed him.

Darius only nodded, before pulling her close again. As Selena cradled his face against the soft crook of her neck, the look in her lovely eyes was a picture of worry and sadness.

The following morning, Selena was rushing around getting ready for work. Thoughts of the party the night before hindered her progress though. When Darius had dropped her off at home, she was disappointed by the fact that he didn't ask to stay. It made her feel a bit better to think he was simply trying to abide by her request that they abstain.

Just as she was about to walk out of the door, the phone rang. Hoping it was Darius, she rushed to answer.

"Hello?"

"Hey, babe. How 'bout lunch today?"

"Ramon?" Selena said, her voice going flat.

"That's right. So? How 'bout it?"

"Um . . ." She sighed, wondering what Darius would think. *Wait a minute,* she said to herself. No man had ever told her what to do and none ever would. "All right, Ramon, just tell me when and where."

During a meeting with her top executives, Selena was happy to inform them that the first five issues of *Reigning Queens-Miami* had sold out. To mark the release of the six-month issue, she decided to celebrate with the party they had canceled when the magazine debuted. Of course, the gathering would be held in Miami, Florida.

"So, I know you can't wait to get Darius back down to Miami. Where it all began. . . ." Carla sighed in a dreamy tone, while she and Selena lingered in the conference room after the meeting was adjourned.

"Why would I do that?" Selena countered without meeting her friend's gaze.

"Please, Selena, I've never seen you so caught up over any man."

Selena groaned and tossed her pen to the table. "I just don't know, Carla," she said, leaning back in her chair.

"Well, how's it goin' between you two?"

"Great."

Carla grimaced. "Yeah, you sound ecstatic."

"I am happy. I am, I just . . . I'm concerned about the way he sees me. Those photos . . . I'm around so many men and he already has this hang-up about trust."

Carla ran both hands through her neat braids and glared at her friend. "Honey, listen, Darius McClellan sounds like a brotha who don't scare easy. Besides, your past is just that."

Though Carla's words were valid, they did little to ease Selena's mind. The two friends talked awhile longer. Then, Selena headed to her office where her lunch date was already waiting.

At lunch, Selena and Ramon chatted away. They were

having a wonderful time enjoying their new role as friends more than the one they shared as lovers. At least, Selena was enjoying the friendly role. Ramon, however, had other motives for inviting her to lunch.

"Selena, I want you back."

"Back for what?" she absently inquired, her attention focused on the huge chicken Caesar salad she'd ordered.

Ramon leaned across the table and covered her hand with his. "I wanna work out our problems and have a relationship with you again."

Selena stared at Ramon for a minute before she spoke. "No way, Ramon."

"Why not?"

"Now, the answer to that question is a long one. How much time do you have?" she asked, her hazel eyes widening.

Ramon pulled his hand away from hers to run it through his short dreads. "Honey, I know things between us were screwed up, but I want to make it up to you."

"I doubt you'd know where to begin," Selena told him, rolling her eyes.

"You could show me," he innocently suggested.

"Ramon, if I were even considering getting back together with you, which I am not, I hope there would be somebody that would slap some sense into me."

"Selly—"

"You must think I'm crazy. But, I'm not surprised. You know I'm seein' someone else and here you are still tryin' to ease your way back in." Selena realized how cold she sounded, but she didn't care. It angered her to know that Ramon thought she was naive enough to simply forget all that he had put her through.

Ramon was watching her with an unwavering dark stare. "Look, I don't know this guy you're seein' now, but he sounds pretty damn controlling from the times I've talked with him on the phone."

Selena ran both hands through her hair and rested her elbows on the table. "It's called being interested in *one* woman. I wouldn't expect you to understand," she accused, watching as he winced in response. "Now, if you want to keep this sad excuse for a friendship, then I suggest you drop your notions of us getting back together. It ain't gonna happen, love."

"I can't help the way I feel, Selly."

Selena shrugged. "Look, I'm tryin' to be nice here. I don't want to fight about this or the past. You'll have to work out your feelings on your own."

"You drive a hard bargain," Ramon said, watching her close her eyes. "I'll take it, though. I'll take whatever I can get."

Selena nodded and settled back in her seat. Her eyes left Ramon's to travel around the room. She couldn't have been more surprised when she saw Darius. From across the crowded dining room, it appeared that he had already spotted her and Ramon. Even at such a distance, she could see that his stare was murderous and unwavering. Selena almost laughed at her luck and bad timing. She knew, though, that if she smiled or waved she would make things that much worse.

"Ramon, are you ready?" she asked, her appetite for the rest of the delicious salad vanishing. She could have kicked herself for being such a coward, but that didn't stop her from hurrying out of the restaurant.

"There's a call waiting for you in your office."

Selena glanced at Anna and frowned. "Did you tell 'em I was at lunch?"

Anna Edwards shrugged. "I did, but he said he didn't mind waiting."

Selena had a fine idea of who it was and had no desire to prolong the inevitable. Tossing her keys to the desk, she picked up the receiver. "Darius?"

"Meet me at my house for dinner," he said. The words sounded more like an order than a request.

Selena closed her eyes and pressed a shaky hand across her forehead. "I don't want to fight," she whispered.

"Neither do I. I'll see you at seven."

"Fine," she accepted, before the connection ended.

"Come on, damn it, you haven't done anything wrong," Selena was telling herself as she sat in her car. She was parked outside Darius's brownstone. She was almost an hour early for their dinner date, but she wanted to get it over with. Knowing that she had all the courage she would be able to muster, she left her car and made her way up the wide, brick stoop.

She rang the doorbell quite a few times and her spirits rose slightly in hopes of Darius not being there, but the door opened just as she was about to walk away.

It was impossible to control the look on her face when she saw Darius. There was a towel wrapped around his lean waist and drops of water glistened on his muscular chest.

"You're early," he said, his clear deep voice holding just a trace of breathlessness.

Selena finally managed to drag her eyes back to his face. "I must be hungrier than I thought," she grumbled, rushing past him.

Darius followed her into the large, comfortable living room and watched her for a moment. "Well, make yourself at home," he finally called, pulling the towel away to dry his hair. "I'll be right back."

Though she'd seen him nude many times, Selena's mouth fell open from the sight. Her eyes followed Darius until he disappeared up the stairs. Then, she busied herself reading magazines in an effort to calm herself. Of course, nothing helped.

When Darius finally returned downstairs, his composure was relaxed, but reserved. He pulled one hand from the deep pockets of his saggy gray cotton sweatpants and waved it in the direction of the dining room.

Selena hesitated, not believing the charming host routine for a moment. "What's this all about, Darius?" she asked, her voice clearly suspicious.

His long brows rose slightly. "Didn't you say you were hungry?"

Selena watched him a moment longer, then nodded and followed him into the dining room.

They were well into the delicious meal of roast beef, broiled potatoes, and steamed vegetables before any words were spoken.

"I take it you didn't have enough at lunch today?" Darius asked, his stare trained on her nearly empty plate.

Prepared for the conversation, Selena had already settled on what she was going to say to him. She slammed her knife to the table with such force, it caused the rest of her silverware to clatter.

"Now you listen to me," she began, pointing one finger in his direction. "I am so sick of this! You saw me with Ramon and immediately started assuming the worst. I shouldn't have to reassure you like this. It's almost a daily thing with you."

Darius propped his chin on his fist and watched her. "I don't recall mentioning Ramon."

"Drop it, Darius. You didn't have to mention him. I mean, I've been going through this with you since we met—even after we've said we love each other. I can't believe I defended you today when Ramon called you controlling."

Darius appeared intrigued by the statement, but offered no response regarding it. Instead, he lowered his gaze and began to tap his fingers against the tablecloth. "You know, when a person sees the need to explain without anyone questioning, it ususally means he has somethin' to hide."

Selena smoothed her hands across her jean-clad legs. "I have nothing to hide and you know that," she said, managing to keep her voice steady.

Finally, Darius uttered a heavy sigh and covered his face in his hands. "Selena, I'm just as sick of this as you are," He admitted.

She leaned forward. "Then stop it, there's no need."

"I know, I know. I just need you to understand where I'm coming from."

Selena pulled her napkin from her lap and placed it on the table. "You know, Darius, I'm sick of hearing that too. So here it is, either you cease the mistrust and the jealousy . . ." She paused when he looked at her. "Yes, I said jealousy 'cause you're pullin' that crap too. You either stop it, or it's over. The working together on this case, everything!"

Darius was speechless as he watched her gather her things and leave.

Selena spent the next hour or so driving around the city in hopes of venting off more of the frustration from her dinner with Darius. Of course, she knew that driving in such a state would solve nothing and would most likely result in a traffic ticket.

"And with the luck I'm havin' right now, they'd probably wind up throwing my butt in jail too," she grumbled, brainstorming for other ideas.

There was a small pub a few blocks away from her office. She considered it, but with her anger at such a fever pitch, she'd be in no condition to drive once she left.

Choosing the smartest and safest route, next to home, she decided to head into the office. There was always something there that needed to be done. With her personal life in such a shambles, work would definitely be a welcome outlet.

The impressive building that housed the ten floors of *Reigning Queens* magazine was practically dark. Its headquarters at that hour was the complete opposite of its usual noisy, bustling state.

Selena relished the quiet, using the private elevator to the executive floor, which opened right in her office. Without bothering to turn on her lights, she went to the desk and switched on the computer. The desktop screen appeared shortly after, but Selena stared blindly at the row of icons lining the left side of the screen. There, she began to recap her evening with Darius. Her *disastrous* evening with Darius.

She couldn't believe that with everything else going on, he could possibly be so upset about Ramon Harmon. She understood how hurt he'd been by Tenike, but how long would he punish her for the horror of that relationship? It wasn't worth it, she kept telling herself. She'd spent long enough downing and berating herself for the mistakes of her own past. She wasn't going to allow someone else to come in and bruise the self-esteem she was fighting so hard to hold on to. Still, there was some part of her that argued Darius McClellan was worth the effort. He was a man very well worth the effort.

The phone buzzed and she was about to let the service handle it, but hoped whoever was on the other end would relieve her mind of thoughts about Darius McClellan.

"Selena Witherspoon," she answered in a light, inviting tone. Her greeting was followed by a brief silence.

"Hello, Selena."

Selena's heart slammed quick against her chest, then up to her throat when Francine Johns's voice came through the line. "Calling to state your terms, Fran?" she asked, surprised by the cool quality of her voice.

Another brief silence.

"I didn't mean for it to go this far, Selena."

"What?" Selena never expected to hear those words.

"You know I'm involved in this and . . . I am . . . partly to blame, but I—I was so damn mad about you and Jay and I wanted to teach you a lesson. I lost my nerve and it was all supposed to end though, way before those pictures of you two came out," she said.

Selena was almost too stunned to breathe. "So what? Are you trying to tell me you never meant to send those pictures to me?"

"At first I did, but later . . . later I—"

"Aw, Frankie, please! Those photos of me and Jay were a great event in this hell you've been putting me through."

"I wanted it to end, Selena."

"You're lying. This is perfect revenge since you've hated me—you've all hated me since college . . . when all those lies were started about me."

"Selena, I swear to you—"

"Frankie, I never slept with your husband. I was upset and he was comforting me. I didn't ask him to, he just did it. There was never anything more to it. Still, you knew he was attracted to me. Now do you think I believe you never meant to get back at me, to make me pay for whatever you think I did? And what do you mean about being partly to blame?"

"There's someone else. Someone else involved in this," she admitted in the softest of voices. "They concocted this whole mess. They're the ones who want to keep this thing going. Not me."

"Who?" Selena inquired, her voice losing some of the edge. She could almost hear the woman's fear. "Fran?"

"I can't say," she whispered as though the person were right in the room. "I can't say. I just had to call you so—so you'd know whatever happens, I'm not to blame. I'm out of it."

"Not until you give me this person's name," Selena demanded. Knowing it was important that she remain calm didn't stop the quivering of her voice. "Francine?" she called, when the silence lasted a bit too long. She could hear the woman breathing over the line. "Fran, if you don't call this person out, it's like you're still in business with him. Is that what you want, Frankie? To go down with this fool? 'Cause that's exactly where you're headed."

"I'm so sorry, Selena. I'm sorry I ever went along with this," Francine whispered, before the connection ended.

* * *

"Well, if she's smart, she's already skipped town."

"That doesn't really ease my mind, Max."

"Sorry."

Selena rested her elbows on her knees and raked all ten fingers through a hoard of loose coffee-brown curls. "So, I guess this means we won't be able to get any other information on who she's workin' with either?"

Max rubbed his bald head. "Unless they make contact with you directly."

"Which you doubt?" she asked, seeing the skepticism in his dark gaze.

Max could read her emotions just as easily, taking note of her mounting agitation. "We're gonna solve this thing. Just don't worry about it."

"That's easy for you to say!" Selena cried, bolting from her chair before Max's desk. She raised her hand then, bowing her head as she grimaced. "Sorry, Max, I just . . . I need somethin' to take my mind off all this mess."

"Thought about takin' a trip?" He voiced the suggestion tentatively, showing surprise when she fixed him with a radiant smile.

"Funny you should ask that," she drawled, sauntering back toward the desk. "I almost forgot that I'm going to Miami."

Max was both confused and amused. "Miami?" he inquired.

"To celebrate six months of a very successful Miami *Reigning Queens*."

Max closed his eyes, throwing back his head as though he'd suddenly remembered. "Congratulations, then," he said, while standing. "Hope you have a good time. You sure worked hard enough to get that thing together."

"Well, I plan to have a good time, even with those two giants following my every move," Selena noted, jerking her head toward Max's office door where the "two giants" waited.

Max chuckled. "They can't be that bad."

Selena raised her hand. "Nah, they're sweet, very discreet . . . they don't crowd me at all. If you guys hadn't told me about them, I probably wouldn't know they were there."

"Well, you know . . . we could probably cut it down to just one giant, if D was goin' to Miami with you," Max coyly remarked.

Selena knew he was only teasing, but she tensed anyway. "I know that's not possible. And so do you," she added, gathering her things.

"I didn't say that to send you running, Selena."

"I know, but it's time for me to head out anyway. I only wanted to hear what you thought of the tape."

"Don't you wanna talk it over with D? I know he'll be up here shortly," Max said, massaging his neck as he watched her.

Selena was already shaking her head. "I'll leave that to you."

"Selena—"

"I need to get out of here," she interrupted, the thought of running into Darius quickening her actions. "Just call me if you come up with anything." She was already walking out the door.

Selena headed toward the elevator corridor. She never saw Darius, who arrived in the hallway to see her leaving.

Fourteen

Darius was seated behind his desk going through mail, when he came across a gold-embossed, gray envelope. Frowning, he tossed aside the other correspondences and concentrated on the tiny package. Inside, he found an invitation—airline ticket included—to Selena's celebration of Miami *Reigning Queens* sixth-month issue. A sense of relief washed over him as he held the invitation in his hands.

They had been so distant for the past couple of weeks. Darius could never remember being as scared as he was the night Selena stormed out of his home. He realized then how easy it would be for him to lose her and he knew he couldn't let that happen. He didn't think he'd ever fall so much in love with her, but he did. The last two weeks had also given him time to really think. Though he had much work to do in changing his way of thinking, he had managed to gain a handle on many of the issues involving Selena. True, she was a very appealing and dynamic woman. Of course the opposite sex would be attracted. It certainly wasn't her fault and he had been punishing her for it. Besides, the last thing she needed was his scrutiny. Francine Johns's call had made them more alert than ever. Darius and his staff had been unable to locate her and had nothing to go on. There was nothing to aid them in locating the woman's elusive accomplice. Where Selena was concerned, Darius knew if he felt anything it should be pride over the simple fact that she was in his life.

* * *

Selena was in her office wondering if Darius would accept her invitation. She truly hoped he would, but decided not to worry herself thinking about it.

She was in her office going over last-minute preparations for the party by phone, when Secelia Rogers waltzed into the office.

"Grammy!" Selena cried from across the room, both shocked and elated to see her grandmother. She ended the phone call quickly and rushed over to hug the lovely older woman.

Selena was the image of a younger Secelia Rogers. Selena could only hope she looked half as wonderful as her grandmother when she reached the age of sixty-three.

"How are you, sweetie?" Sess asked, toying with her granddaughter's bouncy, chocolate curls.

"I'm fine," Selena tiredly responded. "Trying to tie up a few things before this party."

Secelia nodded and perched her petite form on the edge of Selena's desk. "And how is everything else going?" she asked.

Selena groaned and braced her hands on the opposite end of the desk. "I haven't seen Darius in about two weeks and we have no more leads in the case."

"Ah, honey, I'm sorry. Especially about Darius."

Selena waved her hand. "I keep saying to myself, 'You weren't wrong about him,' but every day I go without seeing him I start to doubt that even more."

"Well, all I can say is I've never seen you so serious about any man. Not even that Ramon," Secelia noted.

"Hmph, I hope it's all worth it," Selena grumbled.

Secelia leaned over and patted Selena's hand. "It will be. I promise."

Selena took her grandmother's hand and came around the desk to hug her. "Thanks, Grammy Sess," she whispered.

"Now," Secelia said, pulling away and cupping her granddaughter's face, "are you gonna invite me to this party or do I have to beg?"

A look of pure surprise crossed Selena's beautiful light caramel-complexioned face. "You wanna go to the bash in Miami?"

Secelia smoothed her hand across her sleek, short hair and sent the younger woman a humorless stare. "Yes. *And?* Is there something wrong with that?"

Selena raised both her hands and shook her head. "Not a thing, Miss Sess. So tell me, do you want first class or coach?"

Of course, Selena decided to book a different hotel than Velma Morris's Paradise Halls for her crew's stay in Miami. Not that she had much choice in the matter, since the hotel was under new management and undergoing renovations. Selena didn't see much need to go overboard for accommodations since the party would be taking place in just two nights.

"Baby, how in the world could you leave this to go back to New York?" Secelia Rogers was asking as her hazel eyes feasted on all the gorgeous men walking around the hotel.

"Cool down, Miss Sess," Selena warned, though she was amused by her grandmother's allure. Even in her sixties, Secelia Rogers could still catch a man's eye.

"I mean these men are simply—"

"Excuse me, miss?"

Secelia turned and found a very handsome young man gesturing toward the small duffel bag near her sneaker-shod foot.

"May I take this bag and show you to your room?" he asked, extending his hand toward Secelia.

Secelia spoke without even wasting a glance in her granddaughter's direction. "Baby, I'll see you later," she called, already taking the man's hand.

"Mmm-hmm." Selena grimaced, shaking her head at the woman. Though she agreed that the men were as gorgeous as they were when she last visited, this was primarily a business trip. Still, that didn't stop her from looking over her shoulder for Darius.

The night of the party arrived so quickly, Selena felt caught up in a whirlwind. With the sellout success of Miami *Reigning Queens*, the city was ripe for an over-the-top celebration.

Selena tried to call Darius before leaving her suite, but was unable to reach him after trying his home, office, car, and cell phone. She cursed herself for her fanatical attempts to track him down. He was obviously a man who disliked ultimatums, she decided. He hadn't tried to reach her since their disagreement more than two weeks ago. Now Selena believed it was way past time she stopped fooling herself.

Chic, classy, and seductive were just a few accolades possible to describe the party. Everything lived up to Selena's expectations and she thrived on the scene. Because the weather permitted, the bash was held on the top floor and spilled out onto the rooftop of the publication's headquarters. It took a while for Selena to believe the high-rise and everything inside was actually her property. From the beginning, she'd forced herself not to indulge in the fast life. Extravagant homes and luxurious cars weren't all that important to her. With this new magazine, though, she'd wanted to do it right and she was glad she had.

Selena had been sharing a dance with Thomas Jordan, her advertising vice president for Miami *Reigning Queens*. He was so in awe of everything he saw, they'd been dancing for almost five minutes before he said one word.

"So? Are you impressed?" she finally asked, her hazel eyes glistening with happiness.

Thomas uttered a short laugh. "I think you know the answer to that. You have outdone yourself this time, girl."

Selena shrugged and threw her head back. "Thanks, I know." She sighed, joining Thomas when he laughed.

Thomas and Selena burned up the dance floor for at least

twelve minutes. Selena was completely in her element that evening and it showed. She was breathtaking in a tan silk frock that barely reached midthigh. The long sleeves of the dress flared elegantly at her wrists. Tanned, strappy heels completed the sensual, lovely outfit.

"I think I better let you go now," Thomas decided, as he smiled across her shoulder.

"What?" she asked, cutting herself off to follow the line of his gaze. Finding Darius behind them rendered her motionless. "Okay, Tommy," she whispered.

Darius nodded as Thomas stepped past, and then his warm brown eyes turned back to Selena. He was utterly gorgeous in mocha Maurice Malone trousers and a matching jacket over a collarless cream-colored shirt and vest.

Selena's light eyes roamed the devastating length of his lean, athletic frame. Her legs threatened to give out beneath her at any moment. Thankfully, Darius made the save.

"You came," she breathed, staring up at him.

Darius smiled as he eased his arm around her small waist and held her tight. He loved her awed little-girl expression as she struggled to overcome her surprise over seeing him.

"I'm hurt that you would think I wouldn't be here," he murmured against her ear, when he dipped his head.

Words seemed unnecessary after that. Selena surrendered to the smooth R&B, the relaxed atmosphere, and the tall, dark, incredible man holding her in his arms. With a sigh, she rested her forehead against his chest, comforted by the steady, strong beat of his heart.

Their dance was so slow and heated that it was impossible to mistake them as anything other than two people who knew each other on an intimate level. Selena rested her palms flat against Darius's chest as her lips slid across the smooth line of his jaw. In response, Darius lowered his head to give his searching mouth more access as his hands smoothed over her back to cup her full bottom.

"Darius . . ." she breathed, feeling him squeezing her

gently. She couldn't stop the moan that escaped her lips when he pulled his hands away. She was so totally immersed in him that it took a moment to return to reality. When she did, there was another shock.

Darius was pushing the lovliest, pear-shaped diamond ring onto her finger. He stared at it for a moment, before looking back into her eyes.

"Please say you'll marry me," he said, cupping her chin in his hand.

Selena tried to say the word, but it just wouldn't come. "Do you know what you're asking?" she whispered.

"I know all too well."

"It's only been six months."

"And in that time we've learned what it takes most people six years to find out."

Selena closed her eyes torn between elation and disbelief. "Yes, Darius. Yes. . . ." She sighed, not caring whether it was too soon for such a commitment. She moaned when his head lowered and he thrust his tongue smoothly into her mouth.

Later, Selena realized that she didn't even remember the rest of the party. All that mattered was the one exquisite moment that was about to change her life.

Loretta McClellan owned a well-known soul food restaurant in Newark, New Jersey. When the woman retired from thirty years of elementary school teaching, her energetic nature would not allow her to sit by resting on her laurels. She decided to use her entire savings and begin the establishment. It proved to be a wise move. In the time the restaurant had been in operation, Loretta had become independently wealthy.

The restaurant had been converted from a small department store it once housed. Loretta's Tavern was the sight of Darius and Selena's engagement party. Old friends, employees, and family attended the gathering.

Lovely could only begin to describe the event. The warm,

cozy interior of the restaurant was decorated by flaming candles and beautiful flowers situated all across the dining room. The food was set out on long, curving glass tables. The spread was abundant and inviting. Dishes included succulent roast beef, baked chicken seasoned to perfection, fried turkey, stuffed au gratin potatoes. An array of sliced and marinated vegetables as well as three cheese macaroni pies, quiches, muffins, ice creams, cakes, and other delectables were all on hand.

Selena and Darius were in awe when they saw the lengths Darius's grandmother had taken to make the party a success. They only spent a few moments together before guests began pulling them away from each other.

"I must say, I am truly shocked."

Selena almost screamed when she turned to find Harry standing a few feet away. He was the picture of success and confidence, but that did nothing to quell his boisterous personality.

"Well, I'm surprised to see you here," Selena admitted, as she stepped closer. "I didn't think you'd show up to my little affair," she teased.

Harry waved his hand. "Aw, save it. You know how busy I've been with this line."

"I know. I guess that show in Miami did it for you, huh?"

"Hell yeah," Harry drawled, closing his eyes as he recalled the event. "Girl, I had so many orders after that thing, I tell ya, I'll never be able to repay Velma." He sighed.

Selena noticed Harry's preoccupied expression when he mentioned his cousin. Smiling, she took his arm and pulled him along with her. "Let's dance," she ordered.

"So how is Velma? Have you seen much of her?" Selena was asking after she and Harry had been on the floor awhile.

"Well, you know she had to answer for what happened with the hotel."

Selena's eyes widened. "Did she spend any time in jail?"

Harry sighed and tightened his hold around Selena's waist. It was clear that the entire situation still aggravated him. "She was able to work something out with the cops. Gave up a few names and they went easy on her. I don't know where she is now. Until the trials, they've got her someplace for protection in case . . ."

"My God," Selena breathed.

"Plus she lost the hotel."

"Yeah, I know," Selena said as she smoothed her hands against Harry's chest. "Lord . . ." she breathed.

Harry was silent for a few moments before he cleared his throat. "Why'd you ask me to come to this mess? I wasn't tryin' to get you down on your big night?"

"Please, you should've known I'd be concerned about what was goin' on," she argued.

"Well, there was a bright side to it all." Harry sighed, and patted her waist.

"What?"

"Hell, it appears you got your man."

"Hmph, yeah . . . I only hope I can keep him."

Harry frowned. "Excuse me, but what kind of talk is that at your own engagement party?"

"Harry, I love Darius and I know he loves me."

"But?"

"It's this case and how overprotective he is of me. Which doesn't go hand in hand with his suspicions when he has to deal with other men approaching me. He went through a lot of rough stuff in another relationship and that's made the situation even more frustrating. I—I just don't know sometimes," she admitted.

"Well, he asked you to marry him, didn't he?"

"Yes, he did. It doesn't make me forget all the arguments we have about this, though. I can only pray we're past it all, but with this case still hanging over our heads I just feel the worst is yet to come."

Harry cupped her face and stared into her hazel eyes.

"Selena, this is your engagement party. Act like it. You shouldn't be talking like this."

Selena still appeared uneasy. "Thanks, but you don't know what I've been goin' through with Darius. It's good for a while, and then . . ."

"Then why are you marrying him?"

Selena rolled her eyes. "Oh, Harry, don't misunderstand me here. I love Darius very much. I love him and I know he feels the same. All I'm saying is that love and trust are two very different things, and Darius's trust is very hard to obtain. I can't stand the way he changes when he puts that guard into place."

"So what are you gonna do?"

Selena shrugged and shook her head. "I don't know. Praying always seems to help."

Later that evening, Darius shared a drink with Stephan and Nelia Cannon. Darius was anxious to leave the table since all the Cannons could talk about was their disbelief over his upcoming nuptials.

"So have you and Selena set a date yet?" Nelia asked, her black eyes twinkling mischievously.

Darius stirred his drink and refused to look at Nelia. "You know we haven't."

Nelia appeared to be confused. "How would I know?"

"Please, Nel, Selena tells you everything. You probably even know about me proposing to her in a crowded party."

"Mmm, as I recall, it was a crowded rooftop."

Darius extended his hand toward Nel and looked over at Stephan. "This is *your* wife."

Stephan laughed and tapped the smooth hairs lying along his temple. "Nothin' surprises me tonight. I'm still trying to get used to the fact that you and Selena are 'bout to jump the broom."

Darius grinned, the action causing his neat mustache to twitch. "Well, you'll be there in November to see for yourself."

Nelia slammed her glass to the table. "Selena didn't say a thing about November!"

Stephan looked at Darius and the two friends shared a laugh at Nelia's expense.

The threesome continued to laugh and talk over their drinks, when Darius spotted his fiancée across the room. His intense, rich brown eyes narrowed and his head tilted as he watched Ramon Harmon walk over and pull Selena into a snug embrace.

Closing his eyes, Darius was determined not to ruin the evening for any reason. His temper was being tested to the limit as he watched the man pull Selena to the dance floor. Darius looked on as they laughed and twirled to the music. That was all fine, but when Ramon dipped his head and kissed her, Darius lost his restraint. As though they were viewing a movie, Nelia and Stephan watched Darius storm away from the table and bound across the room.

Ramon had released Selena and was leading her out to the terrace. "Let's go somewhere private," he suggested.

"Ramon, I only agreed to a dance, nothing more. Now, you're drunk. Stop it," she warned.

"Drunk on you," Ramon slurred.

"How'd you get in here anyway? I know you weren't invited," she said.

Unfortunately, Ramon had no chance to respond. He was jerked away from Selena as Darius caught him by the collar of his shirt and landed a vicious blow to his face.

"Darius!" Selena cried.

A few people noticed the commotion and went to help. It took a while, but they were eventually successful in pulling Darius away from Ramon.

Selena went to check on her friend, but he was unconscious. With the assistance of the men who stopped the fight, they led Ramon away from the scene. Selena fixed Darius with a look of pure disgust before she left the terrace.

* * *

"For such a successful business man, you sure are stupid sometimes!"

Darius pressed the ice pack to his bruised knuckles. "Granny . . ." He sighed.

"Don't 'Granny' me!" Loretta McClellan shouted as she strode around the large state-of-the-art kitchen that had cleared the moment she walked in. "What the hell possessed you to act like this tonight of all nights!"

Darius leaned back in his chair and kept his coffee gaze trained on the floor. Minutes later, Selena walked in.

"Miss Loretta, could I talk to Darius for a minute?" she asked.

"Of course you can, baby," Loretta said, patting Selena's shoulder before she left.

A few moments of silence filled the kitchen. Slowly, Selena stepped over to the small wooden table where Darius sat. "Can't you even look at me?" she asked.

After a while, Darius raised his brown eyes to her face and watched her expectantly.

Selena tapped her index finger against the tabletop. "You know, I thought—or hoped—we were getting past all this. But, I guess you're never gonna be able to let it go, huh?"

"Don't try making all this my fault, Selena," Darius said, his deep voice sounding unnervingly calm.

"Well, whose fault is it, Darius? You were the one who walked in and started pounding the man!"

"I had my reasons."

Selena slapped her hands to her sides. "What reasons, Darius? What reason could there be for you ruining our engagement party?"

"I saw him kiss you, Selena. Right on the dance floor. I saw him kiss you and I didn't see you do anything to stop it."

An uneasy look flashed in Selena's eyes and she leaned closer. "It wasn't what it looked like," she whispered.

"Oh . . ." Darius said, his stare murderous.

"He was drunk and he didn't know what he was doing."

"Mmm-hmm . . . you sure that's all it was?"

"What are you getting at?"

Darius stood and pushed his hands into the deep pockets of his black Versace trousers. "You claim it's over between you and this guy, but I'll bet he wants you back. That's probably all he talks about," he said, uttering a sound of pure frustration when he spied the guilt spark in Selena's eyes.

"Hmph, sometimes I feel like I really don't know you at all," Selena defeatedly said, watching him turn his back on her. Still, she maintained her composure. "Darius, I swear that my love for you is real. It seems I'm always trying to reassure you of that. You talked to me about Tenike once before, but there has to be more to it than what you told me. It's obvious that you still have a very long way to go before you're ready to be with me."

With a strength she didn't know she had, Selena pressed her lips together and tugged the dazzling ring off her finger.

"You know where I am when you're ready to give me a *real* chance," she said, then walked out of the kitchen.

Darius voiced another impatient sigh and glanced at his wristwatch. "Granny, how much longer do I have to listen to this?"

Loretta leaned back in her chair and threw her grandson a surprised look. "You'll listen until I'm through talkin'."

"Granny, it's over, can you just let it go?"

Loretta shook her head. "I've never been so disappointed in you."

Darius rolled his eyes toward the ceiling. For the past three days he had had to listen to his grandmother express her displeasure at his behavior. Little did she know that she couldn't be any more disappointed in him than he was in himself.

* * *

"Sweetie, please cheer up. This can't be any good for you," Secelia Rogers was begging Selena. The woman's gaze was worry-filled as she watched her granddaughter sit slumped down in a chair.

Selena groaned and braced her elbows on the crisp white tablecloth. "How'd things get so messed up, so fast, Grammy?"

Secelia patted her arm. "Honey, things will work out between you and Darius if it's meant to be."

"But what if it's not?"

"I'll bet some ice cream will make you feel better, little girl," Secelia said. "I know having something good in my mouth always makes me feel better," she wickedly added.

A slow smile spread across Selena's lovely face as she shook her head. "You're a dirty old woman, you know that, right?"

Secelia pretended to be shocked, but eventually began to laugh as well. As Selena wiped the tears from her eyes, she saw Darius seated with his grandmother across the dining room.

Their gazes locked and held for a long while. Darius was the first to look away. His pained groan captured Loretta's interest. She knew he was hurting greatly over his argument and subsequent breakup with Selena. It was clear that he loved her, but there was still so much he had to do to heal the scars of his past.

"Honey, why don't you go get the car? I'll pay the check," Loretta said, patting his hand.

Selena hadn't taken her eyes off Darius since she'd spotted him. When he walked out of the dining room, she held back the sob rising in her throat.

"Granny, I think I'm gonna go speak to Miss Loretta."

Secelia glanced over in the direction Selena had been looking. "Oh, Loretta's here? Well, I'll go with you."

Loretta's surprise turned to happiness when she saw Selena with her grandmother. "Baby, what are you doing here?"

Selena leaned down and embraced the lovely woman. "Just out to lunch. We saw you and decided to come speak."

"Well, I'm glad you did," Loretta said, taking Secelia's hand and holding it tightly.

Secelia pressed a kiss to Loretta's cheek. "How are you, girl? Are you here alone?"

An uneasy look crept into Loretta's brown eyes. "Well, I—"

"You ready, Granny?"

The three women turned toward Darius, who had just approached the table. Selena grew speechless and fought to keep her cool. Likewise, Darius could not keep his eyes off Selena. Still, neither made the effort to speak.

Thankfully, Secelia cleared her throat and eased her hand into the crook of Darius's arm. "How've you been, sweetie?"

Darius dragged his eyes away from Selena and smiled down at her grandmother. "I'm good, Miss Sess. Tryin' to make it," he added, looking back at Selena.

Unable to stand there any longer pretending things were normal, Selena said her good-byes and rushed from the room. Darius's warm gaze followed her until she was out of sight.

"Darius, there's a Ramon Harmon out here to see you."

Darius's brows drew close as the name registered. "Send him in, Melissa." Curious, Darius threw down his pen, leaned back in his chair, and waited.

Ramon strode into the dark, intimidating office with unnerving confidence. Though his handsome light-complexioned face was badly bruised, he looked as though there were nothing out of the ordinary.

"Nice office," he noted, taking in the impressive stark atmosphere. "A little overbearing, though," he added.

"What do you want?" Darius asked, his tone clearly warning.

A short, slightly shaky laugh escaped the man. "Right to the point, I see. All right, I messed up with Selena a long time ago, but I want her back."

Darius's only response was to raise his brows a few notches. Ramon cleared his throat and continued. "I still love her. I had a funny way of showing it before, but I wanna make that up to her."

Darius's silence was more unsettling than his words. He did an admirable job of keeping his temper in check as he let Ramon have his say.

"I know she's agreed to marry you, but I don't think she'll go through with it considering what happened at your . . . engagement party. I think a jealous fiancé would be of little consequence."

"Selena broke the engagement," Darius said when Ramon grew silent.

A wicked smirk tugged at Ramon's mouth as he stared down at Darius. "See?" he said, making a hasty exit when the man rose from his chair.

A few weeks later, Nel and Stephan held a dinner party. Since they lived on a large beautiful estate out on Long Island, the gathering was to be a weekend affair. Several people had been invited and the event promised to be very enjoyable.

"Selena, girl, I'm so glad you decided to come out!" Nel exclaimed, as she hugged her friend close.

Selena pushed her hands into the pockets of her gray sweatsuit and sighed. "Nel, what's Darius doing here? You didn't tell me you'd invited him."

"Sweetie, you know he and Stephan are best friends."

Selena sucked her teeth and massaged her aching temples.

"Look, there're a lot of people here this weekend. You two probably won't even see much of each other," Nel consoled, trying to sound convincing.

Nelia didn't exaggerate when she talked about how many people would attend the gathering. It appeared that well over twenty guests were there and they all seemed to be coupled off. Selena and Darius saw each other constantly and tried to ignore each other. It was impossible to do, considering the sexual tension that seemed to charge the air.

On Sunday afternoon, Selena decided to enjoy some quiet time away from all the merriment. The weather that weekend was warm enough to enjoy a nap under one of the huge elm trees in a secluded area of the estate.

Selena didn't know how long she'd napped beneath the shady tree. When she awakened, Darius was right next to her. *I'm dreaming. I have to be,* she told herself, as she squeezed her eyes shut tightly. When she opened them, Darius was still there. He lay over her with his elbows resting along either side of her head.

"Darius . . ." she breathed, staring up into his soothing gaze. Darius simply lowered his head and pressed his mouth to hers. Selena's lips immediately parted and his tongue slid smoothly into the waiting cavern of her mouth. With every thrust of his tongue, the kiss deepened. Darius grasped her smooth, bare thighs beneath the short wraparound denim skirt she wore and pulled her legs apart. As his heavy body settled, Selena ground her hips against him in a purely erotic fashion.

Darius broke the kiss to trail his lips along the smooth line of her neck. The gentle friction from his mustache sent shivers through her as she arched into his unyielding frame. She rubbed her fingers through his close-cut hair as Darius's perfect teeth expertly unfastened the buttons of her thin cotton shirt.

He kissed the soft skin that bubbled over the tops of the lacy red bra she wore. His tongue slid down the deep cleft of her breasts, before he stopped and raised his head.

"What?" she whispered, her breaths coming in rapid spurts.

"We need to talk."

"Now?"

"We were engaged a month ago," he reminded her.

Selena blinked. "I know . . . now we can barely speak to each other."

"I hate this."

"So do I, and I'd like to blame it all on the stress we're

going through with this crazy case, but it's more than that. I can't make you trust me. I mean, do you really think I'd invite my ex-boyfriend to my engagement party and then carry on with him right in front of you?"

Darius toyed with a tendril of her coily hair. "No, and I was stupid to think it. Baby, it wasn't you I was mad at."

"Maybe not, but it affected me just the same."

After a moment, Darius gave a short laugh. "You know, at this moment, I don't much trust myself either. I *do* know that I still want you to marry me. I realize I probably blew it."

"I still want to marry you too. Can we just forget all that mess at the party ever happened?"

Darius grinned. The twinkle in his brown eyes had returned. "I'll be happy to," he said, bringing his face closer. "I want you with me always, Selena. I know one of us should be suggesting we wait until I get my act together."

Selena pressed her to his chest. "One of us could also suggest we wait until I do the same."

"But I don't want to wait."

"And I don't want to wait to be your wife."

"What do you have in mind?"

"Something small. We should let our grannies handle it," she suggested.

Darius gave her a humorously skeptical look. "You sure 'bout that?"

Selena rolled her hazel eyes and sighed. "I'm sure I want to take the chance," she whispered, pressing a kiss to his mouth.

Fifteen

Even Darius and Selena didn't know what to expect when a limousine picked them up that morning and transported them to the pier. Their grandmothers had summoned them there by way of a messenger. The two of them appeared to be late arrivers and were obviously quite shocked by the lavish sight before their eyes.

"What have y'all done?" Selena questioned when her grandmother rushed toward her.

"We know you said simple, but Loretta and I had a great idea," Secelia explained, glancing over at her partner, who was hugging Darius.

"Yes? . . ." Selena asked, watching her grandmother expectantly.

"Well, we've rented this yacht," Secelia said, gesturing at the huge vessel behind her. "And we're going to cruise down to Jamaica."

"Who's we?" Darius asked, mimicking his fiancée's thoughts.

"The four of us and a few of your closest friends. We wanted the both of you to have something small yet unforgettable."

Loretta slapped her hand against her grandson's back. "That, plus we figured if we made it special enough, y'all would stick together."

"Loretta!" Secelia chastised. "Anyway, we planned you a wedding at sea. Now there's no way you can say no to that."

Selena smoothed her hands across her figure-flattering denims and shrugged. "Do we have a choice?" she asked.

* * *

The wedding was to be the culmination of the exotic cruise to Jamaica. Loretta and Secelia had spared no expense for their grandchildren. The yacht was equipped and well stocked with every food and drink imaginable. An experienced wait staff had even been hired.

"You sure about this?"

Selena turned and saw Darius leaning against one of the poles along the deck. "Positive," she assured him.

Darius pulled the black hood to his sweatshirt away from his head and joined her where she leaned against the railing.

"Are *you* sure?" Selena countered, watching and enjoying the determined look on his handsome dark face.

"I haven't worked through any of the mess that makes me behave like such a jackass, but that hasn't changed the fact that I love you and very much want you to be my wife," he promised her, propping the side of his face in his palm.

Selena rested her chin against his shoulder. "I don't want to lose you," she whispered.

"You won't," he whispered back, rising to his full height and taking her with him.

The wedding itself was as beautiful as everyone knew it would be. The beachfront gathering was held at sunrise, but everyone was wide awake and totally entranced by the exchange of vows.

Afterward, a fantastic breakfast was held along the sparkling waterfront. All sorts of omelets, muffins, and fruits contributed to the outstanding feast.

Selena and Darius barely ate anything at all. They gathered a bowl of fruit and carried it to a high rock overlooking the reception. From there, Selena fed her gorgeous husband and he returned the favor for his beautiful wife. They were fully involved with each other and couldn't wait to be alone.

Instead of remaining in Jamaica for their honeymoon,

Darius whisked his wife away to a secluded mountaintop where yet another surprise awaited.

"Can I take this thing off now?" Selena asked, gesturing to the silk scarf covering her eyes.

"Hold on," Darius ordered, setting down their bags before he untied the scarf.

It took a moment for Selena's eyes to adjust to the sunlight bouncing off the pearly white snow. When her vision was back to normal, a loud gasp escaped her lips.

"Darius! Tell me there're other people here," Selena ordered, her fingers shaking as her eyes grew wide.

Darius looked around the huge log cabin, before he shook his head. "Nope, we're all alone."

"You own this?" she asked, slowly making her way toward the beautifully breathtaking structure.

Darius leaned back against the gray 4Runner and nodded. "I own this and I want to share it with you," he confirmed.

"With me?" she queried, peeking through the frosty windows covered by heavy hunter-green drapes. "I don't believe this," she whispered, awed by the beauty surrounding her.

Darius headed up the snow-covered brick steps. He didn't stop until he'd turned his wife away from the windows and lifted her against his chest.

"Do you know how long it's been since I've had you?" he asked, pressing her against the house and lifting her higher so he could stare directly into her hazel eyes. "I don't want any interruptions."

The thick logs crackled as the fire roared to life. A huge, fluffy white carpet was situated before the fireplace.

Selena sighed her approval when Darius placed her down gently in the center. They hadn't bothered to unpack since there would be no use for clothing. Darius settled his heavy, solid frame across Selena's silky, voluptuous form. He began to rain kisses on the top of the smooth column of her neck.

Selena's long nails grazed the flawless dark skin of his back as his kisses traveled lower.

His tongue traced an erotic pattern across her chest and down the cleft between her full breasts. Finally, his lips closed around the nipples, which had hardened beneath the merciless teasing of his fingers.

Moaning softly, Selena arched her back, pushing her breast deeper into his mouth. Darius didn't mind, eagerly taking all she had to give. He left her begging softly for more when he moved on to lavish her flat stomach and belly button with his heavenly kisses. Selena unconsciously writhed, beckoning him to focus his attention near her hips. Darius curved his large hands around her buttocks to hold her in place as he pressed his mouth to the curly tendrils above her womanhood.

"Darius!" she cried, when his lips tugged at her throbbing need.

Darius didn't veer from his task. His grip tightened as he thrust his tongue more deeply inside her. Selena threw her arms above her head and cried out repeatedly in response to the pleasure she was receiving. The skill and mastery of the intimate caress was incredible. Darius groaned as his tongue thrust rhythmically in the moist heat of her body. Even when Selena was in the throes of a powerful orgasm, Darius continued the relentless onslaught of the exquite caress.

Selena would have dozed off, but Darius wasn't about to let that happen. Rising above her, he buried the long, steely proof of his arousal inside her body.

Bracing his arms on either side of his wife, Darius took her with passionate, possessive force. The expanse of his back was sleek with sweat in the firelight as a result of his efforts.

Surprising her, Darius pulled Selena from the floor and continued his driving thrusts. She wound her arms about his neck and threw her head back. Wanting to take control, she pushed him on his back and assumed the lead.

Darius kept his hands wrapped around her waist as she rode him. Her hips rotated and lifted over his dark body as her nails traced the heavy muscles in his chest. She felt incredible power each time he groaned the satisfaction that was mirrored on his handsome face.

Satisfied, however, could only begin to describe how wonderful Selena was making him feel. Each time he felt her creamy heat engulf his length, he called her name.

When their ravenous appetites had been somewhat sated, they cuddled close before the fire and drifted off to sleep. Their night of love, though, was far from over.

The remainder of the honeymoon floated by like a dream. They used the solitude to learn more about each other and, in the process, fall more in love.

The fantasy-filled honeymoon was brought to an end once business began to require their attention. Selena's new Miami magazine had been doing exceptionally well, but still demanded much of her time. Though her staff there was very competent, Selena always liked being right in the center of things. She'd hoped to avoid it, but a trip to Miami appeared inevitable.

"A phat career, good marriage, gorgeous husband. How do you do it?"

Selena giggled and tossed her napkin at Nelia. The two decided to get together for lunch one day and catch up on things.

"Stop it. You have everything I do."

"But you're the woman who said you'd *never* have it," Nelia reminded her.

"Yeah, that was me," Selena grudgingly admitted.

Nelia popped a piece of ice into her mouth and crunched it. "So, how is it?"

Selena let her eyes slide up to the high ceiling and tilted her head back. "I'm so happy. Everything is going so good and Darius is so . . . mmm." She stopped herself then, disappointing Nel. "But, I have to admit it . . ."

"Admit what?"

"I don't know . . . sometimes I feel like I'm walking a tightrope—wondering when my blackmailer will rear his ugly head again or when Darius might snap again."

"I thought y'all had all that stuff about his jealousy settled."

"Well, we never really *talked* about it. We just sort of forgot about it."

Nelia set her glass down and leaned forward. "Selena, what is there for him to flip over now? Y'all are married."

"There's Ramon."

"What about him?"

"He's been calling, talking that tired mess about wanting to get back together even though he knows that's completely out of the question. I haven't seen him or anything, but who knows when we'll bump into each other? And if Darius is around, well . . ."

"Listen, I advise you to just forget about that crazy brotha. You'll just add fuel to the fire if you don't."

Selena and Darius survived. After being married almost eight months and knowing each other considerably longer, they were still surprised at how new everything seemed. They prayed it would last forever.

Darius was becoming an even more powerful force in his field. His workload had become so heavy that when Selena informed him that she needed to visit the Miami magazine again, he didn't argue.

"Did you have enough?"

Stephan Cannon smiled wickedly as he grabbed his wife by her waist. "I had enough to eat."

"Mmm. . . ." Nelia sighed, enjoying the kisses Stephan rained over her neck. "Down, boy, you've got customers."

"Mmm-hmm, that's what my employees are for," Stephan informed her as he pressed her to the penthouse bed.

When Stephan finally allowed her to leave, Nelia was feeling so wonderful that she almost missed Ramon Harmon entering the store.

"Hey, Nelia," Ramon greeted, as he browsed through a rack of shirts. "Where's Selena been hidin' lately?" he asked.

Just walk out, Nelia ordered herself. She had never cared for Ramon, especially once things crumbled between him and Selena. She knew there was no way she could simply walk away without saying anything.

"Selena's married, or hadn't you heard?" She asked, turning away from the double glass doors.

Ramon looked up. "I heard. I can still see her though, can't I?"

"Not when you want to break up her marriage."

"Nelia—"

"You know what? You ain't changed a bit after all these years. You're still the same dog today that you were then. You know the woman's married, but you won't listen. When she gets back from Miami, I suggest you cool it."

Ramon's dark eyes widened slightly at Nelia's outburst. *Miami, hmm?* He had no intentions of taking the advice just thrown to him. Selena Witherspoon was whom he wanted. Married or not.

Though Darius was bogged down in work, that didn't stop him from missing his wife terribly. They'd been playing phone tag since that first night she left for Miami and it was driving him mad.

"Hello?"

"Hey, love."

Selena shivered at the welcome deep voice on the other end of the phone. "Hey, baby, what's goin' on?"

"Missin' you."

"Me too," Selena drawled, her voice sounding slightly groggy since she'd managed to take out some time for much needed rest.

"So, how is it down there?" Darius asked, leaning back in his suede office chair.

"Oh, everything's—" She paused to yawn. "Everything's fine. Hectic, though."

"Well, I only called to hear your voice," Darius said, once silence had dominated the conversation for a few moments. "Talk to you soon."

"All right, bye, baby," Selena said, and then she was gone.

It was almost impossible, but Darius managed to keep himself from making plane reservations to Florida. More than anything, he wanted to see his wife.

Three days later, Selena was the picture of energy. Her business in Miami was almost finished and it appeared that she would be heading home sooner that she'd expected.

Selena left the door to her suite open, waiting for her bags to be collected by the bellman as she wrapped up her phone call.

"Anna, it's me. Look, track down my gorgeous husband and tell him to call me. I'll be home tonight."

"You're leaving now?"

"Yeah, they're comin' to get my bags in a few."

Anna jotted down Selena's hurried instructions. "He can reach you there in your hotel suite?"

"Yes, I've got some last-minute things to handle on this end and I should be here about twenty more minutes."

"All right, I'll get on it for ya."

"Thanks, Anna."

"Selena?"

Selena whirled around and her eyes widened. "Ramon? What are you doin' here?"

"I came to throw myself at your feet."

"Why?"

"Baby, I can't get you out of my head. I miss you so much. I know I messed it up, but I want back what we had."

Selena rolled her eyes. "Damn, what is it with you? You know it's way too late for any of this. Besides, what we had was me giving you all my time and you giving all your time to everybody else."

"Selena—"

"Ramon, I'm married," she said, waving her dazzling wedding band before his eyes. "I've been married for months."

"I don't care about that," Ramon said, with a wave of his hand.

In a split second, Selena lost her temper. "Now you listen to me, you jackass, I've had it. I've tried to avoid this for a long time, hoping that we could salvage a friendship out of that tired relationship. But you can't even allow that. So I'm done. I have hated you for so long, I can't even remember all the terrible things I've wanted to say to you. In fact, I'm glad you came here today so I could tell you just how much I hate you and how little I want a friendship with you. You're not even good enough to lick the dirt off my tires." She sneered, relishing his shock. Grabbing her purse, she stormed out of the room.

Ramon waited in the room for several minutes after Selena's departure. His hands clenched and unclenched as he struggled to quell the anxiety siezing his heart. He was about to leave the suite, when the desk phone buzzed.

Darius was returning his wife's call. A murderous gleam illuminated his face when he heard the male voice on the other end of the line. "Harmon?" his voice grated.

"That's right," Ramon sang.

"Where's Selena?"

Ramon let Darius hear his smug laugh ripple through the line before he offered a verbal response. "She can't come to the phone right now."

Darius commanded himself not to overreact. He set the receiver down gently, then left his office.

* * *

When Selena arrived at her office in New York, her earlier energy had completely evaporated. The scene with Ramon had totally drained her.

Anna rushed into the office behind her boss with her hands spread wide. "What are you doin' here? Isn't Darius waiting for you at home?"

Selena yawned and ran her hand across the tight chingon she sported. "I didn't talk to him before I left. I'll just see him when I get home. Everything'll be fine."

"Darius? Sweetie, you home?" Selena called as she searched the impressive, spacious Bedford home. Her husband was nowhere to be found. She had tried reaching him again from her office, but she'd had no luck. Melissa informed her boss's wife that he'd left the office a while earlier and made no mention of returning.

Selena decided not to make too much out of it and had no problem waiting for her husband to return home. She settled in from her trip, unpacking, showering, and enjoying a nice light supper. Still, the hours crept by and when Darius never arrived, worry began to set in. The aggravation of the day, however, had worn her down more than she realized and she eventually opted to go to bed.

The next morning, Selena rushed downstairs hoping to find her husband asleep on the sofa. Before she could make it off the stairway, the front door opened and he walked inside.

Selena could tell by the cold, guarded look on his dark handsome face that now was not the time to bother him. Unfortunately, he had scared her terribly by not calling or coming home and she felt an explanation was in order.

"Where have you been?" she inquired simply, propping one hand against her hip.

"Do you care?" Darius snapped and kept walking.

"Darius, what is it this time?" she said, following him into the den.

"You know what, Selena? I'm gettin' real tired of goin' through this with you and Ramon Harmon," he snapped.

Selena bowed her head. "Not this again." She sighed.

"Yeah, again, Selena!" he roared, his murderous expression taking on an even more sinister gleam. "Every time. *Every* time I turn my back, there he is! And there *you* are tellin' me nothin's goin' on!"

"But, there isn't—"

"Stop!" he thundered. "It'll be a lot better if you don't tell me that again."

"Better for who, Darius? You? I'm tired of walkin' on eggshells tryin' to keep you from flyin' off the handle over this," she whispered, though her tone was furious.

"I thought this crap was behind us, but how can it be when it's always staring me in the face? The last time I overlooked it and wound up lookin' like a fool. I won't let that happen again."

"What are you talking about?" Selena asked, sounding weary and completely confused. "You know what? Forget it!" she hissed. "I can't take this. I don't believe I was such an idiot to believe you could change."

Darius shrugged his wide shoulders as though he cared little. "Well, I guess we were both idiots since I don't believe I got involved with someone like you."

Selena's gasp seemed to echo in the room. Her hazel eyes filled with tears that could not be supressed. "Someone like me?" she repeated, her voice barely audible.

Darius turned his back, squeezing his eyes shut tightly. Lord, he couldn't believe he'd just said that. Suspicion and the pride that controlled him wouldn't let him admit his mistake.

"I think we need to end this, Selena," he suggested in the softest tone. "I thought we could make it work, I thought marriage would . . . change things, but I know now that it won't."

Selena used the back of her hand to wipe away the tears streaking her face. "I think you're right," she agreed. Though she was hurt and devastated, she wasn't about to beg. Bolting out of the room, she raced upstairs and slipped on clothes before storming out of the house. She cried the entire time.

Darius took a long, hot shower that seemed to clear his mind a little. Afterward, he pulled the drapes in his study and settled on the sofa with a bottle of bourbon. As long moments of silence passed, he reflected on the past eight months of his marriage to Selena. There were good and not so good days. But, one thing had remained constant—his appreciation, desire and love for his wife. He had been a stubborn fool, wallowing in a past heartache that was too old to waste time thinking about. Still, Selena had remained. She had held onto him—believed in him—believed in what they could have together. That fact should have overruled any doubts and all untruths. Ramon Harmon had lied and he had believed him. Once again, he had allowed his suspicions and past mistakes to get the better of him. This time, however, he had lost Selena for good.

Lord, how could I let this happen? he lamented, though he knew there was no one he could truly blame but himself. With the pain and aggravation making it hard to sit still, he got dressed, packed a few things, and headed out.

Selena was near to hysterics when she arrived at Crystal's, a bar located not far from her office. After driving around for nearly two hours, she decided she needed a drink—quite a few of them. For the twentieth time that day, she replayed the horrible argument in her mind. She'd known things weren't completely resolved where Darius's suspicions were concerned and feared another blowup was in the air. Still, nothing she'd imagined compared to what really happened. When she remembered the harsh sound of his voice . . . the hate in his eyes . . .

"Selena? Girl, what are you doin' in a bar in the middle of the day?"

Selena didn't bother to look up when she heard Nel's voice. She'd called her friend an hour after she'd ordered her first drink. "Thanks for coming."

Nelia blew Selena off with a wave of her hand. "You knew I would. What happened?" she asked, taking a seat at the small, round, high table.

Selena took a shot of Courvoisier and grimaced as the smooth brandy burned a path down her throat. "My marriage is over," she whispered.

Nelia tapped her long nails to the table. "What are you talkin' about?"

"I knew somethin' else would go wrong. Now I'm tired of it. I'm just sick of the entire thing," Selena snapped.

"So you're just ready to give up your marriage over this argument?" Nelia asked, unable to believe what she was hearing.

"It was about Ramon," Selena explained. "Nel, how many times am I supposed to listen to that crap?" Her voice rose, sounding slightly slurred due to the amount of alcohol she had consumed.

"What happened?" Nelia slowly inquired.

Selena flopped back in the high chair and placed her hand flat on the bar top. "I don't know. Darius didn't come home last night. This morning was the first time I'd seen him since I got back from Miami. I haven't had time to do anything to set him off."

"Hmph," Nelia grunted and smoothed her hand across her short, dark hair. "Ramon probably did," she grumbled.

"'Scuse me?"

"A few days ago I saw Ramon at Stephan's store. He asked about you and I let him have it. I told him to cool it when you got back from Miami. I got the distinct impression he was up to something then. Maybe he said something to upset Darius."

Selena closed her eyes and covered her face with both hands. "I don't know about that, but he did make a special trip down to visit me in Miami."

Nelia rolled her eyes. "You think Darius found out somehow? Maybe he got the wrong idea again."

"I don't know, I—" Selena stopped herself as realization dawned. "Yes . . . yes, he definitely got the wrong idea and I know exactly how he got it."

Selena talked with Nelia for another hour over a few large cups of black coffee. Afterward, Selena spoke to Ramon at his hotel and asked him to meet her at her office. Of course, Ramon was only too happy to oblige.

"Selena, Ramon Harmon's out here for you."

"Thanks, Anna, send him on in." Selena stepped from behind her desk and walked over to open the door for her guest. The man was all smiles as he strode into the office with blatant confidence.

"Selly, baby, I knew you'd come around," he cooed, his arms spreading wide.

A purely seductive smile crossed Selena's lips as she stepped into the waiting embrace. The smile remained when the back of her hand connected with his cheek.

Ramon's arms hung limply at his sides as he watched her with confusion and rage. "What the hell—"

"You conniving fool," Selena breathed, placing her index finger less than an inch from his nose before she backhanded him again. "Do you know I could kill you for what you've just put me through?"

Ramon's nervousness was clear. "Selena, what—"

"What? You know what, jackass! Admit it! For once in your miserable, tired life be a man and admit what you've done."

Ramon played the confused role for a few minutes more. Finally, he accepted the fact that Selena would not be convinced of his innocence. "He called right after . . . after you walked out of the suite the other day."

"And?" she persisted, her stare murderous.

"He got the wrong idea and—and I . . . I didn't correct him," he explained, growing even more uneasy beneath her glare. "Selena, I—"

"Save it. You have ruined my marriage. I only hope it's not too late to try and salvage something from it. Ramon, if I ever see you again, you will suffer. I swear it," she vowed. "That night at my engagement party, I should've let Darius have his way instead of running in to defend you. I've done that for the last time. Now get the hell out of my sight."

Ramon offered no argument. He kept his head held high and left the office.

Selena took a deep breath once she was alone. All she could think of was going home—praying Darius would not be there. Her plans were to go and pack a few things and get away for a while. Of course, she had no intentions of losing her husband. Although she understood what drove him to say the things he had, she couldn't completely excuse him. There was so much more she needed to know, so much more they had to talk about. Nothing would change until that happened. It had to happen. The survival of their marriage depended on it.

Sixteen

"Man, what the hell are you talkin' about?"

"I can't think of a better way to handle it."

Stephan gave an aggravated sigh, and silence descended on the conversation after that point. Nelia had shared the story of their friend's troubles, relaying all that had taken place between Darius and Selena and the bleak outlook for their marriage. Stephan had been trying to reach Darius for several days, but had no luck. Finally, he'd received a phone call.

"So, you're just gonna throw away everything you have with her?" Stephan asked after a while. He couldn't believe the man was simply going to give up.

Darius made a fist and pounded it lightly against the wicker table. "Hell, man, didn't you just hear what I said? I've put her through this mess too many times," he groaned, his deep voice sounding weary and hoarse.

"I don't know what to tell you, man. I can only hope you'll think before it's too late," Stephan advised.

Darius rolled his eyes. "It's already too late. I can't keep doin' this to her. I think I'm gonna sell the cabin," he suddenly said.

Stephan uttered a disgusted sound. "What for?"

Darius's deep set, coffee gaze scanned the deed to the romantic mountain cabin that had become a regular hideaway for him and Selena since their honeymoon. "I've messed up with her over and over again. I wouldn't expect her to forgive me again." *I don't think I'd want her to,* he silently admitted.

"Well, I hope you talk to her again before you do anything stupid," Stephan added, trying to sound encouraging.

Darius sighed and leaned back in one of the front porch rocking chairs. He had decided to return Stephan's phone calls and told his friend that he'd gone to the cabin only after the man refused to end the call unless he revealed his whereabouts. As his thoughts filled with memories of all the wonderful times he and Selena had shared there, Darius was suddenly overwhelmed by all that had happened.

"There's only one way to handle this," Darius murmured.

After Stephan left the cabin, Darius set out for a walk. Ten minutes after he left for his walk, Selena arrived at the cabin. Though she'd never felt so alone, she prayed that memories of happier times there would lift her spirits while offering the reassurance that her marriage was worth fighting for. She hesitated before going inside, taking a moment to lean against the hood of the black Volvo station wagon she'd rented. The area was so beautiful, she thought, watching the snow drift from above. She'd always marveled at how untouched the place always appeared. Each time she visited the snowy mountain getaway, she grew more convinced that time had no effects there. If only everything could remain so perfect.

With a sigh, she moved off the hood and went to gather her things from the backseat. As she made her way toward the wide, snow-covered steps, she thought of lounging in a hot bath and forgetting the darkness of the last few days.

The instant her bags hit the polished hardwood floor in the foyer, she began to head upstairs.

The lengthy walk had given Darius the chance to do some serious thinking . . . and reminiscing. So many mistakes he had made with Selena could have been avoided had he been honest with her from the beginning. The situation with Tenike Harris had really ruined his ability to trust, but it was his responsibility to get past it. Unfortunately, it may have been too late and he still believed Selena would be much better off without him and the baggage he carried from that doomed relationship.

He had exited the cabin from the rear, but returned through the front. Upon entering the house, he noticed the bags near the door. The trail of clothing along the carpeted staircase caught and held his sensuous gaze. A curious frown clouded his gorgeous face as he made his way up the stairs. His heavy steps grew slower as the garments on the steps became flimsier. When he arrived at the open bedroom door, his voice had completely deserted him.

Selena had just left a brief, yet enjoyable bath and was smoothing lotion over her body. The steamy, comforting soak had been exactly what she'd needed. She longed for a cup of cocoa and a seat before the fire. Just then, the oak bedroom door creaked, sounding as though it was being pushed open. Selena turned and her lovely eyes widened at the sight of Darius standing there. The moment was awkward, yet intensely erotic as they stood there studying each other.

After a long moment, Selena became more aware of her appearance. She quickly rushed to cover herself.

"I'm so sorry," she breathed. "I, um, I didn't know you'd be here," she explained, reaching for a robe from a nearby armchair.

Darius waved his hand, his eyes never leaving her beautiful form. "It's no problem," was his only response, as he watched her slip into a thick, gray Chenille robe.

Knowing they needed to talk, but not knowing where to begin, Selena headed for the door. "Excuse me," she whispered, attempting to rush past him.

Darius caught the sleeve of her robe in his strong fingers. "Selena . . ."

"I don't want to fight with you again," she said, her voice sounding weary and hoarse.

Darius let his fingers fall from the sleeve. "I don't want to fight either."

Selena's hazel eyes widened slightly as she turned to face him more fully. "Darius—"

"I think it's better for you not to stay married to me," he softly interrupted.

"What?" Selena felt her heart dropping even as her pulse was pounding harshly in her ears when his words sank in. "Darius, you can't—"

"Baby, I can't keep doing this . . . hurting you this way," he decided, walking on into the bedroom.

Selena slapped away her tears with the back of her hand. "But, we haven't even been married a year yet."

"Exactly and look at us," he pointed out, his brown gaze focused out the windows.

"I love you," she whispered, watching as he bowed his head.

"I don't know why," he replied, turning to face her. "I feel insecure when I see you talking to other men and my suspicion is at an all-time high when you're around someone who knew you as well as Ramon Harmon, and none of that has anything to do with the case or your past or any of that mess."

Selena dropped to the edge of the bed. "Darius, Ramon was never anyone for you to be jealous of. At this point I can't even be friends with him."

Darius's gaze narrowed a bit more. "I take it you didn't know about my conversation with him."

"I know now," she confirmed in a lifeless voice.

"I'm sorry I came off that way. Again," he quietly admitted, smoothing one hand across the back of his neck. "After it happened, I realized how stupid I was to believe that crap."

Selena rested her elbows on her knees as she leaned forward. "Then can't you get past it so we can work this out?"

A humorless smirk tugged at his mouth when he looked over at her. "Do you realize how many times you've asked me that since you've known me?"

"And I'll keep asking," she vowed. "I won't lose you over something this petty."

"Hmph. Petty things have a way of turning into all-out battles. Believe me, I know."

Selena lowered her eyes and thought for a moment before she spoke. "Well, I don't know. At least, not what you've been through. I'd like for you to tell me about Tenike."

The hate-filled, murderous expression crept into Darius's brown eyes. "I told you about her."

"You gave me an overview," Selena corrected. "I don't think you ever told me all of what really happened."

"This isn't the time for me to go into it."

"It's exactly the time!" Selena cried, bolting up from the bed. "I'm about to lose my husband because he can't get over a woman who hurt him in the past! I at least deserve to know everything that happened."

Darius stared at her for a long moment. Then he collapsed to a cushiony dark beige arm chair. "You're right," he admitted, but didn't continue.

Selena decided it was up to her. "You told me she messed around on you. A man like you doesn't let that affect him alone. Something else had to have happened. Something more relevant."

"There was a baby." His deep voice was barely audible.

Selena heard every word.

"Everybody—all my friends and family—they told me to be sure before I made any solid commitments. But, I wouldn't listen. I trusted her so much. I mean, I had my suspicions, but I never let them get in the way of our relationship."

"What happened?" Selena softly prompted, seeing his pain.

Darius took a deep breath before he answered. "She had the baby. I kept asking her to marry me, but she wouldn't. She wasn't even going to have the baby. I guess she changed her mind. . . . Anyway, the baby was sick. Tenike, she . . . she didn't take care of herself at all during the pregnancy. It was my child, though, and I went through hell worrying about my son. It wasn't until he needed blood that I found out he wasn't mine at all. I loved him still. He held on for two months before . . ."

Selena came to kneel before him in front of the chair. "Darius . . ." she whispered, resting her head against his knee.

"Tenike was very good at sneaking around. I told myself you were the same because of all the men you knew, your business; then with the case . . . I had many opportunities to allow my suspicions to control my thinking."

Selena looked up at him, her eyes filling with tears. "But you know I love you. You have to. If it were any other man, I think I would have left you alone after our first argument in Miami. But I couldn't because . . . I knew there was more, I felt it. I know we can make this work. I know you want to as much as I do."

Darius smiled when she sniffed and wiped the tears from her cheeks. "Don't you ever give up?" he asked, brushing his thumb across her temple.

"Not when I want something as badly as I want us."

"You'd still want this marriage even after all this we've been through?"

"That's precisely why. We've invested too much into each other to let this ruin us. What Tenike did to you was unforgivable. Learn from it, but don't let it rule you and continue to hurt you," she pleaded.

"This is obviously going to take a long time for me to get through. Do you really believe I can do it?"

Selena's smile was bright and reassuring. "I think *we* can do it. Besides . . . I like to take things slow," she softly teased.

Darius curled his hands around her upper arms and lifted her onto his lap. "All right." He sighed, his expression sharpening. "I'll understand if you want me to move out while we're trying to—"

Selena was shaking her head. Her eyes never left his face. "No, sir, I want my eyes on you at all times."

Gradually, Darius's confidence returned and he trailed his fingers along Selena's bare thigh. "All times, huh? I see nothing's changed," he teased, leaning close to fasten his teeth onto her earlobe.

Selena moaned and snuggled more comfortably into his lap. When Darius pulled back, she frowned her disappointment.

"Um . . . I don't want you to think that I believe our problems are solved if we do this," he slowly explained.

Selena nodded. "I know that."

"And, like I said, I can't sit here and promise you that my getting past my . . . hangups will be a quick thing."

Again, Selena nodded. "As long as you promise to try and promise to trust me—to love me."

Darius pressed the softest kiss to her temple as he inhaled her sweet scent. "Always. . . ."

With Selena focused on a renewed commitment to her marriage, not to mention the mystery of the case still looming in the shadows, Carla, Joni, and Synthia assumed the responsibility of running the New York magazine. The publication never missed a beat and Selena's absense was only felt during the larger meetings. The staff and the magazine's advertisers had been somewhat advised of the situation, and all applauded Selena's courage.

The success of the Miami publication gave the staff and its owner another boost. Miami *Reigning Queens* was even rivaling its sister magazine. Of course, the competition was all friendly. The executive branch team in Miami had taunted their colleagues into creating new features in the New York periodical to challenge its own which featured Miami's sexiest men.

Synthia was on her way to dinner with Joni and Carla to discuss a few possible ideas in addition to the agenda for next week's executive conference. She used her pass key and entered her cousin's darkened corner office. There were a few notes on items Selena wanted to have covered during the meeting, and Synthia had forgotten to take them along when she left that afternoon.

"All right, I just saw you a few hours ago. Where'd you disappear to?" Synthia whispered as she leaned across the desk and looked for the elusive notes. The search was unsuccessful, considering Synthia had an upside down view and the office was quite dark. She was about to move to the other side when a pair of hands closed over her upper arms and jerked her back.

"Hey, baby," the intruder whispered close to her ear.

The rough grating of a man's voice and his hot breath against her cheek sent Synthia's heart pounding in her throat. She opened her mouth to scream, but there was no sound.

The man smiled as fragrant waves of her brown curls slapped his face. "Yeah, Selena," he groaned, enjoying the feel of her bottom nudging his erection.

Synthia ceased her struggles when she heard the man speak her cousin's name. She snapped to her senses when his hand ventured to her blouse and he began to undo the buttons. Her elbow connected with his ribs and he grunted.

"Oh, we want it rough, huh? You know I can handle that," he boasted, grabbing a fistful of her hair and shoving her toward the sofa.

Synthia landed facedown against the cushions. She quickly resumed her struggles. Unfortunately, they were useless in her disadvantaged position and only seemed to spur him onward.

The man wrenched her skirt up with one hand, while undoing his jeans with the other. Synthia tried to raise her head in an effort to scream, but her heart was pounding so fast, her breath came in rapid pants. She ordered herself to calm, then lifted her head once more.

This time, a terrified cry ripped clear of her lungs. He tugged at her panties, but the terror in her scream seemed to startle him and he hesitated. Suddenly, he was struck on the back of the head. The pain sent him reeling in agony and he rolled away from Synthia to land on the floor.

Carla pounced, dropping the figurine she'd used to immobilize him. Her heavy-soled boots landed punishing blows to his ribs, abdomen, and buttocks.

"Rank jackass! Get up! Get the hell up!" she viciously taunted, kicking him as she yelled.

The intruder tried to ward off the more serious blows by covering his head. When Carla stepped around for a different angle, he seized the opportunity to reach out and grab her ankle, causing her to fall near an armchair that flanked the sofa. Carla quickly regained her faculties, but he had already left the office.

"Sweetie, you all right?" she whispered, rushing over to Synthia, who sat shivering and crying on the sofa. "Shh . . ." Carla urged, pulling the woman into a protective embrace.

He had knocked Joni to the floor when he raced out of Selena's office. She hurried into the room, not hesitating to grab the phone and dial the police. Then she too joined Carla in comforting Synthia.

"You don't wanna do that."

"Why not?"

" 'Cause then, I can do this," Darius said, moving the majestic, polished, carved black king piece to corner Selena's king. "Check."

Her soft mouth formed a pout in response to his announcement. "Jerk." She hissed.

"That's how the game is played, love," he drawled, rubbing his hands together as his gaze twinkled with glee.

"You're a shark," Selena accused, tapping her finger next to the short mahogany card table in the den. "You know I haven't played chess before."

Darius shrugged. "Best way to beat a shark is to be taught by one."

"Mmm, and you're gonna teach me all your secrets?"

"Course not. That's why I'm a shark."

Selena's laughter lilted across the room and she was tossing a throw pillow at her husband's gorgeous face when the phone rang.

Darius sighed and stood from the furry red-and-black checkered rug they shared. "Can you be trusted?" he asked, fixing her with a suspiciously playful stare.

Selena raised her hands. "I think you're safe."

"Hmph," Darius said, but headed across the room to answer the phone on the bar. "Darius McClellan."

"D, man, it's Max."

"What's up?" Darius greeted, turning to cast a watchful eye on Selena, who was trying to devise a way to avoid a checkmate.

"Sorry to interrupt y'all over there, man, but somethin' happened tonight."

"Tell me."

"Synthia was attacked."

"What!"

"There's more. It happened at the magazine in Selena's office."

"Shit," Darius hissed, smoothing one hand across his hair.

Selena had already crossed the room. She stood a few feet behind Darius and waited for the call to end.

"All right, man," Darius was saying, "I'll just meet you there. Yeah."

"What happened?" Selena asked before the receiver touched the cradle. She'd twisted her Million Woman March T-shirt into a mass of wrinkles.

Darius took a deep breath, then turned and closed the short distance between them. "Shh . . ." he urged, noticing her bottom lip trembling and knowing she was moments away from crying. "Synthia was attacked tonight at the magazine . . . in your office," he calmly told her.

"Oh God," Selena breathed, covering her mouth with both hands as her eyes widened.

"Shh . . ." Darius urged. "Come on now."

"Darius, what—who would do this? Synth's got nothin' to do with this," she moaned, amidst her sobs.

"Shh . . ." Darius continued to console his wife, his hand stroking her back methodically while he brushed his mouth across her temple. "We're gonna find out who's behind this. I promise you that."

"But—"

"Baby, listen," Darius whispered, bending a little to look directly into her eyes. "Now, I need you to calm down and get dressed so we can get over to your office."

Selena swallowed and began to nod. "Right," she agreed.

Darius cupped her cheek. "Good girl. Now, hurry up so I can drop you off."

Selena stopped and frowned. "Drop *me* off? Where are you going?"

"I'm going to track down Francine Johns."

"Come 'ere," Selena whispered, pulling her cousin close for the tenth time since she'd set foot in the office.

Synthia had just finished recapping her earlier nightmare. "I'm sorry, Selena," she whispered, her voice muffled against her cousin's shoulder. "Sorry I didn't see his face, but it was so dark—"

"Don't you dare apologize for one thing that happened tonight, you hear?" Selena ordered, squeezing Synthia's arms. "We're gonna catch the jackass that did this, but in the meantime we're gonna get you out of town. Someplace safe."

"Sel—"

"I don't wanna hear it, Synth. I know Max'll agree with me too. This person's trying to get me by going after my family and friends," she explained, her delicate features tightening to a hard mask. "I'll be damned if I let anyone else get hurt because of me."

"Sel, wait," Synthia said, clutching Selena's hand. "I don't think that's it. I don't think he meant to attack me."

Selena watched her cousin in disbelief. "Synth? I know you're not makin' excuses for this fool."

"No, no, Sel, what I mean is, I think he thought he was with you. We never saw each other's faces and he called me by *your* name."

"Oh God . . ." Selena breathed, afraid to voice the realization racing through her mind. "Oh God . . ." she repeated, burying her face in her hands.

Synthia pressed her lips together and glanced across her shoulder. "Could you guys give me a minute with my cousin, please?" She asked Carla and Joni.

"Thanks," Selena whispered, when the door closed behind her friends. "They don't need to see me like this. They're worried enough about me as it is."

"Sel, I'm so sorry. I am so very sorry." Synthia shuddered and her voice grew hoarse.

"Would you please stop telling me that? None of this had anything to do with you. This fool has gone too far this time."

"Maybe, but—"

"No buts, Synth! Damn! I can't spend the rest of the night reassuring you here, all right? Now we're gonna get you out of here, get you safe, and—"

"Damn it, Sel! I don't need you to protect me! You've always done that and I never asked for it. Who the hell told you you always had to be the strong one?"

Taken aback by the outburst, Selena patted her cousin's knee. "Synth?"

Synthia left the sofa. "I have a lot to answer for."

"Not this."

"Especially this."

"You're scaring me, Synth."

"And you don't deserve that. I never should've allowed you to be scared a day in your life."

Selena's eyes narrowed as she watched her cousin's back stiffen. "What are you talking about?" she slowly inquired.

Synthia bowed her head and hesitated only a moment. "When you told me you were scared all those years ago— scared that your parents were gonna turn their backs on you—I should've stopped it. I should've said something then—"

"Synth, Synth, what in the hell are you saying?"

"I'm saying that I'm the person who changed your life, Sel. I'm the woman who turned your parents against you."

"Synth . . . no, Synth. You don't expect me to believe you made my parents believe that gossip?"

"But it wasn't gossip, remember? It was true. It was all true."

"So? That had nothing to do with you. My parents never saw those pictures, they were just stupid enough to believe the ones who did. All this started because some girl—"

"Some *girl* who looked just like you."

"A girl who—" Selena stopped herself, her body turning dead cold as her eyes widened. "Some, some . . . other girl . . ."

"No. No, Sel."

"Synthia? Synthia, what . . . Synthia?"

"It was me. Sel, the girl was me."

"No," Selena stated firmly, shaking her head. "No, I don't believe that."

Synthia bent a little at the waist as she tried to look more directly into her cousin's face. "Why not? Why can't you believe it? Because I was always good, little Synthia? Never did a thing wrong? Always acted like a lady, with her below-the-knee skirts, boring pageboy hairstyle, and bifocals? Synthia Witherspoon who was nothing like her glamorous cousin Selena with all the boys hanging on to her every word?"

At that moment Selena barely recognized her own cousin.

"Synthia, where is all this coming from?"

"It was so easy to be you. Nobody even knew I existed on the yard," Synthia went on, referring to their college campus. "They certainly didn't know you were my cousin. I knew guys met after hours in the canteen. I'd seen them playing cards with the cleaning crew every night when I walked back to my dorm from the library. I don't know what made me dress up and walk in there to let them . . . Anyway, after some drinks, I was wonderful company."

Selena's tears fell too quickly for her to wipe them away. "Synthia, why?" she whispered, unable to believe she had never suspected the one person who so closely resembled her.

"Because I could . . . Hell, maybe because deep down I'd always wanted to live the kind of life everyone *thought* you led."

"And when . . . all this came out and everyone thought that I . . ."

"I almost died. I had no idea I was being photographed. When I saw what was happening to you, I—I wanted to come clean, but I couldn't. Selena, I was so scared. Especially when I saw the way your parents reacted. I knew I'd never be strong enough to stand something like that. Still, it killed me to see you go through that. I would've given anything to be able to change it."

"Anything, except the tight relationship you shared with your own parents, right?"

"Selena—"

"And what about now, Synth? What about these crazy messages and the photos I've been receiving? What about how it affected my relationship with Darius? You aren't the same timid little girl, Synt. Why didn't you come forward before?"

"Because then there was Max. Finally, a man who not only thought I was beautiful in my own right, but who hung on to *my* every word. It sounds heartless, I know. That's why I didn't come around as much after the pictures came. I couldn't stand to see what you were going through because of me."

"You couldn't stand what I was going through? Or maybe you couldn't stand that I might realize that the reason the girl in the pictures looks so much like me was that it was you!"

"Selena, I'm so sorry. I know that's weak, but it's all I have. That and these words I'm saying to you now. Words that I'll be saying to your parents, my parents, and anyone else who asks. You don't ever have to forgive me, Sel, but I'm damn well gonna spend the rest of my life making this up to you."

Selena watched as her cousin gathered her belongings and walked out of the office. Alone, she leaned against the desk, burying her face in her hands as tears wet her palms.

Seventeen

"You really think she'll be here, man?"

"There's been no contact from this guy in a long time. She probably thinks she's in the clear," Darius reasoned with a light shrug. "Let's hope she feels comfortable enough to come back," he said, slipping his key into the pocket of his hooded burgundy sweatshirt.

Max sighed. "I hope this pays off, man. I want this guy," he muttered.

"So do I. So do I," Darius heartily agreed, then opened the door and left his truck.

Francine Johns was indeed feeling calm and relaxed. Reassured. She answered the door of her Queens home wearing an inviting smile. A smile that faded the instant she recognized her unexpected callers. Finding the two tall, dark, imposing men on her doorstep immediately had her cursing the fact that she had not bothered to ask who it was.

"I've told you everything," she said, a defiant glint in her green eyes as she focused on Darius.

"And you know that's not the truth," he slowly disputed. "Now, either you talk to us now or our friends from your local precinct will be here next."

Visibly shaken, Francine retreated. Darius and Max stepped inside and headed down the long corridor that led to the sitting room.

"Maybe I should be talking about this with Selena," she suggested, rubbing her damp palms against the front of her casual, money-green pantsuit.

Darius chose his place on an armchair next to the fireplace. "Thanks to you and your friend, my wife and I have no secrets. Talk."

Realizing there were no more excuses to be made, Francine bowed her head and pressed clasped hands to her mouth. "James—my ex-husband—knew Selena in college too. He always wanted her but Selena was never interested in him in that way. I was around whenever James needed a shoulder to cry on and eventually we married. Even then I knew James was still in love with Selena but I thought he'd eventually love me. I was wrong."

"Ms. Johns," Darius said, after clearing his throat, "some fool just attacked my wife's cousin and I'm willin' to bet it's linked to you. Now, I really don't give a damn about your husband's feelings for Selena. All I want to know is who. All I want is a name."

"Ramon Harmon," Francine announced, watching Max and Darius exchange glances. "I see you know him," she added, perching on the edge of the long, padded windowsill. "It was Ramon Harmon who brought me those pictures of Selena and Jay. I knew that nothing happened between them and even if it had, we'd already been divorced several years. I was tired of living in her shadow. I wanted to ruin her life the way she ruined mine. Luckily Ramon wanted her, too."

"Why? What reason did he give?" Max inquired.

Francine was shaking her head. "He didn't—not really. He told me he'd been friends with Jay after Selena introduced them. He was a photographer and did some professional shots for Jay. He did say that he wanted Selena back when he approached me with those photos. They were his way of getting her to need him and welcome him into her life."

"Need him!" Max snapped.

Francine massaged her arms with shaking hands. "Ramon

figured I'd be so bent on revenge because of jealousy or whatever that I'd stop at nothing. He'd swoop in as her great comforter while I had my day. He didn't factor in Selena's new relationship with Darius and when he realized how serious it was, he got angry and wound up wanting revenge himself."

"God . . ." Max breathed, leaving the sofa.

"I was only out to pay Selena back for the hurt she caused me. Even though Jay and I were divorced . . . I meant what I said before though, I never meant for it to go this far," she uttered in the fiercest whisper, wringing her hands as her nervous gaze shifted from Darius to Max. "Ramon Harmon is a cruel, vindictive man. He's caused a lot of problems for you and your wife." She looked at Darius. "But, I'm sure you're aware of that," she tacked on, when he looked away. "Ramon went crazy when you and Selena worked out everything. I guess that's what prompted his actions tonight."

"That all happened at least a month ago," Max argued, turning back to Francine. "Why would Harmon pick *now* to attack?"

"He's very patient. Very methodical," she explained, appearing to shudder. "Tonight was very out of character for him, though. He must be desperate."

"He's insane," Darius bluntly surmised.

"He's dangerous," Francine warned. "Get your wife out of town, Darius."

The long-awaited jog in Prospect Park was marred with talk of Ramon Harmon. The McClellans voices carried like echos as they debated the tense issue.

"I'm not lettin' that crazy fool run me out of town!" Selena raged, when her husband suggested she leave with Synthia, who was on her way to their grandmother's Long Island home.

Darius ran his fingers through his soft hair, while bracing one elbow against the trunk of a tree. "What can I do to convince you of how dangerous this situation is?"

Selena leaned against the tree opposite the one Darius was perched next to. "Baby, I'll have to come back sometime and what then?"

"We'll have him by then," he vowed.

"And if you don't?" she challenged. "Darius, that fool attacked Synthia thinking it was me. He could have raped her, and *that* could have been me."

"It's admirable of you to stand up for your cousin after she put you through so much nonsense," Darius noted, his voice sounding cold and accusing.

Selena let her gaze falter as she shrugged. "She was scared and did a stupid thing," she acknowledged. "What happened hurt me, but I'd always been misunderstood for whatever reason, be it my personality . . . looks . . ." She shook her head quickly. "But, none of what's going on now changes the fact that she's my cousin and I still love her," she declared, fixing her husband with a steady gaze.

Darius reached for Selena's hand and gathered her close. "You're an incredible lady, Selena McClellan," he whispered, pressing his forehead next to hers as his expression sobered. "I'll die before I let anything happen to you," he vowed.

Selena finally took heed of the fear she saw in her man's gaze. "Sweetie, come on . . ." she soothed, standing on her toes to kiss his mouth as she spoke. "Let me help you get Ramon."

Darius pulled away, his long sleek brows drawing closed in a fierce glare. "How the hell could you suggest somethin' stupid like that?"

Selena raised her chin a bit higher. "I can get him. I know I can."

"Get him? To do what, Selena?"

"Do you trust me?"

"With my life."

"And I trust you with mine. So back me up, will you?" she urged.

Darius closed his eyes and massaged the bridge of his nose. "I must be crazy."

Selena tugged his hand away from his face. "No, you're not crazy. You just love me," she whispered, puckering her lips for a kiss her husband was all too willing to give.

"Where is that son of a bitch?" Selena hissed, pacing the luxurious Manhattan hotel suite like a caged cat.

Darius chuckled. "Relax, you were the one who wanted to play Pam Grier's role tonight, remember?"

"Hush," Selena ordered, smiling at the sound of her husband's voice. "Are you sure he won't be able to hear you when you speak to me through this thing?" she asked, tapping her nail against the earpiece she wore.

"He won't hear a thing. I promise."

The doorbell chimed then and Selena gasped before swallowing past the lump lodged in her throat. "He's here," she whispered, making her way toward the front of the room.

"Easy," Darius cautioned. "Remember we're right in the next room."

"Mmm-hmm," she acknowledged, taking a deep breath before opening the heavy white oak door.

"Selena, baby," Ramon Harmon purred, though his expression was slightly wary when he stepped inside the suite.

"Glad you decided to respond to my e-mail." Selena was saying as she pushed the door shut.

"Sounded urgent," he remarked, still inspecting the room as though he were looking for someone. "Where's your man?" he asked, fixing her with his probing dark eyes.

Selena fanned the chic, gauzy material of her blouse away from her skin. "Not here," she pointedly replied. "Thank God."

"Trouble in paradise?"

"You should know."

"Excuse me?" Ramon drawled in pretend confusion.

"Well, thank you anyway."

"You're thanking me?" he asked, obviously intrigued by the gesture.

Selena made dramatic motions with her hands. "Oh, Ramon, I tried to make it work with that man, but I just got so sick of havin' to apologize to him all the time."

"I knew y'all wouldn't make it," Ramon smuggly observed, slowly moving toward her.

Selena shrugged. "He couldn't handle me or my past, so forget him."

"Good for you," he applauded.

Selena tossed her glossy curls across her shoulders and fixed him with a look of cool innocence. "I just needed someone to vent to, Ramon," she purred, "but . . . if you can't or don't *want* to stay, I'd certainly understand."

Ramon dragged his fingers through his thick hair. "Did I say I wanted to leave?" he asked, gracing her with the devilish grin that used to send her swooning.

"No . . ." she breathed, turning to lean against the back of a cushioned chair. "But I haven't been very nice to you lately."

"Are you tryin' to make up for it now?"

"Ramon, I'm just so frustrated! So tense!" she fretted, sashaying around the suite in the gorgeous blouse and form-fitting flare-legged pants. She trailed her hands through her hair and across her body, appearing like a feline on the prowl and aware that her actions were having the intended effect on Ramon.

"Maybe you need to do something to take your mind off it all," he suggested, his steps steady, a determined gleam enhancing his expression as his eyes raked her curvaceous figure.

"Something to take my mind off it all?" Selena questioned, tapping her fingers to her chin as she pretended to consider the advisement. "Like what?" she asked, setting her mouth into a pout.

Ramon closed the remaining distance between them. One arm snaked around her waist, while he cupped her chin in his free hand. He kissed her. Hard. Selena felt nauseated and faint as his tongue slid into her mouth. She moaned out of disgust, but Ramon took it as a sign of her pleasure.

"That fool can't do it like me, can he, baby?"

"Mmm . . . what fool?" she asked, purposely misunderstanding.

Ramon chuckled, then moved in to kiss her again.

"Ramon, really, I—I want to thank you for everything," she said, moving away before he could touch her again. "I only wish I had wised up before I married Darius."

Shrugging, Ramon smoothed his hands across the silky texture of the tight, turquoise T-shirt that emphasized his muscular physique. "I tried to get you to see what he was like, baby," he said, taking full credit for his schemings.

Selena hoped she was doing an adequate job of masking her hate. "I'm glad our . . . bad past didn't stop you from caring."

"Hmph," he grunted, pacing toward the French doors leading to the balcony. "I didn't even realize I still cared, till Velma called."

"Velma?"

"Velma Morris. Your boy Harry's cousin," he flippantly clarified, never noticing the shock registering on Selena's face. "She got in touch while you were down in Miami workin' on the new mag. Told me about you and McClellan."

"But how? How'd she know about—"

"'Bout us?" he interrupted, then waved his hand. "Said she knew you'd been without a man for a long time. She got all the tidbits from her cousin, who was always worried about how our breakup affected you. Of course, I didn't mind confirming how stormy we were. I told her we just had some misunderstandings."

Selena felt her stomach rumbling. "Misunderstandings? But . . . why would she call you. If it was like that she could've just set me up with somebody else."

Ramon shrugged. "Guess I was a sure thing."

"A sure thing?" Selena asked, her voice flat.

"That's right. Anyway, she wasn't too happy with you bein' down there once Darius got hung up on you. See, he was down to satisfy *her*, not you."

"He was there on business."

"Yeah, but ol' Vel planned on takin' it further later. If Darius hadn't figured out she burned down her own damned hotel, they'd be screwin' on a beach somewhere right now," he predicted, chuckling heartily while Selena turned away.

"What did Velma expect you to do?" she softly inquired.

"Well, McClellan got hooked on you fast, so Velma figured I could come down and take your mind off him so she could get some quality time."

Selena clenched her fist to keep her hand from shaking. Her fear reasserted itself with the knowledge of how carefully the ordeal had been planned. "So, what happened?" she asked, surprised by the strength of her voice. "You never showed up," she recalled.

"I couldn't get away at the time, but damn! I wanted to," he said, his eyes trained on her chest as though he could see right through her blouse. "Hearin' your name and then findin' out you were gettin' busy with some new fool made me see how stupid I was to let you go."

You didn't let me go. I left, you pig.

"Anyway, I remembered that crap with the pictures and Francine thinking you'd slept with Jay. I thought we could use it to put a little scare in you and by the time I saw you, you'd stick to me like glue and allow my charms to win you all over again. Wasn't until I found out McClellan lived here in New York and that y'all was still real into each other since Miami that I realized I'd have to come up with something better than those little notes if I planned to end that relationship."

"So you did this?"

"Hey, *this* is my insurance." Ramon clarified, his dark eyes snapping with a sudden fire. "I get you, your connects, and your plush lifestyle or you get your rep tossed to the wolves. Again."

"And what about Darius?" she asked. "I'm still married to him, remember?"

"Not for long. Don't get any ideas about workin' it out,

either," he warned, pointing his index finger in her direction. "You file for divorce in the morning or I'll bring out all those pictures and all that ugliness. I'll even send a few to your grandma's church and see if she'll stick by you. Then, you'll *have* to depend on me," he said, studying her expression closely. "Nah . . . on second thought . . . maybe I should bring it all out anyway."

"For insurance?" Selena guessed.

"Now you're gettin' it."

Selena's hazel stare narrowed and she didn't bother to hide her emotions. "It was you who attacked my cousin, wasn't it?"

Ramon's confident grin faded, then quickly reappeared. "Tell Synth I'm sorry. Y'all always did look too much alike. Can't tell you how many dreams I've had 'bout the two of you. With me, of course."

Selena's smile was tight. "Of course," she whispered.

"I tell ya though, Synth's got it goin' on with that body. Maybe we can work out somethin' to make my dream come true."

"You know, Ramon, after all the hell you put me through, I was still fool enough to consider letting you walk away from it all. Then, you put your hands on my cousin, so now it's payback time."

Ramon's laughter was like the roar of a well-fed lion. "You must be forgetting that I got the upper hand. Finally. It's not about you anymore, Selena, baby. You with all your clout and money and men. It's about me. Me gettin' mine."

"And you will," she promised, placing her hands on her hips while she set her neck at a rebellious angle. "See Ramon, after you attacked Synthia—"

"I didn't attack her. I thought it was you."

"Oh? So you meant to attack me?"

"Just wanted to put a lil' scare in you."

"Well, Synth thought she was about to be raped. We called the cops and they treated it as a crime scene, which means they dusted for prints and guess whose they found?"

"Please! Everybody knows I was up in there to see you plenty of times."

"Yes, but my office is cleaned every evening. Besides Synth's prints, yours were the only others they found."

Something flickered in Ramon's midnight stare, but he wasn't bested yet. "Why would I leave prints if I was up to no good?"

Selena shrugged. "Whatever you were there for won't look good. Especially since you just admitted to blackmail for money, and sexual favors no less. Money and sexual favors you would never have collected since the woman in the 'gang bang' wasn't me."

"Say what?"

"You heard me."

Ramon smirked and waved his hand. "Save it, Selly. Anybody would think—"

"Would think it's me. The woman in the other photos is owning up to her performance and she's all too ready to come forward and back me up when I need her. Then, on top of *all* that, you tried to rape my cousin."

Ramon's confidence dwindled. Having Selena take the upper hand enraged him. "Synth tried to act so scared, but she liked it," he eventually said out of spite, wanting to remove the smug smile from Selena's face.

"What did you say?"

"You heard me. I could feel her grindin' her butt against my stuff the whole time."

Selena's smug grin transformed into something more wickedly seductive. She strolled toward Ramon and smoothed her hand across his jaw and cheek. "I think that says it all, don't you, love?" She whispered, her words meant for her husband who was listening in to the conversation. She watched Ramon's expression turn curious. "Come on in," she instructed, then balled a fist and smashed it into Ramon's cheek. She followed the blow with a backhand slap and a knee to his groin.

SIGGLING ROMANCE BY
ROCHELLE ALERS

ABOUT THE AUTHOR

South Carolina native AlTonya Washington published her debut romance *Remember Love* in April 2003. In addition to raising her two-year-old son, she works as a library reference associate. AlTonya enjoys creating stories filled with secrets and surprises. She is a fanatical reader and writer with hopes for continuing her writing career for many years to come.

Dear Readers,

I thank you all so very much for your comments and support of my debut effort. My second novel, *Guarded Love* was an enjoyable challenge. I pray that the emotionally charged love story of Darius McClellan and Selena Witherspoon held your interest, roused your tempers, fueled your fantasies and satisfied your desire for a sexually charged, mysterious love story.

As always, I welcome your comments, whatever they may be. Please feel free to e-mail me: altonya@writeme.com. I promise to respond in a timely manner. I love you guys for supporting me. You've made this new author feel welcomed and very much appreciated. Please visit my Web site: altonyawashington.com

May God Bless You All,
AlTonya Washington

Darius smirked. "Hmph, stress, hurt, anger . . . it was a lot to handle. I love you so much for sticking by me."

Selena's intense stare was riveted on his. "I love you so much for doing the same."

Darius pulled her into a tight hug and chuckled when his wife squeezed him back just as tightly.

"What you doin', girl?" Loretta McClellan playfully whispered, seeing her cohostess at the den door.

Secelia Witherspoon positioned her index finger before her lips, before motioning for Loretta to sneak over.

Peeking into the room, Loretta saw her grandson and his wife. Quietly, she closed the door and secured the lock.

"Think we'll be great-grandmothers by next Christmas?"

"Do I?" Secelia raved. "I already have some baby catalogs in my bedroom."

"Well? What we standin' here for, girl? Let's go take a look," Loretta ordered, following Secelia down the hall.

"Where would we go?"

"Lock ourselves in our room."

Selena turned in his arms, easing her own around his neck. "I wouldn't be opposed at all."

"I love you," Darius said, his gorgeous brown eyes relaying the sentiment more deeply than words ever could.

Selena searched his soothing stare, before pressing her lips against his. "I love you. So much. All you've done to work through the pain that was eating away at you. The pressure of that and the jealousy it created. Talking to me about how you're feeling—being honest about it all . . . you show me every day how important our life together is to you," her expression turned humorous. "I'm especially impressed by your 'assistance' with the Heavenly Bodies issue," she commented. Her husband had taken to offering his opinions on the candidates for the steamy edition.

Darius shrugged. "I figured I should have an idea of whose getting my wife's time," he teased.

Selena scooted up to kiss his cheek. "Not *getting* only *borrowing* between the hours of nine and five."

Darius nuzzled her neck with the tip of his nose. "I meant it when I told you that I always want you with me. I had to make you believe that I really meant that. This entire situation . . . Ramon Harmon showing up in your life—"

"Ahh Ramon, enjoying a few years in jail . . ." she teased, then her expression clouded as the reality of his downfall set in. "Sometimes I still can't believe he did something so stupid with such dangerous consequences."

Darius shook his head. "But you know, everything that happened, I needed to go through it. To me, it proved how much I valued our marriage. We both realize now that we probably jumped into the commitment too soon." He looked to her for confirmation.

"You're right," Selena sighed, "we loved each other, but we had so many demons to get past. It wasn't fair to us to start a marriage under that kind of stress."

Epilogue

Christmas, one year later

Secelia Witherspoon's gorgeous Long Island home was a vision of everything that epitomized holiday warmth and cheer. Each window glowed with golden rays from an electric light figurine. Aromatic candles burned, filling the house with fragrances of apples, cinnamon, and vanilla. Every fireplace roared with a crackling flame and there was not one tree, but three—each decorated with a loving touch.

In the second-floor den, nestled away in their own private corner of the darkened room, were Darius and Selena. They sipped creamy eggnog and enjoyed the tree lights from their spot on the fluffy copper-colored rug near the sofa. They were silent—each thinking over how far they'd come and how much they had gained.

Darius set his mug on the food-laden tray they had prepared before leaving the Christmas celebration on the first floor. He tugged Selena back, enfolding her more snuggly against his chest. Her lashes fluttered down over her eyes as complete contentment soothed her entire body.

"Second Christmas," Darius announced, brushing his lips against her temple. "Still love me?" he whispered.

"More than ever," she drawled, without a moment's hesitation.

"Does that mean you wouldn't be opposed to *not* going back down to the party?"

A side door opened and a hoard of men rushed out, a few dressed in police uniforms.

"Did you get everything?" Selena asked her husband.

"Got it all. You all right?" Darius questioned, concern etched across his dark handsome face as he pulled her close. Selena let her eyes drift shut and relished the serenity of his hold. "I'm fine," she said, opening her eyes to glare at Ramon. "That jackass kissed me. I think I need to gargle with some disinfectant."

"You set me up?" Ramon acknowledged, while he was being read his rights.

"And with Francine Johns's testimony and this police wire," she said, extracting the earpiece and pulling the mike from beneath the collar of her blouse, "we won't be seein' you for a long time. I think they still put blackmailers and rapists in jail. Don't they, baby?" she asked, snuggling back into Darius's arms.

"Damn right," he growled, his scathing gaze fixed on Ramon, who looked away with unease clouding his face.

"Pretty boy, prima donna like you should fit right in," he added.

"Let's go," one of the officers ordered and Ramon was forcibly escorted from the room.

Amidst the commotion, Selena remained tucked away in Darius's secure embrace.